Murder
on the Moon

Mark Robinson

First published in 2018

All characters and events in this publication, other than those clearly in the public domain, are fictitious and any resemblance to real persons, living or dead, is purely coincidental.

No part of this publication may be reproduced, stored in a retrieval system, or transmitted, in any form or by any means, without the prior permission in writing of the author, nor be otherwise circulated in any form of binding or cover other than that in which it is published.

To Claire, Archie and Toby

1. Bedrooms – Cheng, Lonnen, Wrycroft
2. Bedrooms – Ellis, Medvelev, Nash
3. Bedrooms – Daley, Velasquez, Yuridov
4. Control Centre/Common Room
5. Lab 3 (Roscosmos – under construction)
6. Lab 2 (European Space Agency)
7. Lab 1 (NASA)
8. Video conference room
9. Maintenance Pod 1
10. Maintenance Pod 2
11. Lunarsol Pod 1
12. Lunarsol Pod 2
13. Lunarsol Pod 3
14. Lunarsol Pod 4

ACKNOWLEDGMENTS

I must give a special mention to my writing group buddies. Thank you Stella, Janet, Nick, Henry, Frank, Shaun and of course our tutor Tom for your invaluable support and encouragement and for letting me use your names for characters in the book!

Thanks also to my old uni friend Dr Dave Cowlishaw for the suggestions on murder methods. If my subsequent internet searches set off any red flags with the authorities then I'm naming you as an accomplice.

1

Nash took a deep breath and released it slowly, savouring the silence. He scanned the horizon, waiting eagerly for the sunrise. After fifteen days of darkness he was surprised how much he was craving natural light.

'Sixty seconds,' announced his commander's voice through Nash's earpiece. The Russian was one of the unfortunate few to remain indoors that morning; most of the crew had scheduled work outside to give themselves an uninterrupted view of the sun's arrival.

The white circle suddenly appeared, illuminating the barren landscape. Nash allowed himself a minute to enjoy the abrupt change then resumed his journey, keen to see what effect the long cycle of night and day might have on his experiments. Four months into a two year programme he already felt like time was racing away.

A lock of hair fell across his forehead, prickling his skin. He blew upwards, annoyed that he'd let it get so long. With no way to soothe it he tried to put it from his mind, continuing the loping march to his destination. He was distracted by a deep rumbling sensation beneath his feet.

'For God's sake,' he muttered. The presence of the solar engineers was a constant irritation, and he worried about the damage they were doing to the lunar surface before it was fully understood.

'Everything okay, Richard?' came Lydia Ellis's voice through the headset.

'All fine apart from those bloody cowboys drilling too close again. They're meant to keep a kilometre beyond the perimeter.'

'They hit some hard rock below the surface. Commander Yuridov approved their request to relocate.'

Nash checked the comms settings on his arm display. Doctor Ellis was the only crewmember on this channel. 'Did he? I'll have words when I get back.'

'Don't go too hard on him. You know what they're like. They'd have gone ahead with or without Yuridov's agreement. We'll have to keep an eye on them though. Us proper scientists need to stick together.'

Nash smiled to himself. She always had a way of cheering him up. 'How are your worms?' he asked, cringing slightly at how forced his change of subject sounded. One of Ellis's experiments involved monitoring earthworm survival rates in different atmospheric conditions.

'All still alive at the moment. I'll be taking one of the tanks down another notch tomorrow. My focus today is the seedlings. The roots have taken despite the low gravity, and they've survived the darkness of the last two weeks. I want to see how much they perk up now we've light overhead.'

'That's great,' said Nash. A successful plant growth programme would have far-reaching implications for the long term viability of their base. He'd like to look at the results in more depth but with hundreds of his own experiments, some requiring daily attention, he was already stretched. 'That reminds me, I must check how the sun's affecting the colloids. And the algae. So much to do...'

'... So little time, I know,' Ellis finished. 'Good luck, you can tell me how it's all going over dinner.'

At eight o'clock Nash completed his report on the bone density of his medaka fish and saved it to the European Space Agency server. Walking into the living quarters he greeted Ellis, Daley and Medvelev and went to the food store to select his meal. Fish and chips with mushy peas, why not. It had been a successful day and a treat was warranted. After rehydrating then heating it he joined the others.

Daley eyed the plate suspiciously. 'And I thought beans on toast was weird.'

'You don't know what you're missing. Try some.' He held out a forkful of peas.

'No thanks man. I'd rather eat my own snot.'

'I will,' said Ellis. She took the fork from Nash's hand, closing her eyes in mock pleasure as she ate them. 'Mmm, delicious.'

Daley laughed and shook his head. 'You're a nightmare Lydia. What about you Sergey, tempted?'

Medvelev, his deathly pale skin contrasting sharply with the deep black of Daley's, looked up and considered the offer. 'They would taste better in vodka I think.'

Daley grinned. 'That's your answer to everything. I'm still shaking off that stuff they gave us when we launched.'

'Traditional Russian toast before liftoff.' He held up his cup of water. 'Nasdarovje!'

They were interrupted by the arrival of the remaining Lunarsol engineers. Cheng was as neat as ever but Lonnen, Velasquez and Wrycroft all looked sweaty and exhausted.

'Oo-ee. What a day,' said Lonnen in his strong Texan accent. 'Ah sure could do with a beer.'

'How'd it go?' Daley asked.

'Tough,' Lonnen replied. 'Bad start hitting that granite,

cost us a coupla hours abandoning the site and setting up again.'

'That move could jeopardise the base and my experiments,' said Nash. 'You're meant to stay well outside the exclusion zone.'

'Look, Nash – ,' started Lonnen.

'Let him speak,' said Velasquez, sitting down and putting his hands behind his head. 'Get it off his chest, then we can all ignore him and get back to our dinner.'

Nash glared at Velasquez, then stood and picked up his plate. 'Fucking cowboys,' he muttered as he stormed off to his quarters.

Five minutes later he heard a knock on his door. Still angry, he braced himself for an argument. The sight of Doctor Ellis disarmed him immediately.

'You certainly have a way with people Richard,' she said, leaning against his doorway.

Nash pinched the top of his nose and sighed. 'I know, that was foolish. It just winds me up sometimes how they act like they're running the show.'

'Well, let's face it, that's not far from the truth. Look at it from Yuridov's perspective. He's outnumbered and has enough of his own work to do. He'll step in if necessary but would rather we sorted out our own differences.'

'You're right. I'll go and see Velasquez, try to clear the air.'

Ellis smiled and made to leave, then turned with one hand on the doorframe. 'Look on the bright side. At least you don't have to spend all day with them. They're under a lot of pressure. If you play your cards right they'll start arguing among themselves soon and will forget you're even here.'

'Now that would be good. I swear I could murder them sometimes. I'll speak to Gabriel but will keep my head down for the next couple of days, or I might do something I'd regret.'

The second day of the lunar sunrise was another busy one, particularly for the Lunarsol team. Although an expeditionary mission with a skeleton crew, the hope was that proving the concept of solar harvesting would lead to operations on a far greater scale. All were desperate to get the project delivering as soon as possible.

'Okey-dokey, let's see what's on the shopping list today,' said Lonnen, settling his slim frame into the driver's seat of the large mining rover. 'Aluminum for the arrays. The charts reckon there should be a sizeable deposit about four clicks away. Let's go see.'

Wrycroft, the bigger of the two men, had already completed the safety checks and indicated to Lonnen they were set to depart. The sunlight disappeared as they moved deeper into the large crater beside their base and they were thrown into darkness. It would take another few days for the sun's slow ascent to reach this far. Bright headlights automatically came on.

'Estimated power consumption up two percent,' announced Wrycroft. 'We'll get six hours on site before we need to turn back, more if we're careful.'

'Let's not risk it. Do you want to be the one to call Jonathan for a tow back to base?'

The creases in Wrycroft's skin from years spent outdoors deepened as he smiled at the thought. They had plenty of people on Earth telling them what to do but Jon Daley was the boss up here. With a dry sense of humour, the concern was more that he'd never let them live it down.

'I'm showing a rocky patch ahead', he answered, absent-mindedly scratching his day's worth of stubble as he scanned the gloomy terrain. 'Turn left twenty degrees and continue on that line for 500 metres'.

'Aye aye, cap'n.' Lonnen looked thoughtful. 'You think Gabe and Nash are gonna sort themselves out?'

Wrycroft winced at the mention of the previous night's

incident. 'It's not just the doc. Gabe seems to be rubbing everyone up the wrong way. He'd better get it out of his system soon or it'll be a long two years.'

'I don't get why he's so uptight,' said Lonnen. 'We're on track, everything's going smoothly. He should be pleased.'

'Probably frustrated,' replied Wrycroft. 'He's gagging to get that first cell up and running. Maybe things'll improve now we've more room.' The astronauts had initially been confined to the landing module while the base was constructed. Tough inflatable shells had been positioned before three manoeuvrable 3D printer robots covered them in a protective layer of regolith, the dust and rock found on the moon's surface. Life had become more comfortable as the structure grew and they'd been able to move in. 'We're past the rough patch. You can turn thirty degrees to starboard now and that'll take us straight to the hotspot.'

While the two miners drove deeper into the crater, Gabriel Velasquez set off in a smaller lunar buggy in the opposite direction. He glanced at the two robots still working on the base. The third had been repurposed and was finally being used by Cheng to construct the cells that Velasquez would soon be moving into position. Then the main objective of harvesting solar power for transmission back to Earth could begin. That would be a big day indeed, and Velasquez was determined to make sure they didn't fall behind. The non-mining crew were becoming an annoyance, sapping their resources. The robots were a perfect example. He watched as one of them slowly climbed another laboratory, gradually encasing the inflatable in regolith. Velasquez shook his head. This had always been the plan, and he knew he shouldn't be so discouraged, but he was eager to push on and disprove the sceptics by exceeding the predicted yields.

Back inside the base Yuridov and Daley were running through the current status report with NASA.

'Ok, moving on to maintenance,' came the voice of Henry Heffer, NASA's chief communications officer, or Capcom as he was known to the crew. An astronaut himself, he was able to communicate clearly and concisely with the team on the moon. Moreover, they trusted him to always have their back. Heffer would liaise directly with NASA, ESA, the Russian agency Roscosmos and their corporate colleagues at Lunarsol, giving the astronauts a single familiar contact and sparing them from enduring too many meetings.

'You're scheduled to run full diagnostics tomorrow on the secondary Oxygenator, H_2O reclaimer and CO_2 filters,' Heffer continued. 'However, as Lab Three is ahead of schedule we're thinking you can hold off until that pod's online. You'd only end up having to redo the tests anyway.'

'I concur,' replied Yuridov. 'Primary and secondary systems are functioning perfectly so the risk is minimal. I can spend the time finalising the site survey for the gym pod.'

'That's what we thought,' said Heffer. 'Jon, I take it you're in agreement?'

'Fine by me,' said Daley. 'The sooner those robots complete the build the sooner Cheng can have them.'

'Okay, good. That's it from me. Anything else to report? Everyone happy?'

Daley and Yuridov looked at each other. Since this was a voice only call Heffer couldn't see Daley give a small shake of his head. Yuridov nodded in agreement. 'All's well here, thanks.'

'Excellent,' replied Heffer. 'I'll let you guys get on. Houston out.'

Daley made sure the line was disconnected before speaking. 'No sense letting them know tempers have been a little frayed lately. We'd only have to go through extra counselling which is the last thing my boys need.'

'Da,' agreed Yuridov. 'We can sort it. Maybe I'll have a

word with Richard while your team are out.'

'Lydia said he was going to keep a low profile and crack on with his work. He'll be hidden away in his lab with his beloved Petri dishes. He can be a single minded son of a bitch sometimes but he knows his stuff.'

'I'll keep an eye on him. Can you ask your guys to go easy for a bit?'

'Will do,' replied Daley. 'They're big boys, I'll make sure they behave. Okay, I'm going to see Cheng and find out how the solar cells are progressing. Buzz if you need me.'

Daley took a couple of slow bounds over to the coffee machine, made two cups and took care to ensure the lids were firmly secure. Carrying drinks in low gravity took some getting used to. He left the command centre and set off for the four pods that made up the Lunarsol manufacturing wing. Raw materials were refined into the base elements before moving to pod two where precision equipment produced basic monocrystalline silicon wafers. The apparatus was in full flow but with no sign of Cheng Daley continued to the third pod. This one was cleaner than the previous two, and he had to don additional overalls before entering.

Here the silicon wafers were transformed, before passing through to the final assembly area where they were fixed in larger panels that Velasquez would place out on the surface.

'Brought you a coffee,' called Daley as he approached. 'How's it going?'

'Jon, don't bring liquids in here,' Cheng said wearily. 'This place needs to stay as sterile as possible. It's hard enough keeping the dust out.'

Daley paused and half turned, unsure whether he should retreat with the drinks.

'They're here now,' said Cheng, looking awkward at having admonished his boss. He took one of the cups and placed it carefully on a desk. At one metre sixty-five Cheng was the shortest of the astronauts, noticeably so when standing next to Velasquez and Wrycroft. What he lacked in height he made up for in muscles, not that strength was an issue here with everything weighing a fraction of what it would on Earth.

'Everything's running smoothly,' reported Cheng. 'We've three batches of the unrefined silicon wafers. Pod Two is already working on the fourth. I've just loaded batch three into the texturing process to reduce their reflectivity. Batch two is in the diffusion furnace receiving their phosphorous coating. And over there the silicon nitride is being applied to batch one. Only a couple more stages and they'll be ready to move next door.'

'Any issues?' asked Daley.

'Not really. I've set the carriers between stations to move slower than they would on Earth. No sense bouncing them out of line. Once they're loaded everything's been tickety-boo. I'm running quality control at each stage and performance has been spot on.'

'Fantastic, great job Sying. Make sure all the data's on the server so the folks back home have something to look at.'

'It'll be easier once I get that second printer. I need it next door constructing the frames or we'll fall behind very quickly.'

'I know, I know. There's too much research going on in this place, it's hampering our work. Can't be helped, we needed them to get up here. Do the best you can, okay?'

After inspecting pod four, where little was happening, Daley continued down the access passage directly to the laboratory wing. The connection provided an alternative escape route in an emergency, but also had the small advantage of giving him a shorter journey to complete his round trip.

He rejoined Yuridov who was alone in the control room checking the air quality in each pod. Daley spent the rest of the day completing paperwork and monitoring the three Lunarsol employees out on their EVAs. As the afternoon progressed one or two of the other astronauts came and went, usually to grab some food or a drink, but otherwise it was a normal day.

Closing his laptop, he went to sit with the two Russians. Medvelev, waiting for his laboratory to be constructed, had drawn the short straw and was still based in the landing module. He'd been speaking in his native tongue but switched to English when Daley joined them. Only the NASA and ESA astronauts had learned Russian during their training and Daley appreciated the gesture.

Medvelev continued to describe one of his experiments. Daley quickly lost comprehension and was relieved when the rest of his team appeared. Wrycroft and Lonnen had hit the jackpot and had brought back enough aluminium for two arrays. Velasquez, back from his site, had helped them unload before they called it a day.

Ten minutes later a freshly showered Ellis joined them. Everyone had had a productive day and it wasn't long before they were all laughing and enjoying the relaxed atmosphere.

'Where's Doctor Nash?' asked Yuridov a little later.

Lonnen and Velasquez both groaned. 'Be nice,' said Ellis smiling. 'He's probably lost track of time, I'll go check.'

The seven remaining astronauts idly watched her go. Wrycroft casually examined his fingernails, while Cheng leaned back and stretched. Lonnen leaned over and poked him in the side, ruining his enjoyment of the yawn and causing the others to laugh.

'Son of a –', said Cheng, chuckling along with the others. 'You wait, I'll get y –'

He was cut off by a shout from the direction of the labs. Daley and Yuridov were quickest to react, jumping up and running out, closely followed by the others. They arrived at the open door of Lab Two to find Ellis leaning over Nash who was lying on his back in a puddle of water.

She was frantically trying to administer CPR. Yuridov grabbed an emergency defibrillator from the wall and powered it up as he skidded to her side. It was already clear they were too late. Nash was dead.

2

The grey estate car pulled up outside the rundown block of flats. Switching off his engine, Detective Inspector Tom Blake put both hands on the steering wheel and peered into the darkness. The nearby streetlamps had been smashed by vandals, but the night was clear. The moon was particularly bright and he could even see a few stars, a rare sight in the city. He sighed then turned to face the occupant in the back seat.

'I'm breaking a lot of rules bringing you to a crime scene. Touch nothing. Say nothing. If my boss finds out you were within a hundred metres of this place she'll lock me up. Understand?'

Two small eyes stared straight back at him, contemplating these demands, before finally responding.

'Yes, Daddy.'

'Good. Put your hat on, it's cold out.'

'Ok.' Olivia thought for second, then added 'Daddy? What's a crime scene?'

Blake sighed again. This was a bad idea. 'I'll show you, come on.'

He stepped outside and opened the rear door. His five year old daughter hopped down to the ground and took hold of his hand. They walked to the flats and Blake pressed the buzzer for number 52. The name Chappell was neatly written next to it on white card beneath a plastic cover.

'Hello?' came a crackly voice on the other end.

He leaned in closer to the intercom. 'It's Blake.'

'Come on up, sir. Fifth floor. The lift's out of order I'm afraid.'

'Of course it is,' Blake said to himself as a buzzer sounded and the door clicked open. A light flickered on as the two of them stepped inside. Blake glanced around the foyer, noting a couple of lightweight buggies, some cardboard boxes and a broken chair. A notice optimistically asked residents not to leave items in the hallways, next to a handwritten sign telling people 'Do NOT throw dogshit out the windows'. Blake decided he'd rather not know what had pre-empted that one.

Walking past the abandoned possessions he paused at the bottom of the staircase. 'Right, Livvie, we're going to play a game. How many stairs do you reckon to the next floor?'

She stood there looking at them disappear round the corner after the first half a dozen. 'Um. Twenty?'

'Let's find out.'

They counted their way up to the first floor. 'Eighteen...nineteen...twenty!' they said together, laughing as they got to the landing. 'Amazing, well done. I bet you can't guess how many there are to the second floor though.'

'That's easy,' Olivia replied confidently. 'Twenty again.'

'Same again? Are you sure?' She nodded emphatically. 'Let's see if you're right shall we?'

He almost made it to the third floor before the game

wore off and he had to carry her. Still in his arms, Blake walked down the corridor until he reached the right door.

'I mean it Livvie, you have to be a really good girl now. You mustn't touch anything, just sit quietly and afterwards we'll go for a hot chocolate, sound good?'

He took a moment to get his breath back, then knocked twice on the door. A uniformed constable opened it, startled by the sight of his superior carrying a small girl.

'Evening Christian,' said Blake. 'Olivia, this is Constable Morgan. Constable Morgan, this is Olivia, my daughter. Slight childcare issue,' he added sheepishly.

The younger man grinned. 'Of course, sir.'

Blake bent down so his daughter could reach the floor and pointed her towards a chair against the wall. He wished he'd brought a colouring book to distract her but there hadn't been time. Emily was so much better at that side of things. He felt around inside his pockets and found a notepad and a pen. Handing it to Olivia he suggested she do a drawing then turned to Morgan.

'What have we got?'

'Armed robbery, sir. A bookies on The Wells Road just after ten this morning. We've a suspect in for questioning, but he didn't have any cash on him and isn't saying a word. We think he handed it off to Chappell sometime today so we've brought him in too. They've been associated in the past. No money here either though. We don't have much to hold him with so he'll likely be released shortly. I've been through the place and found nothing. I was hoping you might come up with something.'

'Don't get your hopes up, it's been a long day.'

Blake looked around the room. Everything was exceptionally tidy, certainly more than his own house. The coffee table had a photography magazine and a couple of books neatly stacked in one corner. Blake noted the titles. A Disreputable Scandal and Balkan Poetry Today. Otherwise the surfaces were clear. He called Olivia over and picked her up so he couldn't be accused of leaving a child alone in a suspect's flat, then went through to the bedroom.

Again, everything was spotless. The duvet and a sheet were neatly in place on the large double bed, and three cushions were placed delicately on top. A chest of drawers had a few picture frames on, and beside the bed was a small unit with a lamp and a single book, The Trunk by Claire Seagrave. A solid old wardrobe was the only other furniture.

'Does he have an alibi?' Blake asked.

'Says he didn't leave the flat all day.'

Blake opened the wardrobe.

'That's not very nice,' said Olivia.

'Mmm?' Blake said, only half paying attention. 'What's that Livvie?'

'He's got a dog. I saw a basket in the kitchen. It's not very nice that he hasn't taken him out all day.'

Blake looked at Morgan. 'A dog?'

'Yes, sir. A German Shepherd. It was here when we took Chappell in for questioning. Constable Harker took it to the animal shelter for safekeeping until Chappell is released.'

'That's a big dog to be inside all day. Are they even allowed pets in these flats?' As he said it he thought back to the sign in the foyer. Maybe Chappell was the cause of the complaint, although given the cleanliness of the flat it didn't seem likely.

'Doubt it, sir, but that doesn't stop some of the residents.'

'Maybe he employs a dog walker. Is he mobile?'

'He looked fit enough to me. Once he accepted there was no choice he stormed out saying –' Morgan consulted his notebook. '"Let's get this over with then" '. He glanced at Olivia. 'Words to that effect anyway, sir.'

'So he's a healthy guy with a big dog who claims he hasn't left the place all day,' Blake said as he walked back into the lounge. 'Sounds unlikely to me. Especially as he clearly likes to keep the place spotless. Unless he's managed to train it to use the bathroom I'd say he's not being entirely truthful.'

'Yes, sir.'

'Get his shoes off to forensics. They'll be able to tell if he's been out. Netham Park's closest, see if you can get any CCTV.'

They were interrupted by a knock on the door. Morgan opened it and Blake's heart dropped as Detective Chief Superintendant Stella Whiteley walked into the room, wearing a long, yellow coat and carrying a black woolly hat. She was known for turning up during investigations but Blake would have chosen any of his other cases to be scrutinised over this one.

'Sorry, guv. Emily got stuck at work and I'd just picked Olivia up from school when the call came through.'

Olivia looked nervously up at her father, missing the withering look he was currently receiving from his boss. Blake's face turned red. This was going to mean a proper bollocking.

'Don't worry about that now,' Whiteley informed him, much to his surprise. 'Something's come up, we need to go. Can you arrange a babysitter?'

'Er, yes, Emily will be home by now, I can drop Livvie off on the way.'

'I'll follow you, we can drive up together.' She nodded to Morgan then turned and left the flat. Blake raised an eyebrow then followed. He paused in the doorway, looking at a packet of dog poo bags on a side table.

'How often do you reckon they empty the dog bins round here?'

'Dunno, sir. Not often enough probably.'

'Get someone to check them out. If he's savvy enough to know the council's timetable he might have hidden the cash in one of them.'

'Will do, sir. Shame my shift's just finished, I'll have to get one of the other lads to do it.'

Blake smiled. 'Don't blame you. Make sure do it tonight though. Okay, you,' he said, turning back to Olivia. 'A hundred stairs wasn't it? How many can you manage on your own this time?'

Whitely didn't say anything on the journey, other than telling Blake she knew very little and it would be best to wait until they got there. He didn't push her, but when they arrived at a building on the outskirts of Didcot with the European Space Agency logo above the entrance his curiosity was instantly aroused.

A tall, athletic looking man was waiting for them in reception. 'Formalities first, I'm afraid. Would you mind looking into this camera?' He pointed a lens towards Whiteley and tapped a few keys on his computer and handed her a pass, then repeated the process for Blake. 'All done. This way please.'

He led them down a wide corridor, his shoes clicking loudly on the hard surface as they walked, then swiped a pass and led them into a conference room. Its only occupant, a smart middle aged woman with auburn hair falling a few centimetres below her shoulders, looked up and greeted them.

'Chief Superintendent. Inspector. Thank-you for coming out at this hour. I'm Janet Higgins, the Programme Director for the Helioselene Mission. You may have heard of it?'

Blake glanced at his boss then back to Higgins.

'The moon colony, of course. Nine astronauts aren't there, including one of ours? It's a joint undertaking with several other countries to farm solar power. It was in the news often enough when they first went up.'

'Yes. They've been there four months, setting up the base and starting their work. Some are aligned to the commercial side who, let's be blunt, are the ones paying the bills. Others are there for research, including as you say our own astronaut, Richard Nash. Until today, that is.'

Blake raised an eyebrow and waited for Higgins to continue.

'Doctor Nash was found dead in the early hours of this morning our time. It's unclear how he died. Everyone has been very quick to defend their own astronauts of course, and all have offered to head up the investigation into Richard's death, but he's a British citizen and official protocol states we should be the ones to lead on this. Which is where you come in.'

Blake looked again at Whiteley. 'You're kidding,' he said. 'Why me? I mean, I know I've led a few murder enquiries but they were all, well, local issues. This is a bit outside my jurisdiction.'

'Not anymore,' Higgins replied. 'It's true, we have good people within the British Space Agency who are very familiar with Nash, his work and the wider programme. They're not murder investigators though, and besides, they're too close to this. The military were considered too, with their experience of looking into cases on foreign soil, and the Met Police, but like the military, they're a large organisation and we want to keep this low profile. Your name kept coming up, particularly in light of the McClelland kidnapping when you were with the Met, and even though you might think of your past murder cases as routine the files I've seen suggest otherwise. Plus your degree in aeronautical engineering might help.'

'That was a long time ago.'

'Don't worry, I won't test you on it. You never know, some of it might come back to you. At the very least it may help you ask the right questions. Ultimately, your technical background combined with your reputation both at the Met and in Bristol meant your name moved to the top of the list. The final clincher was that Nash lived in Bath, part of your Force's area. It might not have been where he died but it adds weight to the argument that you're the right person for this.'

'And my other cases?' Blake asked, directing the question at his boss.

'Others can pick them up,' Whiteley said. 'Do a quick handover this evening but from tomorrow we'll set you up here.'

'Here?' asked Blake looking around.

'We have offices in a science park on the outskirts of Bristol,' Higgins replied. 'You can base yourself there if you prefer, although I expect you'll want to visit us here in Harwell at some point. There are a lot of experiments which you may need to review. They're almost certainly irrelevant, but you might find a link between Nash's death and something he was working on. We haven't ruled out accident but that will be up to you to determine.'

'I don't suppose there's any chance we can fly a coroner up there?' Blake asked. 'Without access to the body this won't be easy.'

'It won't be. No, we can't fly anyone up there. It takes months to prepare a launch. We can't fly him back either, at least not yet. The entire crew would have to come home and the mission aborted, and given the commercial nature of the operation that's not going to happen. Not until we understand more about what happened anyway. Your hands are tied I'm afraid.'

'That might work in our favour,' Whiteley pointed out. 'If they came back they'd scatter to the four winds and we'd have a hard time getting to them. And if we do solve it, the extradition process could take years. Keeping them all in one place might not be such a bad thing.'

'What about the astronauts themselves?' asked Blake. 'Do they get a say in this?'

'They do,' said Higgins. 'The crew can evacuate if a majority vote to return, for whatever reason. In reality, if two or three chose to leave then Flight Control would evaluate the situation and in all likelihood abort the mission. In normal circumstances,' she added.

'Let's assume they're staying where they are for now,'

Blake said. 'Is there some way I can talk to them?'

'We have video link to the base so yes, you'll be able to interview the astronauts. Going back to your question about a coroner, there are medics among them. The problem is, we can't ask one of them to perform the post mortem in case they were involved in Nash's death. The odds are too high that we'd end up asking them to cover their own tracks.'

'Okay. No body. No post mortem. The suspects all several hundred thousand kilometres away. Different organisations of multiple nationalities all with their own agendas.' Blake shook his head in bewilderment. This was not how he'd imagined spending his evening. 'How big is my team? This'll need a lot of manpower.'

'Sorry, that's off the cards too,' said Higgins. 'We can't risk this getting out. The public cannot know, not yet. You can choose two or three of your officers to support you but that's it. Already too many people know about this so time is critical. You'll have full jurisdiction and, we're assured, full cooperation from every party. You'll probably need to visit some of them in person so a private jet will be at your disposal. We'll do all we can to support you but I appreciate this is an unusual and difficult case. Can we count on you to help us, inspector?'

Blake took a quick look at Whiteley before replying. Now wasn't the time for a flippant remark. 'Yes, of course, we'll get to the bottom of this Ms Higgins.'

'Thank-you. I'll arrange a briefing for you and your team here at 10am tomorrow with Frank Maddix, the ESA Flight director. Now, if you'll excuse me, I need to update the senior operations team.'

They shook hands and stepped back outside. The athletic looking man who'd led him in was waiting.

'I'm Danny Brown. Welcome on board.' Now that Blake was officially running the investigation Brown was far more informal than when they'd first arrived. 'Bureaucracy around here can be a bit of a challenge. I'll be on hand to try and make things as smooth as possible. Those passes will let you into your office in Bristol. Your room will be ready by the time you get there, with laptops giving you access to the ESA network. I'll be based there too in case you need anything. You also have full access to this floor here but the rest of the building remains off limits.' He led them back to the entrance. 'I liked Doctor Nash, inspector, he was a good man. Anything I can do to help you on this just let me know.'

'You knew him well then?'

'Yes, of course. He's worked here for years. A lot of his training took place elsewhere but this was his base. He has an office upstairs where he planned a lot of the research he's been working on.'

'I'll need access to that room too then.'

'I'll get it cleared.'

Blake thanked him and they stepped outside into the cold November evening. He took a deep lungful of fresh air and tried to make sense of all the information swirling around inside his head. 'Insane,' he muttered under his breath.

'I know,' agreed Whiteley as they walked back to their car. 'And for some reason they seem to think you're the best we have. I'm not sure they're right. Don't think I've forgotten about that little stunt with your daughter earlier. They seem determined to have you though, which in itself makes me suspicious. A part of me can't help wondering if they want us to fail.'

'Thanks for the vote of confidence, ma'am.'

'Don't get arsey. I'm just saying, keep an eye on everyone, including Higgins. There could be more to this and we don't know who we can trust.'

'This feels like career suicide.'

'Just try not to do anything to embarrass us. Any thoughts on who you want on your team?'

'Jim and Kathryn, definitely, and if I'm allowed then I'd like Phil Palmer too.'

'I'll get them assigned.'

Blake opened the car door and looked back at the building. 'Beats sifting through bins of dogshit I guess.'

'What?'

'Never mind. Come on, let's get back. I've a feeling tomorrow will be a busy day.'

3

The unmarked police car pulled up outside the ESA office shortly before ten o'clock. Jim Hamilton eased his bulk out onto the kerb first while Blake came round from the other side. They'd travelled from their headquarters in Portishead together and were met on the pavement by Kathryn Bennett and Phil Palmer who'd arrived shortly before them.

'Thanks for getting here so quickly,' Blake said, greeting his colleagues.

'The chief called personally, said it was urgent,' Palmer replied. 'What's this all about?'

Blake glanced around to make sure they wouldn't be overheard. 'Possible murder. Details are sketchy at the moment but I'm told it certainly looks suspicious. Victim is a fifty year old male, body discovered yesterday evening. We'll be briefed inside now. Oh, and you may have heard of him. Dr Richard Nash from the moon colony.'

Bennett's mouth dropped open in surprise and Palmer

let out a whistle. 'Wowser,' he said.

'It's all classified, obviously. The four of us, and DCS Whiteley, are the only ones who know from our side. Let's keep it that way, okay?'

He led them into the building where Brown met them and took photos of the three new arrivals. He quickly typed in their names and produced the passes. 'Follow me please,' he said. Brown led them down the corridor, past the conference room Blake had visited in the early hours, before taking them up a short flight of stairs. The walls were adorned with pictures of space, from the International Space Station to colourful star clusters. Blake admired the beauty of a couple of them, although whether they were some far distant nebula, a pulsar, quasar or some other astronomical phenomena was lost on him. He was already getting the feeling he was going to learn a lot on this case.

Several doors led off the corridor on the first floor. Knocking on the third one along, Brown didn't wait for an answer before opening it and leading the team inside.

'Dr Maddix, this is Detective Inspector Blake and his team.'

The office contained a mass of paperwork, although there was a peculiar feeling of organised chaos about it. The occupant exuded a similar presence. In his late sixties, wearing a creased burgundy shirt, his top button undone and a stained tie pulled down slightly, he had the look of someone who didn't particularly care about his appearance.

'Call me Frank,' Maddix said, coming round from behind his desk to shake their hands. 'Terrible thing, terrible.'

'I'll be outside if you need me,' Brown said, closing the door behind him as he left.

'Thank-you for seeing us,' Blake said once they were alone. 'I understand you're the flight director for the mission?'

'One of them, yes,' replied Maddix, shuffling back between his desk and a side table strewn with papers and dropping wearily into his chair.

Blake sensed that Maddix wasn't quite ready to discuss Nash yet so kept the conversation light as he tried to put the flight director at ease. 'So, you were involved in their journey to the moon?' he asked.

'No, no. It's a common misnomer. I didn't have anything to do with the launch – the flight, if you will. Not as it was happening at any rate. My Russian colleagues took the lead on that aspect. It's a bit of a misleading title. My role is more to do with the lunar base itself. I manage a team of flight controllers whose job it is to make sure the site is operating safely. The title is more of a hangover from ISS terminology. That's the International Space Station by the way. We tend to use the same names to keep it simpler for everyone.'

'Ah, I see,' Blake replied. 'Was it a surprise that ESA were included on this venture? Seats must have been at a premium.'

'They were, yes. I'd say our chance of being represented was as good as anyone's though. Space exploration is very much a collaborative business these days. The base is a British design, and whilst that isn't enough to have guaranteed us a seat, there are plenty of other contributions we've made to the overall project. Both intellectual and financial – we matched the funding provided by NASA and Roscosmos. I have to confess though it was an exciting day when Richard was named as one of the crew.'

'You knew Doctor Nash well then?' Blake asked, seeing his opening.

'Very well, yes. In fact, I know his father William from way back. Young Richard sometimes came along to various events and always showed a keen enthusiasm for anything to do with space. I was very pleased when I saw he'd been accepted onto the astronaut programme.' He looked sadly into distance for a moment, then added 'I'll visit William and Deb later today, break the news to them.'

'One of us will accompany you for that,' Blake said. 'Please let me know when you plan to go.' Maddix nodded absent-mindedly. He was clearly still struggling to come to terms with what had happened.

'It must have been a shock to hear of his death,' Blake said gently. 'Sorry to ask, but can you tell me anything about it?'

'There are more questions than answers at the moment, I'm afraid,' Maddix replied, massaging his temple. 'He didn't show up for dinner yesterday evening. That's not in itself unusual, it's not a formal meal where they all eat together or anything. No one had seen him all day though so Doctor Ellis went to check on him. That's when she discovered his body.'

'Have you spoken to Dr Ellis personally?'

'No, this is all second hand knowledge. From what I gather she found him on his knees with his head inside a fish tank. The assumption is that he drowned.'

'Drowned?' Blake asked, taken aback. 'On the moon? In an environment with no water? Forgive me but don't you find that a touch bizarre?'

'Yes, I suppose it is when you put it like that. It's an extremely hazardous environment and there are any number of potentially fatal scenarios the astronauts could have been faced with. We do everything we can to anticipate these things, to reduce the risk and to train them how to avoid such dangers. You're right though, drowning wasn't one of them.'

'Is there any way this could have been an accident?'

Maddix shook his head. 'Extremely unlikely, I'd say. Nigh on impossible in fact. The tanks Richard was using were very small. The base is well equipped and is exceptionally efficient at capturing and recycling the water they do have. It's hoped that ice deposits suspected in their vicinity will be mined for fresh supplies, but at the moment it's still a rare and valuable resource to them. The tanks would have had the bare minimum for the fish to survive. I can't think of any way Richard would have inadvertently ended up face down in one of them. Besides, if by some bizarre sequence of events he had accidentally fallen in, it would hardly have been difficult to lift his head out again. No, inspector, in my opinion this was most definitely not an accident.'

*

Once Maddix had finished giving them an overview of the mission and a brief taste of Nash's experiments, the two cars took Blake and the others back to their new office on the outskirts of Bristol.

'Where do we start, sir?' Hamilton asked as he closed the door to their large investigation room. Even though, at fifty-two, he was the oldest of the four detectives, he was comfortable serving at the rank of sergeant and had never had the ambition to take the inspector exams. Happily deferring to Blake in the team hierarchy, Hamilton preferred to, as he put it, avoid all that management nonsense and get on with the real work. They made a good team and had completed several successful assignments together since Blake had moved to Bristol.

Kathryn Bennett, with her long dark hair tied back in a ponytail, had also worked with Blake and Hamilton on a number of cases. Originally from Halifax, she'd started her career in the West Yorkshire Police until she transferred to the Avon and Somerset Constabulary five years previously when her boyfriend had been offered a job in the area. The relationship hadn't lasted but she'd settled in well with her new force and was now an established member of the team.

Phil Palmer had grown up on a rough estate in the south of the city. Skilled in computers, with a naturally inquisitive mind and hard working parents, he'd managed to avoid getting drawn into any of the gangs in his neighbourhood. As a teenager he'd successfully navigated the fine line between maintaining his independence and staying in with his school friends, many of whom were now on the wrong side of that line. He'd developed a natural diplomacy when handling volatile situations, which were frequent. Somehow he hadn't even alienated them when he'd signed up to join the Police force, a rare career choice for a black kid from his area.

Blake looked at all three and was pleased he had them with him. He still felt they were woefully underpowered for such a high profile case, but couldn't deny he had the best people he could have hoped for. As much as he might complain to his boss about this assignment, and despite his initial reservations, he knew he was already hooked. There had never been anything like this before.

'Ok. Let's keep it simple to begin with. We've got eight suspects. It seems a fairly safe assumption no-one else could have done it, and it sounds like we can rule out accidental death. Suicide seems unlikely too. I want a photo of each of them stuck to that wall over there.' He gestured to the long bare wall running the length of the room from the door to the window. 'We're going to have to get to know everything there is to know about this lot. Let's do a basic profile on each then start getting into more detail. I want face to face meetings set up with all of them over the next couple of days, and we're going to have to speak to colleagues, family, friends, you name it. You'd better all bring in an overnight bag, just in case. There might be some short notice travel needed on this one.'

The three of them indicated their agreement. They'd all worked high profile cases before and were used to the demands such jobs could bring.

'Jim,' Blake continued. 'You get the initial profiles written up. I want a summary in one hour. Kathryn, can you find out how we go about getting some kind of live feed to the base, and what the availability of the crew is. I know we've been given full access but no sense storming in and, for want of a better word, alienating them. Make polite enquires about when the least inconvenient time would be for them which won't intrude too much on their work.'

'They're still working?' Bennett asked.

'I don't know,' Blake replied. 'I'm told a flight home hasn't been agreed yet so while they're still up there I imagine they'll be keeping busy. We'll have to ask them.'

He turned to the youngest member of his team. 'Phil, you've got Nash. What's his background, what was he working on, what was he like? Remember, his death isn't public knowledge yet so you're going to have to tread carefully when you start digging around. That goes for all of us. The shit'll hit the fan when the news breaks and I don't want any of us to be the ones responsible for that. This'll get a whole lot harder once the press are involved so let's make the most of it while we can. I hope you didn't have any other plans for the next few weeks.'

They shook their heads. A thought occurred to Blake who made a mental note to phone DCS Whiteley later. 'Right, you make a start,' he said. 'I need to make a couple of calls so let's catch up in an hour.'

He watched the three of them turn to the empty desks and pick one each, then turned and left the office. He bumped into Brown in reception.

'Any chance you could rustle up a kettle?' he asked. 'We're going to be putting in some long hours in there.'

Brown had a slight conspiratorial twinkle in his eye that Blake liked. 'Well, it probably goes against several health and safety rules, sir, but I'll see what I can do.'

Blake thanked him and stepped outside, momentarily shocked by the cold air as it bit into his skin. He was going to have to make sure they all escaped the claustrophobia of their room. It was too easy on an investigation like this to pick up unhealthy habits and he wanted his team to stay alert. He glanced both ways then decided to head off to his right, walking briskly to the end of the building to keep warm. He crossed the road and found himself at a small pond with a jetty. Skirting around the edge he found a bench where he sat and called his wife to let her know a big case had come up and he'd be late home. Then he called Whiteley to ask if she could get a fake investigation team set up.

'Why?' she asked.

'So that when the news invariably breaks, they can deal with the media while my team are left alone to get on with it. The last thing we need is the distraction of performing for press conferences every five minutes. Besides, with my boyish good looks they never take me seriously anyway.'

'Fair point. Apart from the good looks bit, obviously. Alright, I'll authorise it. Anyone in particular you have in mind?'

'If you can swing it then Mary Phillips at the Met would be perfect. I've worked with her before, she's good with reporters. I'll have to provide her with updates but she can handle the baying hordes. Better than I would, that's for sure.'

'We'll have to get agreement from Janet Higgins at ESA but I don't see it being a problem. How's it going otherwise, settling into your new digs?'

'It's a bit spartan at the moment but that'll change. I've definitely worked in worse places.'

After ending the call Blake sat on the park bench and contemplated his next move. Deciding it was worth the risk, he brought up Facebook on his phone and quickly tracked down a distant university friend, Shaun McHugh. He sent him a message apologising for the approach out of the blue, and asking if he was free to meet up some time soon. A minute later McHugh replied, sounding surprised but pleased to hear from him. They swapped a couple of messages, agreeing to meet at McHugh's office the following morning.

As Blake sat there he felt a few drops of rain beginning

to fall around him. He pulled his hood up and watched the drops land on the path. How much we take for granted he reflected. Would the astronauts miss this sort of thing? They must, he decided. Sure, they'd have the excitement of weightlessness and countless other new discoveries, but sooner or later they'd surely start to long for simple acts of nature such as raindrops falling on a path. They'd be stuck indoors for weeks at a time. Even going outside would feel reasonably oppressive in their uncomfortable spacesuits. They'd have known that of course, and to some extent prepared their minds for their new environment, but Blake wondered if anything was different that they hadn't anticipated. Perhaps that could be one line of enquiry when he spoke to them.

He looked up at the clouds. The rain had got heavier while he was lost in thought and a big drop landing on his cheek snapped him out of his daydreaming and brought him abruptly back to the present moment. Time to head back and get started.

*

Palmer looked up and grinned as Blake let himself back into the investigation room, lifting his mug in acknowledgement of their new facilities. Blake saw a table in the corner with a brand new kettle and a selection of mugs laid out on it. He wandered over to make himself a cup and was pleasantly surprised to find a tin full of biscuits. A water dispenser had been positioned next to it, with two spare 20 litre bottles under the table, and next to that a fridge in which Blake found not only milk but a selection of sandwiches. A bowl of fruit sat on top.

'Oh, he's good,' Blake said as he helped himself to a biscuit. 'Okay, how are we doing?'

He walked over to where Hamilton had stuck eight photos spaced out along the wall. The others joined him.

'So, what we have is essentially two separate groups,'

Hamilton said. 'There's some overlap on certain roles, and I'm told the guys on the ground made a huge effort to get everyone to gel, but ultimately there's no avoiding the fact they're up there for different reasons. First, we've got the five employees of Lunarsol, the private company which pretty much defined this expedition. Without their capital there would be no lunar base. Or at least, there wouldn't have been one for several years.'

'Yes, I remember the publicity when they launched,' Blake said. 'They want to install solar panels on the moon, collect the solar energy then beam it back to Earth.'

'Is that even possible?' Palmer asked.

'That's the gist of it,' Hamilton replied. 'Got to admit the technicalities go over my head a bit but I'll try to get to grips with it later.'

'The concept is surprisingly simple,' Blake said. 'They'll convert the energy into a microwave laser then transmit it to receivers dotted around the Earth. Those in turn will feed the energy directly into their grids.' They all looked at him. 'Er, did a module on electrical engineering at uni,' he added. 'Carry on Jim.'

'Right. So, we've got these five – Daley, Lonnen, Velasquez, Wrycroft and Cheng.' Hamilton tapped his pen against each of the photos in turn as they walked along the wall. 'All involved in the commercial side of the operation. They're busy mining the raw materials, making the solar panels, preparing the sites and so on.'

He continued to the remaining photos. 'Then we've got these three, or four if you count Doctor Nash. The scientists. Ellis, Medvelev and the base commander, Yuridov. You might think of these as your traditional astronauts. One American, female, obviously, and two Russians, both male. The latter are also the pilots. The whole trip was reliant on Russian spacecraft and although they only needed one pilot for that, the Russians insisted on two of their guys being included. As with everyone up there, they're high achieving, multi-taskers, so now the taxi service is complete they're running an assortment of experiments and studies. So is Ellis, the only NASA representative and, until recently, Nash.'

'Only one person from NASA?' Bennett asked. 'Seems odd doesn't it?'

'A little, but with limited seats and a Russian rocket they couldn't throw their weight around too much or they'd have risked being cut out altogether. I'm guessing from a political standpoint they were satisfied that with Lunarsol involved the majority of the crew are from the States even if they're not part of NASA.'

'And like Maddix said, NASA's funding matched ESA's and the Russians so they have no greater claim to a seat than either of those,' Blake added.

'Of the five Lunarsol employees,' Hamilton continued, moving back to the first set of photos, 'four are American, although Velasquez and Cheng are first generation after their parents moved over from Argentina and Beijing respectively. This whole trip is a bit of a PR machine. Cheng is partly a nod to foreign relations with the Chinese, and his role includes linking into their state media. The same goes for Velasquez, with South America and also Spanish-speaking Americans.'

'And the fifth?' asked Blake.

'Wrycroft's Australian. He has a military background, but that's not unusual. It's a common route into the astronaut programme. He also has a PhD in geology and is leading on the mining side of things. Comes from a family of miners apparently.'

'Good work, Jim,' said Blake, looking along the eight faces staring straight back at him. 'So, one of these is our killer.' He held their gaze for a few seconds then turned to Bennett. 'Kathryn, any joy finding a webcam or something so we can talk to them?'

'Oh, we can do better than that. We've been set up with an interview room next door, complete with high definition widescreen giving us direct access to a private area in the lunar base. When they were designing its layout the boffins figured the astronauts would need a quiet space away from the others. If they had any personal issues or just wanted time with their families they'd want somewhere they couldn't be overheard.'

'Perfect,' said Blake, involuntarily picturing the Big Brother diary room. 'Day a hundred and twenty on the lunar base and Richard Nash has got himself killed.'

'It's not quite as intrusive as that,' Bennett said. 'At one point multiple live feeds to various parts of the base were considered but ultimately rejected. The risk of hackers accessing them and seeing something confidential was seen as too big a risk, but the main reason was the sanity of the crew. Having their every movement filmed and analysed was deemed a step too far. They already have to go through a number of intimate tests, but turning them into twenty-four hour laboratory rats was too much.'

'So, no chance of a quick open and shut case with video footage of the murder then,' said Blake. 'If it even is a murder.'

'Not this time I'm afraid. However, I did speak to Brown,' continued Bennett. 'He's given me the itineraries of the entire team – work schedules, rest time, exercise routines and so on.'

'Excellent. So, now we know where they all were at the time of Nash's death.'

'Unfortunately not. The logs show what they were meant to be doing but it appears things gradually got more relaxed over the last few months so we can't be absolutely sure people were where they were meant to be. And without an exact time of death the window is too big. It's tightened up now of course, so from this point on we should find it more reliable, but don't get your hopes up on the alibi front. I'll go through it to see if we can eliminate anyone but the data is limited so I'm not hopeful.'

'Ok, can't have everything. At least we now know when

we can get hold of them.'

'Exactly. I haven't directly approached any of them yet, as I was curious about which ones might come to us.'

'Come to us?'

'Well, yes. They're all aware that Nash was probably murdered, so I imagine they're now nervous they might be next. All but one of them anyway.'

Blake thought about that for a moment. 'If you were the killer, would you get in first with your police interview to appear afraid for your own safety, or would you think that's too obvious and play the double bluff, waiting to be summoned?'

'Or play the triple bluff and go first knowing that we'd know the killer wouldn't do that,' Palmer said. 'It's all mind games at this stage, I'm not sure we can second guess what they're thinking.'

'No. Still, I'm curious now to see who contacts us first,' Blake said. 'Let's introduce ourselves. Kathryn, can you draft a short message to the crew letting them know we're investigating Doctor Nash's death and that their safety is our first concern. Say we'd like to chat to each of them and could they let us know when a convenient time will be. We can cross check their replies against their known free time, but Phil's right, we can't read too much into it at the moment. Ok, thanks Kathryn. Phil, anything on Nash?'

Palmer pinned a ninth photo to the wall. 'A fascinating guy. He grew up in Salisbury, excelled at everything academically as you'd expect. Got into Millfield, the sporty school in Somerset where he went on to do rugby, swimming and hockey to county level. It was in the sciences he really stood out though, which led to Cambridge and a double first in Natural Sciences and Chemical Engineering. After that came two years at the Sorbonne in Paris, with a Masters in Materials, whatever that means, and additional modules in Philosophy and Robotics. From there he moved to MIT in the States to do his PhD in Biological Engineering, but while there also took a couple of courses in their Aeronautics and Astronautics department. That was his route into the European Space Agency where his academic career, athleticism and fluent French all helped with his application. He's subsequently added Russian to his repertoire as part of his astronaut training.'

'Well, I bet we all feel quite inadequate now,' said Blake.

'He's good looking too,' added Palmer. 'One metre eighty-five tall, athletic build, super fit as you'd expect for his profession. Generally speaking, not the kind of guy I'd put down as a suicide risk.'

'Anything else?'

'From what I gather, although he was sociable enough leading up to the launch he decided the mission duration was finite, and he wanted to maximise the time spent on his scientific work. He avoided social media where possible and rarely gave interviews. All in all, he kept a fairly low profile, which is good for us as it means no one's noticed him missing yet.'

'Let's hope that lasts. Good work, all of you. Ok, let's start building up the profiles on our suspects. We can take two each. Full history, and start a list of contacts we might need to interview. Their boss, doctor, school friends, school enemies. Anyone who might give us a bit more of an insight into their personalities. We'll do what we can by phone but will need to visit some if only to get out of this place, so I want numbers and addresses where we can reach them. We've been promised a private jet to meet these people, it'd be a shame not to use it. Once we start speaking to them it won't be long before people start asking questions about Nash, so I want to have covered as many of them as possible before this gets out. Everyone happy?'

Blake received a couple of 'Yep's and a thumbs up from Hamilton in reply. They broke and the others all naturally migrated to the kettle while Blake picked out a desk and logged into the laptop he'd been given. He blew out his cheeks and exhaled slowly, gathering his thoughts. A mixture of trepidation and excitement stirred inside him. This might be an impossible case but he couldn't wait to get started.

4

The astronauts all gathered in the common room and took seats around the central table. Yuridov had called the meeting to discuss what had occurred, and what people wanted to happen next. The mood was sombre, and Yuridov noted a lot of them were avoiding eye contact.

'Ok, thanks for coming,' he began. 'This is obviously a difficult situation and we need to decide what to do. I'll start with the facts. Doctor Nash's body was discovered by Doctor Ellis yesterday evening. We attempted to resuscitate but without success. It appears he had been dead for some time. Mr Daley and I took some photographs of the scene and have sent those to Control. We left the body in situ overnight but today, following confirmation from Houston, we've moved him to Maintenance Pod Two. That's a temporary measure in case an autopsy is required, which I suspect it will be, and we need easy access. Once that's been decided and completed, he'll either be moved to the descent vehicle and will accompany us back to Earth, or more likely he'll be buried here. Either of those options require an EVA so won't be rushed. We don't have the facilities to perform a cremation so burial is the only option.'

'We'd leave him here?' asked Ellis quietly.

'You all know the protocols. An accidental loss of life has always been a very real possibility, and we've all taken part in the 'death simulations'. The team on the ground are going through all of that now, deciding how to break the news to Doctor Nash's family and so on. If there had been no suspicious circumstances then we would bury the body, hold a memorial, then get back to work. Doctor Nash knew that and agreed to those conditions before we left. As we all did.'

'We never dwelt on the possibility of it actually happening though,' replied Ellis. 'The full protocol states all options will be considered if such an event were to happen. I know the likely outcome is as you've said but it was never set in stone.'

'No, it wasn't. And it would appear this was not an accident, so the existing protocol is redundant anyway. Last night I asked each person here if you knew anything about what had happened, and the answer was no. We've had a night to reflect on it since, although I doubt any of us got very much sleep. So, I will repeat my question. Do any of you know anything about the circumstances regarding the death of Doctor Nash?'

The response was unanimous. Velasquez, often the most vocal of the crew, voiced the loudest denial, while Cheng as usual was quieter. Ellis, as the only female, was clear, as was Medvelev who replied in Russian and Wrycroft with his Australian accent. Daley and Lonnen were equally firm in their replies. The answer was no. Yuridov remained impassive, already fairly sure he knew what the responses would be.

'Ok, I'll confirm your replies to Control for the record. If any of you wishes to speak to me in private then please do.'

No one answered, although a couple of them shifted positions in their chairs. The atmosphere was uncomfortable, and despite exchanging quick glances most tried to avoid looking at each other for any length of time.

'An English policeman has been assigned to investigate,' continued Yuridov. 'Doctor Nash was British so they have jurisdiction in the matter. He will be interviewing each of us in turn. You are free to discuss your work or anything else which comes up.'

'I've spoken to Mr Lomax,' added Daley, addressing the Lunarsol team. 'He's given the same instruction. No subject is off limits, and he'll be assisting this detective with his enquires to try to help him resolve this as quickly as possible.'

'What's there to say?' asked Lonnen. 'We dig for minerals. We dump them at the base. There's not a lot else to tell him.'

'Be that as it may, he'll need to speak to you and will be asking questions, not just about your work but about life here and your relationship with Doctor Nash. It goes without saying that you may, or perhaps I should say must, speak candidly.'

'This isn't going to look good for me then, is it?' said Velasquez. 'You all know we had a falling out the other night. This detective will think I'm guilty before I've even opened my mouth.'

'Don't worry,' drawled Lonnen. 'I'll tell him none of us like you, it wasn't just Nash.'

There was a brief pause before Wrycroft laughed, soon followed by the others. They momentarily forgot the tragic events of the last twenty four hours and the atmosphere in the room lightened slightly.

'Could be worse, I suppose,' said Velasquez. 'At least I have an innocent face. Cheng clearly looks dodgy, and Eric's descended from convicts so will obviously be top of this policeman's list.'

'Dunno about that mate,' replied Wrycroft, overstressing his accent. 'Mr Daley here is the only one of us with a beard. He clearly has something to hide.'

'Yeah, acne,' said Lonnen, prompting more laughter, and causing Daley to scratch his chin self-consciously.

Yuridov brought the room back under control. 'Yes Velasquez, you're a suspect. So am I, so is everyone else. And rightly so. Initial indications are that one of us is a murderer.' He let the sentence hang in the air for a moment. 'The important question now is, was Doctor Nash the only target or is anyone else at risk?'

The rest of the crew shifted uneasily again. The same thought had kept most of them awake the previous night, and there were uncertain looks amongst them as they considered who of their colleagues might now be a threat.

'There's no way of knowing,' said Ellis. 'Not yet. Not until someone figures out the motive.'

'Quite,' replied Yuridov. 'It could have been a personal issue, or it might be something much wider. Or who knows, maybe this will somehow turn out to be a huge mistake and Doctor Nash killed himself, perhaps by accident. We don't know. The point is, what do each of you want to happen next? The obvious answer is to abort the mission and return home. That's completely understandable. I'll go round the room and ask each of you the question. Do you want to abort? Mr Cheng?'

The American, seated directly to Yuridov's left, considered his answer. He looked at the others around the table, then back down at his hands resting in his lap.

'No,' he said finally. 'I came here to do a job. A job that's not done yet. Personally, I can't think of a reason why anyone would want to hurt me so I don't feel threatened. Besides, I can take care of myself. I'm not comfortable knowing it's likely someone round this table has done –', he paused, searching for the right word '– what they did, but I don't think we should pull out until we know more.'

'Noted,' said Yuridov. 'Mr Wrycroft?'

The big Australian didn't hesitate. 'No. Same reasons, including being able to handle myself. Anyone comes at me they're gonna regret it.'

'There's no need to go all alpha-male on us,' quipped Lonnen. 'If you're scared it's ok to say so.'

'I'll show you scared,' said Wrycroft, pretending to throw something at Lonnen.

'It's a no from me too,' added Lonnen looking back at Yuridov.

Velasquez, sat next to Wrycroft, considered his response. 'I just want to see if this works. We're close to having our first array ready. Once that's in position and generating power we can send a small amount of it back home, and it'll mean the whole thing hasn't been a waste of time. I can't leave yet.'

'Thank-you. Ok, Mr Daley, how about you?'

'The unofficial steer from Lunarsol HQ is that it's business as usual until we find out more. They can't force us to stay, but there's a lot riding on this. A replacement crew is feasible but, aside from the cost factor, they're still in training as they're not scheduled to take over for another twenty months. If we go back now this place will be mothballed until they're ready, which'll have a knock on impact for sponsors and could potentially jeopardise the whole project. I haven't spent the last four years of my life on this just to see it fail so soon. I'm staying.'

'Alright. That's the Lunarsol team all in. Doctor Ellis, Commander Medvelev, don't let that influence your decision. The corporate pressures on successful solar harvesting have no bearing on the work you're doing. Please feel free to speak candidly.'

Medvelev shrugged his shoulders. 'I do as ordered,' he said in his thick accent. 'We're military, we follow chain of command. If Roscosmos wants me to stay, I stay.'

'And if Roscosmos say it's up to you?' asked Yuridov.

'Then I stay. This is once in lifetime experience. If we

go home they won't let us come back.'

Yuridov turned to Ellis. She rubbed her face with both hands. It was clear she'd been crying, and with an obvious lack of sleep was looking exhausted. 'I'll stay,' she said quietly.

Yuridov considered pressing her for a more reasoned response but decided to let it go. 'I won't reply to Control yet. Each of you take some time to think this through and if you change your mind come and find me privately. There's no shame in wanting to go back.'

No one said anything. 'For now, we stay then,' concluded Yuridov. 'Jonathan, from a Lunarsol operations perspective I assume there's no change to your schedule?'

'That's right,' said Daley. 'We're a scratch for today but Doctor Nash's experiments were completely independent from our work so there's no impact on us from here on.'

'That leaves the lab schedule,' said Yuridov. 'Control will have to put together a new plan for the three of us,' he said, looking at Ellis and Medvelev. 'No doubt we'll pick up some of Doctor Nash's work. It may mean some of our own less critical studies are downgraded. They'll decide that. I'll let you know as soon as I hear.'

'I'll send a list to NASA of what I consider my priorities,' said Ellis. 'Some of my work would still be able to continue with less frequent supervision.'

'Of course. I think that covers everything for now. Does anyone have any questions?'

No one did so the meeting was ended. Dealing with the fallout of Nash's death meant there wasn't time for the Lunarsol crew to go outside on their scheduled EVAs. Cheng headed straight for the manufacturing pods. Lonnen went with him, ostensibly to support the production line but more so he could get away from the communal area and keep himself busy. Daley and Wrycroft chose to analyse the area surveys, attempting to derive more detail on which minerals might be available to them. Velasquez decided to head back to his quarters.

'It's best to keep busy, right?' said Ellis to the two remaining Russians. She pushed herself away from the table and stood up. 'I'll be in the lab. You can tell this policeman I'm available to talk to him whenever he likes.'

Yuridov acknowledged the offer and as she walked away he turned to look at Medvelev. They held each other's gaze in silence for several seconds before nodding almost imperceptibly, then both rose and went back to their tasks.

5

The four detectives spent the rest of the day glued to their screens. Every now and then one would get up and collect something from the printer, or stick something to the wall below one of the photos.

They'd allotted suspects alphabetically, with Blake picking up the last two, Wrycroft and Yuridov. He took a sip of tea then decided to start with the Russian. Perhaps not unexpectedly everything was perfunctory. His school results were excellent, as were the scores on his university entrance exams. Everything he did subsequently on his route to becoming a cosmonaut was consistently impressive. There was little warmth in his official profile. It simply contained an efficient, though nonetheless exceptional set of academic accomplishments. Blake sighed. Getting to know Yuridov's character from his Russian state files was a futile task.

'How's it going with Medvelev?' he asked Hamilton.

'Hopeless,' came the reply. 'All I've got is a list of exam

scores and postings in the Russian military. Even that's vague, it doesn't go into any detail on what he actually did. There's nothing in here at all about the man himself. I've not got onto his lunar experiments yet but so far the historical stuff isn't telling me anything we couldn't have guessed.'

'Same here,' said Blake. 'We need a different approach for these two. Ask around, see if anyone at ESA knows either of them through the Helioselene programme, or any previous missions. There were plenty of team building exercises, someone must be able to tell us what they're like.'

'Will do.'

Blake saved the few notes he'd made then switched to the Australian. He soon realised this would make much easier reading. Wrycroft's journey from an outback mining town to becoming one of the first people to walk on the moon in nearly fifty years was remarkable. A childhood growing up in the harsh reality of a Queensland mining town sounded idyllic in the way Wrycroft had presented it on his Lunarsol profile. The freedom it offered meant he'd learned to fly by his early teens, and had been forced to learn mechanics even before that.

'You soon learn to become resourceful when you find yourself stranded in such an inhospitable land,' he'd written. His father had spent his life in the mines at Moura and Wrycroft's bedtime stories were of chasing seams of coal deep into the Earth's crust.

He'd breezed through the mandatory exams at school and a desire to see more of the world took him to Macquarie University in Sydney where he got a place studying chemistry and geophysics. At first the over-populated campus had seemed daunting but he quickly adapted. Blake imagined Wrycroft's size and rugged outdoors look wouldn't have hurt. Other guys would no doubt have been wary of taking him on while the girls probably couldn't get enough of him.

He'd joined the university flying club which in turn led him to the Royal Australian Air Force who sponsored him through his PhD after he'd come top in his degree. Blake noticed with interest that Wrycroft's father had died in an accident at the mine while his son had been in his final undergraduate year, and wondered if that had contributed to the young man's drive and ambition to achieve more with his own life.

After university, twelve distinguished years of service followed, until he left the air force and took up a civilian role at a diamond mine in Western Australia. 'Why move out west?' Blake jotted on his notepad. Was it a desire for new experiences or reluctance to follow the family tradition, he wondered. He tapped his pen on the page and tried to think of what might have led him down that route. It was probably as simple as it being where a job had come up, but it would be something to ask when they spoke.

Whatever the reason, that had been Wrycroft's route into Solarcorp. The parent company had mining interests all over the world, including Western Australia where they were also starting to experiment with a solar farm. Wrycroft had taken a job at one of their mines, but by then was senior enough that he got involved in the wider aspects of the company's interests. At first the solar venture was small scale but Wrycroft expanded it hugely, implementing the system of building the solar panels in situ from the raw materials found locally in the land. When the parent company founded Lunarsol Wrycroft had been an obvious choice to join the team.

Blake stood and arched his back. He'd been sat still for too long and suddenly felt a desperate need for some fresh air. He walked over to Yuridov and Wrycroft's pictures and pinned a sheet of his handwritten notes underneath each one.

'I need a break,' he said, turning back to face the others. 'Make sure you guys don't stay staring at your screens in here too long, ok?'

'You used to run a bit didn't you, sir?' Palmer asked.

'Did for bit, yeah. Hard to stick to a routine in this job and I've let it slip lately. You?'

'Got into it the last year or so. A mate and I have just managed to get places for the London marathon next year so I need to do more. Let me know if you want to go out some time.'

'Blimey. Rather you than me. I'd be up for joining you on a couple of short runs but you can do the longer ones with your mate.'

'Nice one. I'll bring my kit in.'

'I might join you, if that's ok?' said Bennett.

'Of course, the more the merrier. Jim, what about you?'

Hamilton looked down at his bulging stomach and made a show of brushing off some biscuit crumbs. 'Nah, you'd only hold me up. Give me a bell when you're in better shape and maybe I'll let you tag along.'

Blake grinned, told them not to forget to take a break, and stepped out of the room. He toyed with heading home. A family dinner then helping put the kids to bed sounded appealing, but he knew he'd be too distracted to be any sort of company. The background on Yuridov was unfinished and he didn't want to set a bad example to the rest of his team by doing anything less than a thorough job on it.

It was only 5.30pm but darkness had fallen and the streets were still damp from the earlier rain. For a moment Blake just stood there and watched the traffic building on the ring road. The freezing autumn weather was invigorating, and as he contemplated what to do next his phone started ringing.

'Good evening, inspector. It's Janet Higgins. Thought I'd check in, make sure you're settled. Have I caught you at a bad time?'

'Not at all,' Blake replied. 'Just stepped outside for some fresh air.'

'I can see why people take up smoking sometimes. It's

good to have an excuse just to stand up for a change.'

'I never was cut out for office life,' Blake admitted. 'The best ideas always come when you're away from your desk.'

'I quite agree. Archimedes didn't get his Eureka moment while poring over textbooks.'

Blake smiled. 'Maybe if I get really stuck I should just take a bath.'

'Worth a try,' Higgins replied. 'Are the offices ok? Got everything you need?'

'Yes ma'am. Brown's doing a great job of looking after us, and we have access to all the systems. The Russians look like they might be the trickiest to crack, their files aren't particularly helpful. If you can suggest anyone we can talk to I'd appreciate it.'

'Leave it with me. I'll set something up with Roscosmos.'

There was a pause on the line and Blake wondered for a moment if she was still there. 'I'm still finding this hard to believe,' she said finally. 'Richard has been such a huge part of my life, all our lives, for the last few years. We all know there are risks with space travel but the worst bits were over and everything had been going so smoothly. His death came out of nowhere and we're all reeling.'

'Sounds like he was a popular guy.'

'He was, for the most part. He could be a little prickly sometimes but only because he was so absorbed in his work and passionate about what might be achieved. I don't understand why anyone would want to... to...'

'Harm him?' offered Blake. 'It's hard to see a motive at this stage, but I'll keep you up to date with our progress.'

'Thanks inspector. I'm glad we've got you on this, it needs an outsider's view. We're all too close to it. You'll have to excuse me though I'm afraid. I'm on my way to brief the Security Council at Number Ten.'

'Good luck.'

'You too,' Higgins replied then hung up. Blake turned

and started walking aimlessly, heading away from the science park. The building they'd been placed in was on a new build development with little else to see or do nearby. He realised it could be all in his head, but apart from the busy road it all felt very desolate, cut off from the rest of the world. Perhaps that would help him get into the minds of the astronauts he thought ruefully. He felt very isolated all of a sudden, the enormity of the high profile case weighing on his mind. He glanced across to the other side of the roundabout in front of him and saw a pub. The Folly. Yep, he thought to himself, sounds about right.

He stifled a yawn and rubbed his face. The passing traffic seemed noisy as the tyres went over the wet ground, and the headlights in the blackness somehow made him feel exhausted. The early start was catching up with him, and he knew that going back in to stare at a screen wouldn't help. He saw an X48 bus approaching with City Centre written on the front. Sod it, he said out loud. He'd end up doing a half-arsed job on Yuridov if he went back in now. A few people were already waiting at a nearby stop, so when the bus pulled in and the doors opened Blake jogged up and jumped on board.

At the back a group of teenagers were talking loudly and throwing chips at each other so he turned and went upstairs. He dropped into a seat then realised across the aisle another young man was also eating some. As the smell wafted over him Blake realised how hungry he was. An image of his local chippy popped into his head. He sighed. There was no point fighting it. He texted Emily. 'On way home. Fish and chips?'

A minute later he received an emoji with hearts for eyes.

Blake let himself into his house and, leaving the food in the kitchen, he jogged up the stairs to look in on the children. They were sound asleep. He kissed them tenderly on their foreheads and stepped back out, gently closing the door behind him. He smiled as he saw the flicker of a candle coming from the bathroom. He went in and knelt down to kiss Emily as she lay in the bath, casually tracing his fingers up one side of her body.

'Need a hand?' he asked as he gently cupped her breast. She smiled as she lifted his hand off and placed it on the side of the bath.

'Go and get me a drink,' she ordered. 'Then you can tell me all about this big case of yours.'

'It's classified.'

'I don't care.' She flicked bubbles at him. 'Now go!'

'Yes ma'am,' he said for the second time that evening.

He returned a few minutes later with two glasses of red wine. The food was warming in the oven, but the sight of his wife lying naked in the bath had made him forget his hunger.

'I mean it. This is serious. You can't say a word to anyone,' he said, handing her one of the glasses. 'Anyone.'

'Ooh, intriguing. Who is it? Someone famous? Politician, sports star or singer?'

Blake paused, but more for effect than because of any doubts about discussing the case with his wife. He knew it was inappropriate and broke many rules, but he'd often found chatting to Emily about a case helped.

'Richard Nash.'

It took a second for the name to register then she half sat up to look at him. 'The astronaut? Dead?'

'Yep.'

'Bloody hell,' she said, leaning her head back and sinking down into the water again.

'Bloody hell,' echoed Blake quietly, taking a sip of his wine.

'Murdered?'

'Looks that way. We don't have a lot to go on yet but yes, it's definitely a possibility.'

She went silent for a minute taking it in. This wasn't the first time she'd heard her husband talk about a death on one of his cases, but the enormity of this one wasn't lost on her.

'Sophie's been doing a project on the moon,' she said finally. 'They watched the landing at school a few months ago. All the kids are fascinated by it, even more than the grown ups.'

'Well, they're going to be talking about it again all over the country once word gets out.'

'I wonder what it's really like, living up there?' Emily pondered. 'It must be quiet. And lonely.'

'And not as glamorous as you'd think. I was looking at some footage of their living quarters earlier. The separate pods have small touches to personalise them but deep down they all have that same clinical feel. There's nothing particularly homely about any of it.'

'I'm not sure I could handle that.'

'It's not all bare walls. It looked like there have been a few attempts to add a touch of colour here and there. There's a print in one of the rooms of a small frog sat on a leaf. Reminded me of our honeymoon.'

'Perhaps that's it. A lack of green. Maybe it drove one of them crazy.'

Blake looked around him. Their bathroom was the complete opposite, with vivid-coloured children's bath toys everywhere. The thought of somewhere more calming didn't sound so bad right now.

'I bet everything up there was ruthlessly thought through by committees and focus groups,' he replied. 'There's nothing random. No variety. I dunno, maybe they need that. There's enough things that can kill them instantly, some monotony might be quite appealing.'

'Doesn't the moon make people here go a bit mad sometimes?' Emily asked. 'Maybe the effect is even worse if you're on it. Perhaps one of them's turned into a werewolf.'

She rolled onto her front as she contemplated this. Blake reached over and stroked her ankle, sticking up above the bath. 'I don't know about that,' he said, admiring her backside. 'But there's a full moon I do approve of.'

*

'Tom! Good to see you!'

Blake stood and grinned as Shaun McHugh barrelled across the reception area. McHugh shook his hand then leant in for a clumsy hug cum backslap. He was a little surprised at how much hair Shaun had lost in the last, what was it, ten years. Jesus, where did that time go.

It had taken Blake an hour and a half to drive to the MoD base at Boscombe Down where his old university friend now worked for a subdivision of the European Space Agency. After a thorough security check, which had even included mirrors being used to look under his car, Blake had been allowed to go no further than the guarded reception area.

'Come on, I'll give you the tour. You can leave your car here and jump in with me.'

McHugh led Blake outside to his car. 'A Tesla?' commented Blake admiringly. 'Nice.'

'Yeah, it's a company car but I can't imagine going back to petrol now. They feel so, I dunno, antiquated.'

He pulled silently out of the car park and drove deeper into the site, took a right turn then stopped at some traffic lights. Blake peered forward.

'There's nothing coming,' he said, looking around.

He jumped as two fighter jets suddenly burst out of nowhere, passed in front of them and took off, roaring into the sky. He shook his head, smiling to himself as the lights turned green and McHugh crossed the runway. 'Not your average commute to the office is it?' he commented.

A couple of minutes later he pulled up outside a non-descript building and plugged the car into a recharging point. Once inside he took Blake up one flight of stairs and into a small office with a view out over the base.

'Thanks for seeing me at such short notice Shaun. Sorry it's been a while.'

'Ah, well, life gets in the way and all that. Make yourself at home.' McHugh gestured to a chair facing his desk while he moved round to the other side. 'Feels a bit formal this, like I'm interviewing you or something. Where do you see yourself in five years time?' he joked. 'I'll take you for a sightsee in a bit, need to get my step count up anyway. We can have a quick chat here first though.'

Blake snorted. 'Your step count?'

'Christ. It's doing my head in, but I'm addicted now. Caroline thought I was starting to let myself go, sat behind a desk all day, so she got me this contraption.' He waved his watch in front of Blake. 'Says I should aim for ten thousand. As if. I'm trying for five though. It's bloody annoying. I catch myself going up stairs one at a time instead of two so I can get a few more in, and the other night I was pacing round the house like a lunatic at ten to midnight as I was a few hundred short for the day. I need help.'

Blake laughed. 'Well, look on the bright side, she could have bought you golf clubs.'

'Dear God. Shoot me now. So, your call has made me very curious. What brings you down this way?'

'It's a case I'm working on, but it's a strange one and I'm not going to make this easy. Pretty much everything about it is confidential, so I'll be asking things without any context, and at the moment will be able to tell you very little. I suspect that will change in a few days, maybe a week if I'm lucky, but for now please bear with me.'

'All cloak and dagger, eh? Well, I'll help you where I can. Fire away.'

Blake paused, considering how best to phrase it. 'It's possibly connected to the Helioselene project. Do you know much about that?'

'Of course. The moon mission to harvest solar power.

They can collect much more up there without an atmosphere to get in the way. It's a play on words. Helios, the Greek god of the sun, and Selene, the goddess of the moon. Any aspect in particular you're interested in?'

'Well, at the moment, all of it. I have a basic grasp of the solar farm side of things – Lunarsol and the mining team and so on. Then there's the other astronauts and whatever projects they're working on. I guess I'm just after a vague sense of how it all slots together.'

McHugh thought for a moment. 'It's all down to Chase Lomax really. He's the head of Lunarsol and is quite the personality. His solar farms on Earth have already made him not only wealthy but massively influential on the renewables lobby. He has huge arrays all over the world, and a few years ago started talking about using the moon to capture solar energy. People were sceptical of course; the overheads would be, well, astronomical if you'll excuse the pun. It's not just the energy side of things for Lomax though. He's become fascinated with rockets and space exploration and all the wonders of the cosmos. I suspect it's more of a pet project to him than anything else, although if it does turn a profit that wouldn't hurt.'

'These billionaires like their toys,' Blake mused. 'Surely a spaceship is too much even for him though?'

'It is. Or I should say, they are. The project flew multiple unmanned missions to drop supplies off in advance of the crew's arrival. You're right though, he couldn't do it alone, which is why he's ended up sharing the base with astronauts from ESA, NASA and Roscosmos. He's technically very smart, obviously, but it's his salesmanship that got this thing off the ground. He went to the Russians and said he was putting together this expedition. Told them NASA and ESA were interested, made them think they'd be missing out if they didn't play a part. Don't forget, Russia never made it to the moon before. Not with an actual cosmonaut anyway.'

'I'd not thought about that,' admitted Blake.

'Yeah, well, the Yanks beat them to it last time and they didn't want to come second again. Lomax needed them more than the other way round but that's not how he played it. They're the only ones with the ability to physically get there. In the end he did such a good job selling them the idea they ended up not just supplying the rocket but contributing to the funding as well. Of course, NASA and ESA wanted in once it became clear this might actually happen. They were falling over themselves to throw money at Lomax in order to get their guys a seat.'

'Couldn't those agencies have done all this without Lomax?'

'They could, yes. And they would have, eventually. They all work together well enough on the ISS, and there's been talk of a combined lunar expedition for years. You know what these big organisations are like though, nothing happens quickly. It needed someone like Lomax to bang their heads together and actually make it happen. He's paid his share too, don't forget, a lot of the funding came from Lunarcorp or their sponsors.'

'Sponsors?'

'Yeah, Lomax's salesmanship again. Look at how much Coke and Pepsi spend on a thirty second ad at the Superbowl, then just imagine what they'd pay to get an image of their products being used on the moon base. They're not the same obviously, carbonated drinks don't go down so well in low gravity, but they came up with a space-friendly version that looks good in the pictures. Lomax got hundreds of product placement deals set up, from watches to toothpaste. Commercialising the whole venture may sound vulgar but it paid for the lion's share. Without it we'd still be a decade away from having a base up there.'

'What do you know about the astronauts themselves?' Blake asked.

'Can't tell you much about the Lunarsol guys I'm afraid, but the other four have been in the space programme for years. I've met Nash a couple of times. He's a smart cookie. Medvelev came here for a few weeks once too.'

'Yeah? What's he like?'

McHugh considered how best to answer. 'Let me show you something.' He stood up and opened the door, gesturing for Blake to go first. As they walked down the corridor McHugh pointed to a photo on the wall. 'That's him.'

Blake looked at the picture, recognising Medvelev from the photo Hamilton had pinned to the wall the previous day. Half a dozen smiling technicians in white coats were flanking the Russian pilot, who was staring impassively at the camera.

'A real barrel of laughs as you can tell,' McHugh added. He continued walking down the corridor. 'We do a lot of simulations here,' he explained. 'Roscosmos have plenty of that for the launch side of things, but we're well renowned for other aspects of the mission once they're on site.'

He jogged down some stairs then led Blake outside. They started walking towards a large structure across the road from the building they'd been in.

'Medvelev was here for a few reasons. Partly he needed to improve his English. It was already good; the Russians are strict teachers. But it was like hearing a textbook being read out loud. Being here gave him the chance to pick up a few colloquialisms and to learn how to relax a bit, to sound more natural.'

McHugh stopped to allow a convertible to pass. 'Probably a pilot,' he said to Blake, rolling his eyes. He crossed onto an immaculately manicured lawn. 'Anyway, Medvelev was also here to look at some of the experiments we're running. He spent a lot of time with Nash going through the ESA objectives for the trip.'

'Why would he do that?'

'Back up, to put it simply. If anything happens to Nash, Medvelev will pick up a fair chunk of his work. So would

Yuridov and Ellis. The experiments wouldn't stop just because one astronaut is unwell or incapacitated. Likewise, Nash had to gain a fairly comprehensive understanding of all of their work in case one of them is hurt and can't perform their tasks.'

'I see,' said Blake. 'Makes sense.'

'Well, in theory, yes, although from what I gather they barely have enough time to get their own work done. Realistically I'm not sure how much they'd be able to take on of someone else's. Let's hope they all stay fit and healthy up there.'

They'd arrived at the other building, sparing Blake any awkwardness in having to reply. McHugh swiped his pass and a security guard let them through after checking Blake's visitor's pass against the system to validate his access level.

'The third reason Medvelev was with us was to practice in here.' McHugh opened a door, holding out his arm dramatically as he presented a cavernous room to his audience. 'Ta da,' he added.

'Wow,' said Blake. Ahead of him was an obviously very deep swimming pool. A variety of space-age looking equipment surrounded it, and mechanical arms extended out over the water ready to move the pieces into position.

'A lot of simulations happen under water,' McHugh explained. 'It's a pretty close approximation of the weightlessness they experience up there. And it helps them get used to their bulky spacesuits.'

Blake grinned. 'I bet that's a lot of fun,' he said. 'I'd love to have a go.'

'Sure, you can if you like.'

'Really?' Blake asked incredulously, turning sharply to look at his friend.

'Yep. All you need to do first is send in your application form to ESA, beat all the other thousands of applicants, and get accepted onto the astronaut training programme. Easy.'

'Git. You got my hopes up then.'

'Sorry. I should warn you it's not all fun and games. Trying to perform complex manoeuvres through thick gloves is almost impossible. They have to put hundreds of hours' worth of time in here. The equipment's not cheap either – it's strictly look but don't touch for the likes of you and me. That's one of the reasons Medvelev left under a bit of a cloud.'

'What happened?'

'He made a mistake. He and Nash were down there simulating an emergency evac. If something goes wrong and they have to get out quickly they can bypass a lot of the gear and all the usual safety checks. Suit up, get the hell out, no messing. Medvelev screwed up helping Nash with his helmet. It could've turned nasty, one wrong move and there's definitely a risk of drowning. It happens, that's why they practice here so they don't make the same mistakes up there. That's not the issue. The problem was he took it badly, blamed the whole thing on one of the techs. It was a heat of the moment thing, frustration tinged with exhaustion, but these guys are usually better than that. It was unfair to pick on the poor lad. Although to be fair to Medvelev it was a bit of a hairy moment. Nash came very close to being seriously hurt, or worse. He took it all in his stride though, smoothed things over once he was out of the water. As far as I know that was the end of it. On the plus side, I hear it brought the two of them closer together. They practiced the exercise again and again after that until they could do it blindfolded. I believe they get on very well now they're actually on the moon.'

'Let's hope so,' Blake said quietly.

6

'All set, sir,' said Brown, poking his head through the doorway. Blake had only been back in Bristol for less than an hour and it was already time for their first video conference with the moon base. The rest of his team followed him out. Blake would lead the conversation but he wanted the others there for this first interview. The situation was highly unusual and when it came to their turn to conduct one of these calls he was hoping the surreal nature of the experience would at least be tempered by being here for this one. Besides, he thought to himself, I don't mind the support myself.

'You've a message from Director Higgins,' Brown informed Blake as he led them into the small conference room next door. 'The jet is being prepared to fly you to meet the general in charge of Russian space operations. I'll accompany you to the airport this evening.'

'Excellent, thanks Danny.' He looked around as Palmer and Hamilton took seats over on the far side of the room.

A small camera pointed at a desk with two empty chairs facing a large screen.

'It's all quite simple really, sir,' said Brown. 'Everything's already scheduled so when your meeting starts the screen will come on automatically.'

'Is there much of a delay?' Blake asked, imagining the conversation was likely to be quite stilted and laborious as the sound and image took time to transmit across the vast distance.

'I believe it's a second or two, sir. It's pretty quick, you probably won't even notice once you're into the swing of it.'

'Really?' Hamilton asked, looking at Brown in amazement. 'That's remarkable. Doesn't seem that long ago you had to wait five seconds just to talk to someone in France.'

'We're getting old though, sir,' Brown replied smiling. 'Things have moved on a bit. I'll leave you to it now. Everything you say is confidential obviously. The call will be recorded and stored in your encrypted folder should you need to refer back to it later, but no one else will have access. Good luck.' He stepped back outside and closed the door behind him. A nervous silence filled the room. Blake glanced at his watch.

'Three minutes 'til blast off.' He placed his notes and a pen on the desk and took his seat. Bennett sat next to him. 'When Doctor Ellis joins us I'll introduce all of you briefly,' Blake said. 'She might as well see the whole team now in case one of us needs to do a follow up call later.'

'I'm not sure she'll be able to see us over here,' pointed out Palmer.

Blake looked at the two men sat against the wall, then at the camera, tilting his head to help gauge if the lens might reach them. The screen suddenly came to life and Lydia Ellis' face appeared, looking back at Blake with a quizzical expression. She angled her head to match Blake's.

'Is everything ok, inspector?' she asked.

'Er, yes, sorry,' Blake replied sheepishly. 'I was just, er, never mind.' He smiled to, he hoped, put everyone at ease. 'Please excuse us, this is the first time any of us have done this. Spoken to an astronaut I mean. In space.' He shifted self-consciously in his chair as he realised how foolish he was sounding.

'Don't worry, you'll soon get used to it. There are a lot of strange things about being here, but talking on a video conference is towards the more normal end of the spectrum.'

'You've done this a few times then?'

'Plenty, on this mission and from your seat, speaking to other astronauts on the International Space Station when I was still on Earth.'

'Ah, of course. Well, let me introduce my team. This is detective sergeant Kathryn Bennett,' Blake gestured to his left. Bennett said hello as Blake went on. 'And, I'm not sure if you can see them, over there are detective sergeants Jim Hamilton and Phil Palmer.'

Hamilton and Palmer leaned uneasily into shot and each gave a little wave to the camera.

'It's good to meet you all. Please, ask me anything. Richard was a good friend and as you can imagine I'm shocked at what's happened.'

'I understand it was you who found Doctor Nash?'

Ellis took a deep breath. Her ash-coloured hair was tied back, she had no make-up on, and she was wearing a simple pale blue jumpsuit with the NASA logo on, but there was no hiding her natural good looks. The sterile surroundings behind her only served to make her presence more vivid. Blake imagined you could put Dr Ellis in any situation and she would naturally command the attention of the room.

'Yes. We usually try to complete our workloads by 8pm. That's Greenwich Mean Time – we stick to a twenty-four hour cycle here. The moon is on such a vastly different rotation the concept of day and night gets distorted. Anyway, Richard hadn't showed up so I went to check he was ok. I assumed he'd simply lost track of time, or was having difficulty with one of his experiments and might need a hand.'

She paused, reliving what had happened next. 'The door to his lab was closed and the light was off. I nearly didn't go in as my first thought was that he'd finished for the day and had gone to his quarters to freshen up. I guess something made me look in and double check. I flicked the switch and there he was.' Her voice cracked as she said the words, and her eyes became moist.

'Take your time,' Blake said gently. 'The more you can tell us the clearer a picture we'll have. Any detail, however trivial it might seem, could be important.'

'Yes, of course.' Ellis paused to compose herself. 'It was so strange. One of the fish tanks he uses for his experiments had been moved from its shelf onto the floor. Richard was on his knees, bent over with his head inside it. At first I thought he must be looking at something, but it was his arms that made the picture look wrong. They were pointing backwards, just hanging by his sides with the backs of his hands resting on the floor by his ankles.' She paused again, looking past the camera. 'The sudden realisation was like being hit by a bus. I think I screamed, I'm not sure. I ran over, nearly slipping myself on the water that was all over the floor. I pulled him out and tried to resuscitate him but it was too late.'

'You believe he drowned?'

'Yes. We haven't performed an autopsy but the signs were all there. His face was distorted, bloated, and had turned blue. His lips in particular. It's possible he was already dead before he ended up in the tank of course, but a lot of water came out of his lungs as I was attempting to revive him which is consistent with him being alive when his head was submerged. He would have swallowed large amounts until his oxygen supply was exhausted.'

'I appreciate you're not a coroner, Dr Ellis, but in your

opinion could this have been suicide?'

'Richard? No. No way. He was passionate about his work and, like most of us, had been driven about becoming an astronaut since he was young. This was the peak of his career and he had so much he wanted to do. I really can't see any reason why he'd want to kill himself. Besides, even if he did there are plenty of easier ways to do it, especially up here. I imagine suicidal drowning is rare. A person's natural survival instinct would take over.'

Blake tapped his pen on his pad as he considered the possible scenarios. 'Were there any signs of a struggle? Any marks on Dr Nash's body or elsewhere in the room?'

'Not on Richard's body. None that I saw anyway. There was one strange thing. His worktop was, still is, covered in foam. Looked like a simple experiment, hydrogen peroxide mixed with yeast and water probably. Perfectly safe but makes a dramatic mess, it's always a popular one to show children how exciting chemistry can be.'

'Any ideas why that would have been there?'

'No, it doesn't make sense. Richard certainly wouldn't have left his workstation like that. I very much doubt he would have even done it in the first place, even if he was doing a video blog for schools. You only do that sort of thing in a classroom or where someone else has to clean up after you, not somewhere you have lots of other important work going on.'

'Curious. Ok, going back to Doctor Nash, could he have hit his head do you think? Knocked himself out and ended up in the tank by accident?'

Ellis thought for a moment. 'No, I don't think so. It would have to be a pretty hard hit to knock him out, and that's not easy in low gravity. If you trip and fall over here it all happens in slow motion. And there was no mark on his head to suggest any trauma.'

'Interesting. Of course, I was forgetting about the weightlessness.'

'Well, we're not weightless. The moon does have some gravity, just under seventeen percent of what you're used to on Earth, so we're not all floating around like we would on the International Space Station. But we're certainly a lot lighter.'

'So it would be no difficulty for someone to pick Doctor Nash up and place him in that position? Even, say, a woman?' Blake had intentionally needled Ellis to see how she reacted.

'As you say, inspector, even a woman,' she replied, not rising to the bait. 'I'm fully aware there are only eight of us up here and any one of us could have done it. Even me. I'm sure it won't surprise you to hear me say I didn't, for what it's worth. Besides, even though I could perhaps have lifted him into that position, I'm not strong enough to have forced him into the tank against his will. He could have easily overpowered me.'

'Someone managed it though,' Blake said thoughtfully. He considered what to say next and looked to his left for support.

'It might help if we can establish the time of death,' Bennett said, subconsciously leaning forwards towards the big screen. 'Can you think of anything which might narrow it down?'

'Rigor mortis had set in, so he'd probably been dead for somewhere between four and twelve hours. Maybe even longer. Conditions here are different to those on Earth and they may have influenced the onset. Usually, with the heart no longer pumping, gravity causes red blood cells to sink, which in turn causes a purplish discolouration of the skin. On the moon that process would take longer so the immediately obvious visual signs are distorted.'

'Ok, thank-you Doctor Ellis,' Blake said. 'So, we have quite a large window of opportunity for the murderer to have acted.'

'You do think this is a murder then,' she asked. 'I keep hoping there's another explanation.'

'I wasn't sure until I spoke to you, but I am now. The light switch. You said the lab was in darkness and you had to turn the lights on when you went in. Nash would hardly have taken the trouble to turn them off before drowning himself. Certainly not if it was some kind of freak accident. No, that's good enough for me to formally make this a murder investigation.' Blake saw the downcast look on Ellis' face. 'I'm sorry,' he added.

She nodded without looking up at him and wiped away a tear.

'Can you describe your movements please on the day Doctor Nash's body was discovered?' Blake continued, keen to keep her talking.

'Yes, of course. I woke at 05:30. I spent half an hour doing a workout in my room then got dressed and came into the common room. That's what we call the main communal area where we eat and have a bit of space to relax. Commander Yuridov was already in there eating his breakfast. I got myself a coffee and a food ration then returned to my quarters to catch up on some mails while I ate it. At around 07:00 I went into Lab One to do my work. I was in there, alone, all day, apart from a couple of short breaks.'

'And was that similar to your normal routine?'

'Yes. I usually stay and have breakfast with the others, although not always. Commander Yuridov and Cheng are both early risers and are often there before me. As it was only Andrei, and he was absorbed in something on his laptop, I just decided on the spur of the moment to head back to my quarters. Other than that it was a typical day.'

'And I suppose no one can confirm you did indeed spend the whole time in your lab.'

'Not really, apart from various communications I had with NASA. If I'd known I was going to need an alibi, inspector, I would have planned something a bit more substantial. As it is, much of my time here is spent alone in the laboratory. It was the same for Richard, and most of the other astronauts. We all have busy workloads, and the very nature of that work means our studies are often solitary.'

'I understand. I'm sorry to have to ask you this, Doctor Ellis. I'm fully aware of your academic credentials and have seen a brief overview of some of the work you're conducting. But, and this is a little awkward, the fact remains you are the only female on this mission.'

'Well spotted, detective,' Ellis replied with a small smile.

'I've done training in that sort of thing,' Blake replied. 'I'm sure this came up from reporters before you left, and probably while you've been up there, but given that murder is often a crime of passion I'm afraid it has to be considered. I'll just come straight out with it. Were you in a relationship with Dr Nash? Or are you in a relationship with any of the other crew members?'

Ellis paused before answering. 'It's a fair question,' she said eventually. 'There's no strict rule against it. Indeed, from a purely scientific perspective, the physical and social aspect of a romantic liaison in space is a serious subject, particularly when it comes to longer missions and the possibility of colonisation of other worlds.'

Blake waited for Ellis to continue.

'I was chosen, I hope, for my scientific abilities, not for the expectation that I might provide any insights into that particular field.'

She paused again, but Blake didn't want to put words in her mouth so waited patiently for her to answer his original question.

'So, whilst not actively prohibited, we were advised that any such activity was strongly discouraged,' went on Ellis, 'although I suspect the people at NASA knew there was a very real chance something of that nature might develop. Which it has. To answer your question, inspector, yes, I'm in a relationship with Gabriel.'

'Thank you doctor. I appreciate the sensitivity of the

subject. Just so I have a clear understanding of everyone's whereabouts, was Mr Velasquez in your quarters when you woke that morning?'

'No.' She hesitated, then decided to add more. 'He was with me the previous evening, but left and returned to his room some time during the night.'

'Thanks. I don't think we need any more details on that right now. Can I just ask, do the other crew members know about you and Velasquez? Or anyone on Earth, at NASA or elsewhere?'

'We're a small team, it's hard to keep secrets. It was inevitable that everyone would find out sooner or later. This makes it sound more official than it is, but we announced it to them just over a week ago.'

'How did they react?'

'Well, boys will be boys. Eric and Chris patted Gabriel on the back, and I imagine he got a bit of stick when I wasn't around.'

'And Nash?'

Ellis thought for a moment. 'He was a bit quiet, but that's not unusual. I don't remember him saying anything at the time. Come to think of it, I vaguely recollect him leaving the room shortly afterwards.'

'And how about your colleagues back on Earth?'

'As far as I'm aware it's only us moon-dwellers that know. I certainly haven't told NASA yet as I'd like to maintain our privacy a little longer. I can't speak for the others but I'm not aware of anyone having gossiped.'

'Well, let me reassure you they won't hear it from me. Unless it ends up having some bearing on the case of course.' Blake decided it was time to change tack. 'Ok, so of our main questions regarding Dr Nash's death, the 'who' remains the biggest unknown. The 'when' could be any time that day or the previous night. The 'where' is almost certainly Lab Two, and the 'how' appears to be drowning although there are some inconsistencies. That leaves us with 'why'. Can you think of any reason, Doctor

Ellis, why someone would want to have done this?'

Ellis didn't hesitate in her answer.

'No.'

Blake waited for more, and when none was forthcoming, he prompted her. 'You can't think of anything at all? However small? It might seem irrelevant now but if there's anything which doesn't feel right it would help us to know it now, if only so we can check up and discount it.'

'I honestly can't think of any reason why anyone would want to harm Richard. Yes, we've all had our moments of frustration with each other. It was harder than any of us expected living in confined quarters while the base was being built, but there was never any real animosity that I saw. If anything occurs to me, inspector, I'll be sure to let you know, but right now I'm still coming to terms with it.'

'Ok, thank-you doctor. I think that covers the immediate scene for now. I'd just like to ask you one last question. How are you holding up?'

Ellis considered her answer. 'I'm not sure. It all feels so unreal at the moment. I think part of me is still hoping this was somehow a terrible accident that can be explained, although deep down I obviously know that's not the case. If you're asking whether I want to come home then yes, a huge part of me does. But then, another part of me wants to finish what we've started. I know that must come across as callous, and believe me when I say I'm deeply upset by Richard's death, but I think he would understand. He was a scientist, and the work we're doing up here is the culmination of a lifetime of study. As horrific as this all is, I'm not quite ready to give that up yet.'

'I sympathise, Doctor Ellis. I think that's all I need for now. Please, do get in touch if there's anything else you think of, or if you have any concerns at all.'

'I will, thank-you inspector.' She reached forward and pressed something which ended the call. Blake was about to speak, but wasn't completely sure if both the picture and sound had been ended. He cautiously put a finger to his lips and indicated they should move back to their investigation room.

'I swear, I'm getting paranoid,' he admitted to the others once they were next door. 'Ok, thoughts?'

'The Velasquez thing is interesting,' Palmer suggested. 'Maybe there's a jealousy factor or some kind of love triangle between the three of them. It could be telling that Nash went out soon after they revealed their relationship. Perhaps it upset him. And, don't forget, Velasquez left her room during the night. Ample time then to see to Nash.'

'Good, yes. Anything else?'

'I find it very odd she can stand being in that place,' Bennett said. 'I get it that she's worked hard to get there, but still, if one of your friends had just been murdered, and you're trapped, a long way from safety with the murderer still at large, wouldn't you want to just get home?'

'It's hard to know, isn't it,' Blake said. 'None of us have ever been in the situation they're in. I can definitely see the fascination with being up there. And as I understand it, it's not particularly clear whether they even have the option of coming home yet.'

'She has a point about the murder itself though,' Bennett added. 'Low gravity or not, there's no way she could have forced Nash down until he drowned. He wasn't just a weedy bookworm remember. What was it? Rugby, swimming? I imagine the training they undergo to become an astronaut means they're exceptionally fit. I just can't see her overpowering him.'

'She was the one who found the body though,' Hamilton pointed out. 'That's always a red flag in my book.'

7

'We are going to rack up a lot of air miles on this trip,' mused Hamilton as he and Blake were escorted by Brown through the private departures hall at Bristol airport.

'And with none of the usual pain,' replied Blake, as they were taken quickly and efficiently past security and led directly out to the aircraft.

'Welcome to your very own Gulfstream G280,' Brown announced reverently. 'Courtesy of Chase Lomax. Lucky buggers,' he added with a grin.

'Lomax?' asked Blake.

'Yes, sir. He's as keen as anyone for this to be resolved so his guys can get on with the solar project. Right from the start he offered us the use of the jet. Just wish I was coming with you.'

Blake smiled at him. 'Don't worry Brown, we'll bring you back one of those Russian dolls.'

'I'll settle for a small bottle of vodka if one happens to fall in your duty free bag, sir. Do svidaniya!' he added as he stepped back from the plane.

Blake and Hamilton walked up the steps and were greeted at the top by a handsome, uniformed man in his late forties.

'Welcome aboard gentlemen. I'm Nick Meyer, your co-pilot on this flight. And your air steward. No frills on this service I'm afraid. Let me take those for you.' He held out his hand and took Blake's travel bag then Hamilton's, turning to stow them in a locker behind him.

'Oh, I'm sure we can slum it just this once,' Blake said, making his way into the cabin and trying not to smile too broadly. This job was getting more surreal every minute. The plane had seating for ten, and even at capacity it would still have been ludicrously spacious.

'Make yourselves comfortable. Captain Berry is just getting us cleared for takeoff so while she's doing that I'll run through the safety briefing.'

They settled into what Blake had to admit was the most luxurious seat he'd ever come across, and fastened their seatbelts while Meyer showed them where the life jackets and emergency exits were. The small audience meant they paid more notice than they might normally have done, but formalities over, Meyer filled them in on the rest of the aircraft's facilities.

'It's six hours to Kazakhstan, and they're six hours ahead of us. We'll land early morning local time and you'll be taken directly to Baikonur Cosmodrome. Captain Berry and I will remain at the airport, ready to fly you out again tomorrow evening. I imagine you'll want to squeeze in a couple of hours sleep but in the meantime, can I offer either of you a drink?'

'Oh, a beer would go down nicely, thanks Nick,' said Blake.

'Make that two,' Hamilton added.

Meyer fetched them both a cold Peroni then excused himself and entered the cockpit.

'Cheers,' said Hamilton, holding his glass up and taking

a swig. 'I could get used to this.'

'Three nights ago I was sitting in a damp shithole all night staking out a flat across the road. Fair to say I never saw the week ending quite like this,' Blake said. 'Might as well enjoy it while it lasts. Cheers.'

*

The following morning, after a twenty minute drive from Krayniy Airport, Blake and Hamilton arrived at Baikonur Cosmodrome. The industrial township was in stark contrast to the open plains surrounding it, and Blake looked on in awe as they passed a huge rocket lying on the back of a train carriage. Their car pulled up outside an ugly brute of a building, where they were greeted by an imposing figure in Russian military uniform. The man, with cropped grey hair, a thick moustache and a stern expression was clearly used to the freezing temperatures thought Blake as he eyed his heavy military overcoat with envy.

'Welcome to Kazakhstan, Inspector Blake,' the man said in English, taking Blake's hand in a vice-like grip. 'I am General Igor Greschenko, director of Roscosmos flight operations. Thank-you for taking the trouble to visit me here in Baikonur.'

'Not at all General. It's me who should be thanking you,' replied Blake. He introduced Hamilton who received a curt nod in reply, then turned to look at the space port. 'This is quite a place to have an office.'

Greschenko glanced at the building disdainfully. 'It's not pretty, but it serves its purpose. I'm usually either in Moscow or at the Mission Control Centre in Korolev. This Nash business may mean the next scheduled launch is brought forward, so I've come here to supervise preparations personally.'

'You must think that's a distinct possibility to have, if you don't mind me saying, someone of your importance

73

overseeing it?'

Greschenko snorted. 'Yes, well, the Americans are looking for any chance to replace us with their own rockets. They've made significant advances in recent years, particularly the commercial operators run by their collection of internet billionaires. They're lobbying hard to take over flight operations to the lunar base. I'm here to make sure that doesn't happen.'

'Ah,' Blake said. 'I see. I was under the impression a launch wasn't possible yet. By anyone. Has that changed?'

'Nyet,' Greschenko replied as he led the others into the building. 'You are correct. The American rockets might be ready but they are untested. Even Lomax wouldn't risk using them yet. No, for the moment we are the only proven option. The next Roscosmos launch to the lunar orbit is an unmanned flight with no surface landing. It is intended to drop supplies only. That's scheduled for two weeks' time, and the rocket is already in position. Over the next ten days it will be fuelled and prepared for lift-off. Completely separate to that is our emergency rescue rocket, a contingency for the Helioselene Project should a critical failure occur and a rescue be required. This is kept ready to launch within seven days. You may have noticed it on your way in.'

'Ah, yes, the one on the train?' asked Blake. 'Surely seven days would be too late if there were a disaster though?'

'The delay is unavoidable, plus it would take a further three days to get there, but that should not pose a problem for the crew on the moon. They have several options if an abort order occurred. The base itself is partitioned so if one part is breached the remainder is still habitable. The landing module can act as a life raft, with enough supplies to sustain the full crew for thirty days. Longer if they ration their food. If all else fails they have the descent rocket.'

'And you need this reserve rocket in case the one they

already have develops a problem?'

'Da,' Greschenko replied as he marched through the building, with Blake and Hamilton struggling to keep pace. 'The problem is not food or living quarters. They can survive for a long time if necessary. A rescue mission is only envisaged if there is a catastrophic failure of both the descent rocket and one of the life support machines – the carbon dioxide regulator perhaps. They have backups of course. Two full systems on the base, plus spare parts for repairs. If those fail there is emergency capability in the landing module but that has a limited lifespan. This is where the rescue rocket comes in.'

'And you think it might be needed now?'

'No. Not for its intended purpose. It was really only thought that a direct meteor hit on the descent vehicle might mean a rescue would be required. That's unlikely, and the base is running to optimal performance. We have an unusual situation though. The death of a crew member in suspicious circumstances was not planned for. If someone decides Doctor Nash's death warrants a manned response then I want to ensure we are ready.'

He reached a door guarded by a young officer who quickly opened it and saluted his General. Greschenko ignored him and walked straight into a sparse meeting room. It felt to Blake like something out of a cold war Soviet film set. A single fluorescent tube flickered slowly to life. Metal chairs and a chipped, poorly laminated desk completed the picture. The officer closed the door, remaining outside, leaving Blake and Hamilton alone inside with Greschenko. He gestured for the two detectives to sit.

'That is not why you are here though, I believe?' he said as he walked round to the other side of the desk and seated himself facing the two detectives. 'You are investigating the remaining crew to find out who was responsible for Nash's murder, yes?'

'That's correct, sir. At the moment all eight of them are

suspects,' Blake replied.

'I appreciate you have a job to do Mr Blake, but I can assure you our cosmonauts undergo the strictest psychological tests before they are passed fit for space travel. There is zero chance that either cosmonaut Yuridov or Medvelev would have carried out this crime.'

'I realise that General Greschenko, and believe me, I don't doubt what you're saying for one moment. But I'm equally sure the same will be said of all the astronauts. I also know extensive profiling was undertaken to ensure the different personalities involved in the mission would gel. As I understand it, that means more than just being able to tolerate each other. The crew members chosen for the trip all displayed an aptitude for proactively supporting other members of the team. I don't imagine that nine humans have ever been more closely analysed before, yet here we are, with a dead body, and all the indications to suggest one of the other astronauts is responsible.'

Greschenko stared back at him coolly, no emotion showing on his face.

'And I don't just mean they may have caused the death by negligence or are trying to cover up an accident,' Blake continued. 'This was pre-meditated and clinical in its execution. So, forgive me, but I must ask you some detailed questions about the two cosmonauts. Their histories, their states of mind while on the moon, in the lead up to the launch and before, going back as long as you've known them.'

'Very well,' said Greschenko curtly. 'Ask your questions inspector.'

'Let's go from the beginning. When did you first meet Commander Yuridov?'

'Our paths crossed many times, probably more than I'm aware of with the various conferences we both would have attended, but we didn't formally meet until we began the recruitment campaign for the 2008 cosmonaut intake. Andrei was, as you might expect, an outstanding candidate.

He'd previously graduated from the Kharkiv Military Aviation School, and had served as a senior pilot for five years. In that time he also studied at the Zhukovsky Air Force Engineering Academy.'

'Yes, I've read his impressive CV, General,' cut in Blake, regretting it instantly when he saw Greschenko's face bristle with irritation. This was clearly a man who wasn't used to being interrupted. Blake hurried on, keen to keep the Russian talking. 'What I'd like to know is more about the man himself. What drove him to become a cosmonaut? Why did he first apply for such a position?'

Greschenko looked at Blake impassively for a few seconds. Blake decided to meet him head on and stared straight back.

'He didn't apply,' Greschenko said eventually. 'We decide who we are going to invite for selection, not the candidates. His service record and academic achievements were exemplary so he was shortlisted and subsequently appointed to the Gagarin Cosmonaut Training Centre. Over the next few years he completed a wide range of training courses and support roles within the space programme. He went on to fly three missions to the International Space Station, the last two as pilot of the Soyuz spacecraft and also as commander of the station. He's a well respected cosmonaut and thoroughly professional. He was an obvious choice to lead the lunar expedition.'

Blake realised Greschenko was determined to only give him the official version of his men's careers. Might as well get this bit out of the way, he figured. 'And Commander Medvelev? Did he follow the same path?'

'More or less,' Greschenko replied. 'He's a little younger of course, so naturally has completed fewer flights. He went to the ISS once before he was assigned to the lunar base. His time up there overlapped with Doctor Nash's as it happens.'

'So I read,' Blake said, unable to hide his irritation that

Greschenko wasn't telling him anything new. 'And he's a well respected cosmonaut too?'

'Of course. I suggest you speak to Commander Jim Brooker and Commander Pete Webb who spent six months on the ISS with Commander Medvelev, but I have no reason to believe he's ever been anything but a good team player as you say, and a popular member of the crew.'

'Even during his training? When he was at the ESA deep dive pool for example?'

Greschenko looked at Blake curiously. 'You're very well informed Inspector Blake. I assume you're referring to the misunderstanding with the support technician?'

'It was more than a misunderstanding from what I heard.'

'It was nothing. Frayed tempers after a long day. It happens. The two men shook hands afterwards and moved on, that was the end of it.'

'Does Commander Medvelev often lose his temper?' Blake pressed.

Greschenko glared back at him frostily. 'No. He does not.'

Blake decided a change of subject might be in order. He didn't want to alienate the Russian or he'd clam up and they would have had a wasted trip.

'Forgive me, General, I didn't mean to imply anything. What can you tell me about the work your men are doing now they're up there?'

'Whatever you like,' Greschenko answered. 'The details of the experiments they're conducting are all publicly available. Both of our cosmonauts are carrying out many studies, in addition to their other roles in the mission. Commander Yuridov was the pilot for Soyuz TP-01. That's the first flight of our new TP-class craft, capable of making lunar orbit. He then piloted the descent module. Once they were on the surface he became Base Commander, ultimately responsible for the entire crew.'

'Even the Lunarsol guys?' Blake asked.

Greschenko snorted. 'Of course. They have their own team hierarchy with Mr Daley as their project leader, but even a man like him knows when to defer to a superior. Commander Yuridov is the most experienced cosmonaut up there, and knows how to run a smooth ship in the hazardous environment they're in. It would take a fool not to accept his leadership, and Daley is no fool.'

'"A man like him"', Blake repeated. 'A curious choice of words, General. Is there a reason you say that?'

Greschenko leaned back and put his hands together, his two index fingers outstretched and coming together at his lips. He gave the impression of a man wondering how much to say, although Blake couldn't tell if it was genuine or whether the whole thing was an act for his benefit.

'Please General,' he prompted. 'I urge you to be frank.'

'Very well,' Greschenko said eventually, sitting forward and leaning his forearms on the desk. 'No, I have no evidence to suggest Mr Daley is anything other than an intelligent, hard-working man who has a reputation for getting results. However –' he hesitated momentarily before going on '– there were rumours. Unsubstantiated, but nevertheless an element of mystery surrounded him.'

'Rumours?'

Greschenko shrugged slightly. 'Minor things for the most part. Overworking the crew on some of his projects, cutting corners on safety protocols. The sort of activity you might get away with on Earth but not what you want in a perilous location such as theirs. The story is he didn't get away with it though. Or at least, he might have but one of his team didn't. There was an incident a few years ago in Botswana, someone died. We looked into it of course when the Lunarsol crew were announced. The official enquiry didn't mention Daley at all. He was apparently several thousand kilometres away on a different site and had nothing to do with it. But occasionally word would come through that wasn't entirely true, that he had been working there and he was, perhaps indirectly, I don't know, but that he was somehow implicated.'

'That's very helpful, thank-you,' Blake replied. 'It's certainly something we'll look into. Have these allegations affected the harmony of the crew do you know?'

'Not at all. I don't believe any of them are even aware. In Yuridov's reports he's always stated how professional Daley is and how well they are getting on.'

'And the same goes for the rest of the crew?'

'The Lunarsol team, yes. And until this week, he's had nothing but admiration for Doctor Ellis. His last report did express some concerns about her demeanour though. Previously she has been a good team member, mixing well with the rest of the group. Since Doctor Nash's death, however, he's noticed some changes in her behaviour. It's probably nothing, simply an understandable reaction to his death and the unusual situation she now finds herself in, but he's going to watch her more closely in the short term.'

'Because he has concerns about her? For her own safety or others?' Blake asked.

'I got the impression it was for her safety, but you'd need to ask Commander Yuridov directly if there's more to it than that.'.

'I will, General. I will.'

8

'What did you make of that then?' Blake asked as the plane lifted off from Krayniy Airport. They hadn't spoken as their driver had taken them from the meeting with Greschenko, each of them lost in thought.

'There's something he's not telling us,' Hamilton replied. 'A Russian general running a spaceport in the middle of Kazakhstan is a bit of a step up from your run of the mill interview, but when it comes down to it there's no difference between him and any number of people we've brought in for questioning. You can feel when something's not quite right.'

'Yeah. The question is, was he just trying to protect his guys or was he deliberately hiding something?'

'Felt like the latter to me. Interesting what he was saying about Daley though. You think any of it's true?'

Blake thought for a moment. 'Probably not. Maybe. Who knows? We'll see if Phil can do some digging. He should be able to track down this Botswana victim's family easily enough. They might be able to tell us more than the official report, especially if it's been hushed up.'

'Even so,' Hamilton said. 'Regardless of Daley's alleged iffy past, there's nothing so far to connect him to Nash.'

'No, but it sets a precedent, shows what he's capable of. If we can find something linking the two of them it'll definitely move him up the list of suspects.'

'What about Ellis? She seemed in control of herself when we interviewed her.'

'Maybe she had a wobble after finding the body. No surprise there, it would shake anyone. Since then she's come to terms with it, or at least, analysed the situation and decided how best to handle it, like any good astronaut would.'

'Hmm,' Hamilton mumbled, sounding unconvinced. 'Still seems a bit harsh to me for Yuridov to report it if it was a simple human reaction to the events. They all must have been shocked by what happened so you'd expect a bit of leeway on that front. Why single her out?'

'Fair question. Maybe she was working on something with Nash and is worried she might be next. She didn't mention anything like that though. I'll ask Yuridov when I speak to him tomorrow. He's first up. Ok, I'm going to try to get some kip, I'm shattered. Night.'

Blake reclined his seat and pulled a blanket over himself. He was asleep in two minutes. Hamilton considered doing the same, but caught sight of the fridge out of the corner of his eye. 'Don't mind if I do,' he said to himself, getting up to fetch himself a beer.

11,000 kilometres away, two men sat quietly in a room listening to the conversation taking place on the jet.

'– should be able to track down this Botswana victim's family easily enough. They might be able to tell us more than the official report, especially if it's been hushed up –'

'Get on to Loveall,' said one. 'The Peppers need to disappear. I don't care if they win a cruise or have to evacuate because of a gas leak. She just needs to arrange it fast. And get me the report from the inquest. I want to see it before Blake does.'

The other man typed a secure message into his phone as he continued listening to the two voices coming over the speaker. They sat in silence until Blake fell asleep. Chase Lomax pondered the conversation he'd just listened to. 'Greschenko is trying to send any suspicion our way. Can't say I blame him. Two can play at that though. See what you can dig up on his two. Make it up if you have to. Ellis too. Your guys must be able to come up with something creative. But verifiable. Don't release anything yet, I want to see everything before it goes out. Let's have something ready in case we need it.'

'You want to send them on a wild goose chase?' asked Lomax's head of security.

'We might have to. The slower this case moves, the better for us. The boys up there need to get Phase One up and running, and we need time to get a relief crew ready.'

'You think they'll be needed?'

'If this detective manages to work out who did it then I think it's inevitable, don't you? They're hardly going to let them stay working up there for the full two years. The Brits will insist whoever it is faces justice. I need any change of crew to be in six months minimum, ideally longer.'

'Maybe we could build a prison cell,' the chief of security suggested. 'Once the culprit is identified they can be incarcerated, pending trial, while the remaining crew get on with their business.'

'Not a bad shout,' Lomax replied. 'It'll be hard sell but let's face it, it's maximum security already. They can hardly run off anywhere.'

'You think one of our guys did it?'

Lomax sat back and put both his hands on the top of his head while he thought about it. 'Who knows. The PR will be easier if not. At least the victim wasn't one of ours.'

He stood up. 'I think I need to meet with this detective Blake. See what you can find out about him too will ya? I know we were sent his official file but I want to know all there is about him.' He looked at his watch. 'There's a crisis call with the joint heads in an hour but I'll do that from the plane en route to London. They can't authorise an emergency launch without my agreement, which they're not going to get. In the meantime you take care of the Peppers.'

*

Blake arrived at his ESA investigation room at 6am the following morning. He'd passed out as soon as his head had hit the pillow the previous evening and had woken early, a bit confused about what time zone he was in but feeling refreshed for the first time since he'd been handed the case. Letting himself into the room he was surprised to see Bennett already there, sound asleep with her head resting on a cardigan she'd folded on her desk. He quietly made two strong coffees and took them over, placing one carefully out of reach so she didn't knock it over. She stirred slowly as she sensed his presence and smelt the drink.

'Morning,' she said sleepily, lifting her head. 'How was the trip?'

He looked at her and grinned. Her unkempt hair and bleary eyes gave her a sultry look that somehow enhanced her features. 'You look well,' Blake said. 'Had a fun night?'

'Oh, wonderful,' she replied deadpan. 'It's been non-stop excitement sat here while you two had to suffer the hardship of your luxury jet. Was it as good as it sounds?'

'Better,' he admitted. 'The flight, admittedly, a treat, but being at the spaceport was one of those dreamlike experiences that years from now I'll still be asking myself if it really happened. Greschenko is a cool one though. It was hard to read him and I'm not sure I'm any the wiser on his two guys. He's given me a few things to discuss with Yuridov when we have our call later but on the whole he seemed more keen to point the finger at the Americans.'

She picked up her coffee and held it close, savouring the aroma. 'No surprise there I guess. Well, I've not been able to dig up anything on Daley or Lonnen yet, both have been clean as a whistle so far.'

'Greschenko mentioned something about a scandal when Daley was working in Botswana a few years back. Know anything about that?'

'Botswana?' she said, looking confused. 'He's never been to Botswana. Not according to his file anyway.' She hunted around on her desk for the right paper. 'Here we go. Born 12th January 1971 in Denver, Colorado. Father is Jonathan Daley –' she looked up at Blake. 'Yes, same name. Our Jon seems to have dropped the Jr. Jon Senior was a fireman, retired ten years ago as head of his station, but still consults privately. He's also on several boards, from the high school to the local baseball team.'

'Quite the pillar of the community,' Blake commented.

'It appears so. His wife, Anne, Jon Junior's mother, is equally involved. She was PA for one of the city's congressmen, but has since moved on and is now chair of a child autism charity. Daley has a sister who's severely autistic and from what I've read Anne has played an instrumental part in improving the quality of care for children with the condition in their area. They're a respectable couple, and having a famous astronaut for a son hasn't done them any harm, either for Jon Senior's networking or for Anne's fundraising.'

'What about Daley himself?'

'Nothing particularly remarkable about his upbringing,' Bennett said. 'He had decent grades but nothing stellar like we've seen from some of the other astronauts. He didn't go to college, again, a little unusual considering where he's ended up. He went straight to work for a food distributor when he was sixteen, and spent the next four years there before the company went bust and he was forced into a career move. That happened to be when there was a recession on and there wasn't much work around. He managed to get himself a job on an oil rig in the Gulf of Mexico, quite a jump for someone who'd never seen the sea before. It suited him though. He spent eight years on the rigs before moving into the logistics division at the company's headquarters in Houston. He was there for a couple of years before he moved to Solarcorp. They were looking to expand their operations and took him on to join the team responsible for setting up new sites. It wasn't long before he was heading up his own section. They'd fly in, scout out various locations then build the solar farm from scratch. Once it was all up and running they'd hand over control to another team, and Daley would move on to the next site. He travelled all over but I don't see Botswana mentioned anywhere.'

'Curious. Keep digging, see if anything comes up. Greschenko did say it was only a rumour so he might have been mistaken. Anything else?'

'Not really. Only that his travels coincided with all the other Lunarsol astronauts at one time or another. He's worked with Chris Lonnen a lot. Both Lonnen and Velasquez were on the same set-up crew with him, travelling from site to site, but given the nature of their work it's no great surprise they also crossed paths with Wrycroft and Cheng.'

'No link to Nash I suppose?' Blake asked hopefully.

'Not that I've found,' Bennett replied. 'The first time they met was two years ago when the Helioselene project brought them together. They had to undergo plenty of astronaut training activities so saw plenty of each other from then on. I'm compiling a list of people who were involved in those courses and will start contacting them later today to see if they can give me a better picture of their relationship. Nash was already a fully fledged astronaut of course, having been to the ISS previously, whereas Daley and the rest of the Lunarsol crew were new to it all. They had an intensive training regime to get them up to standard, but all of them came through it and made the grade.'

As she said the last word, Bennett couldn't help but stifle a yawn as it came out. 'Go home,' Blake said. 'Have a shower, get some sleep. There's no need to pull all-nighters.'

'I know,' she said, finishing off her coffee. 'Didn't actually mean to. I had a call late last night with someone in Lunarsol's HR department, then carried on doing a bit of reading after that had finished. I must have dozed off.' She pushed herself away from the desk and stood up. 'I'll head home and freshen up but will come back in shortly.'

'Don't rush. I'm interviewing Yuridov at eight o'clock so we can –' he stopped as his phone started ringing. 'You shoot off', he said quickly to Bennett, 'we'll catch up later. Blake?' he added, answering the call.

'Inspector? I hope I haven't woken you? This is Chase Lomax here, CEO of Lunarsol Incorporated.'

'Mr Lomax, an honour to speak to you, sir,' Blake said. He raised an eyebrow at Bennett, midway through putting on her cardigan.

'The honour's all mine son,' Lomax replied. 'I just want to say I'm here to support you in any way I can. The sooner we can wrap this up the better. I'm in London so if you have time today I was rather hoping we could meet.'

'You're in the UK?' Blake asked. 'Yes, of course, there are several things I need to talk to you about so I can be available whenever's good for you.'

'Excellent. How about lunch? I'll be at the Savoy-Grill, say, 12 o'clock?'

Blake looked at his watch. 'Twelve at the Savoy. I look forward to meeting you then.' He heard the line go dead and tapped his phone absent-mindedly against his chin as he considered the call.

'The Savoy eh?' said Bennett smiling. 'Just remember, you start with the cutlery on the outside and work your way in.'

Blake grinned. 'Get out of here. See you later.'

*

Half an hour later Blake was sitting alone in front of the camera when the screen suddenly came to life and Yuridov's face appeared.

'Good morning, Commander.'

'Good morning, inspector,' Yuridov replied, his emotionless features giving nothing away. 'We're all devastated by Richard's death. Please, ask me anything.'

'Thank-you.' Blake paused before proceeding. 'What went wrong, Commander? Why did someone kill Doctor Nash?'

Yuridov sighed. 'I keep asking myself the same question. Were there any signs, should I have seen it coming? So far I've drawn a blank. I have no idea why or how this happened.'

'I understand there was occasionally some tension amongst the crew.'

'It's always been a major concern. How will the group get on in such a confined environment. Roscosmos and NASA have done a lot of rehearsals with different groups. The results were mixed. No one really knew how we'd all get on once we were here.'

'Have you experienced any difficulties mediating the different personalities?'

'Minor squabbles, that's all,' replied Yuridov. 'To begin with we didn't have a lot of space, and it soon became apparent there were divisions. Not so much with Commander Medvelev who stayed out of petty arguments, nor with Doctor Ellis who has proven to be a skilled diplomat when it comes to handling people, but certainly there was no great friendship between Doctor Nash and the Lunarsol people. I'm perhaps exaggerating the degree of animosity though. For the most part they were all perfectly civil and at times even seemed interested in each other's work. Only the other day I observed Doctor Nash deep in conversation with Mr Lonnen, discussing the terrain they'd encountered on one of their EVAs.'

'EVA? That's Extravehicular Activity, right?'

'Yes. A moonwalk. Much of my time has been spent in and around the base, but Mr Lonnen and Mr Wrycroft have been venturing further out. They've seen more of the moon's surface, and what's beneath it, than any man in history. Richard was curious about what they were discovering.'

'Can you describe some of the more fractious conversations?' Blake asked.

'They generally stemmed from clashes between the studies Doctor Nash was conducting, and the perhaps less than delicate approach of some of the others. There was an incident a few weeks ago where Mr Velasquez had driven the moon buggy close to an area where Nash had laid some sensors. He didn't hit anything but it may have distorted his readings for a short period. I actually thought Nash handled it well and didn't lose his temper. He just pointed it out and asked Velasquez to be more aware in future. I saw no reason to intervene on that occasion.'

'Any others you can think of?' asked Blake.

Yuridov hesitated, seemingly reluctant to go on. 'The day before Doctor Nash's death, there was an altercation, again between Nash and Velasquez. We all saw it. The problem was really with Lonnen and Wrycroft. They'd tried mining for tellurium but hit a problem and had moved their site. Unfortunately they strayed into an unofficial exclusion zone – we have an agreement they won't dig near the base. Nash wasn't happy. He felt, not unreasonably, that the Lunarsol crew only cared about their project and were not considerate towards his work. And he was right, they're not. I had been planning to speak to him, and them, about it. It would appear I was too late.'

'I don't think you can blame yourself, Commander,' Blake said, keen to keep the Russian from being distracted by guilt. 'So, are you saying Velasquez reacted to Nash's accusations?'

'It was a careless remark,' Yuridov replied. 'Unnecessary, and childish. Nash walked out and things were a bit tense for a while. I spoke to Gabe, and I understand Doctor Ellis went to see Richard. I didn't want to make a big deal of it, much better if they could reconcile between themselves without it becoming a formal, recorded incident. Mr Daley and I decided not to report it.'

'So, you're saying Doctor Ellis was the last person to see Nash alive?' Blake was annoyed with himself for not having asked her that when he'd spoken to her.

'No, Gabriel told me he went to visit Richard later that evening. They shook hands and that was the end of it. I was satisfied I'd made the right decision.'

'So Gabriel Velasquez was the last person to see Nash,' Blake clarified, making a note on his pad.

'As far as I know, yes. The last person before the killer, that is.'

'Of course. You don't think Velasquez is responsible then?'

Yuridov blew out his cheeks and held up his palms. 'I don't, no, but then I don't think any of the others would have done it either. There's no reason for them to, it only causes them problems and, in all likelihood, will curtail their own missions. I find it hard to believe any of them would want that. Except, clearly, someone did. Velasquez is, in my view, no more likely than anyone else.'

'Tell me,' Blake said, deciding on a change of direction. 'How is your relationship with Mr Daley?'

'Excellent. Why?'

'I couldn't help thinking, he's a man who's used to being in charge. Has there been any conflict because of that?'

'None whatsoever. We have a strict segregation of duties here, inspector. He is in charge of the solar project, I'm responsible for the safety and operation of the base. We both know our roles and there is no reason for any conflict, as you say. Besides, we get on very well personally. He's a good man to have with us.'

'So if there is a personal issue, perhaps a disagreement between, oh, I don't know, let's say for the sake of argument Velasquez and Doctor Nash, would it be yours or Daley's responsibility to resolve it?'

'If it involved a member of the Lunarsol crew then I would discuss it with Mr Daley, but ultimately it would be up to me to intervene and mediate if necessary. And that is what happened earlier this week. Jonathan and I discussed the breakdown in the relationship between Gabriel and Richard, and decided to take no immediate action but rather keep an eye on the situation. That may prove to have been the wrong call.'

'Think back, commander. Was it yourself or Mr Daley who argued to take no action?'

Yuridov considered his answer. 'It's true, Mr Daley was keen to avoid the unnecessary attention a formal report would have generated. But the same could be said of myself. More for their benefit than my own, I should point out. It was a joint decision.'

'Thank you, commander. For what it's worth I'd probably have done the same. I imagine you already have more than enough bureaucracy to deal with.' Yuridov gave a small bow of his head in appreciation of Blake's candidness. 'Can you tell me,' Blake continued, 'what your movements were on the day of Doctor Nash's death?'

'Yes. I woke at 5.30, as usual. I had a quick check that all life support systems were running as expected and made sure there were no urgent messages, then left my room and went to get some breakfast.'

'What time would that have been?' asked Blake.

'Shortly before oh-six hundred,' Yuridov replied. 'There was no one else around. I got some food and sat at the table just catching up on the news at home.'

'And did the other astronauts join you later?'

Yuridov thought back to the morning in question. 'I can't remember exactly, but yes, I think so. Doctor Ellis came in first but just grabbed something and took it back to her room. The others started arriving from around six thirty onwards.'

'Did anyone not show up?'

Yuridov rubbed his chin with both hands as he tried to remember. 'I'm not sure, sorry. I can't recall whether Doctor Nash came in or not. I think not, but could easily be wrong. Evidently I didn't notice anything untoward at the time. In hindsight that was remiss of me, I should have paid more attention.' He thought about it for a few more seconds. 'Come to think of it, Mr Cheng was later than usual. He's often up before me but didn't come in until well after seven. I didn't think anything of it then, he probably had something he had to attend to. You'll have to ask him. Beyond that people just come and go in the morning, we don't take a roll call I'm afraid.'

'And the rest of the day?'

'Mr Daley and I had a status call with Capcom. No one else was around at that point, they were all busy with their own assignments. Once that was over Jonathan went to see Mr Cheng in the Lunarsol plant.'

'So you were alone in the control centre?'

'Yes, I spend most of my time there.'

'Can you recollect anyone going to the laboratory wing?' asked Blake.

Yuridov contemplated the question. 'Lydia, obviously. She works in Lab One. That's all. No, wait, Jonathan came back that way after he'd been to see Cheng.'

'Interesting. Can I just ask you about Doctor Ellis. I met with General Greschenko yesterday and he mentioned you had concerns about her state of mind. Would you care to elaborate on that?'

'Yes, she took Doctor Nash's death badly, as you would expect. We're all shocked, obviously, but Lydia was hit particularly hard. She was the one who discovered him after all. I don't think she got any sleep that night, and the next day she wasn't in a good place. To be fair to her, she has recovered quickly. I just felt she might need more support than some of the others. We're all receiving counselling from our home teams, but that's personal and anything said in those discussions is not shared with me. From my perspective I want to make sure she's coping. She isn't involved in any of the critical safety procedures of the base so a lapse in concentration isn't likely to be an issue the rest of the crew need have any concerns about, but still, we're in the early days following a traumatic event so I simply reported that I would keep an eye on her.'

'Has her relationship with Gabriel Velasquez caused any problems?'

Yuridov raised an eyebrow. 'She told you? I wasn't sure whether to mention it.'

'To me? Definitely. It's conceivable it has a bearing on the case. Although am I right in thinking you haven't said anything about it to your superiors?'

The uncomfortable look returned to Yuridov's face. Blake noticed a prominent vein throbbing on the side of his head that hadn't been obvious earlier. Perhaps the stress of recent events was getting to him. 'No, I haven't reported it. Yet. It's a private matter and I felt it did not need to be office gossip, as you say. I must confess I've been uneasy about the whole thing and have been wondering if it was the right decision. Really, they should have informed their own sections by now. I did suggest such an action to them the day they announced it, but it's a relatively new development and I don't believe they have done so. I considered giving them a deadline, but in truth it's a personal situation and not an area where I have any jurisdiction. I can't force them to go public, and any involvement on my part would have been purely in an advisory capacity.'

'I understand, commander,' Blake said. 'It put you in an awkward position. Nevertheless, I am not the public, nor am I involved in either of their organisations. I'm investigating a murder and I must insist you tell me anything which may be relevant to the case. It may seem unlikely but crimes of passion do happen, and people have been killed for much less. Are we clear?'

Yuridov nodded slowly. 'Absolutely, inspector, I understand. My apologies.'

'Thank-you, commander. Now, just to reiterate, has their relationship caused any problems?'

'Not that I'm aware of. I suspect among the Lunarsol team it wasn't a very well kept secret, although it came as a surprise to me and, I imagine, Sergey and Richard. The three of us are similar in our personalities, more studious and less, um, gregarious than our crewmates.'

'Meaning?' Blake asked.

'Let's just say they'd probably be more comfortable in a seedy bar in some outback mining colony than the rest of us would be.'

Blake smiled. 'How did you ever all end up in the same place?' he wondered out loud.

9

'This way, sir' said the young waitress when Blake had arrived at the hotel restaurant. He'd dashed off to Bristol Parkway station immediately after the interview with Yuridov and had arrived in London with enough time to walk the four and a half kilometres from Paddington to the Savoy. He'd never been a big fan of the tube and walking through Hyde Park then along The Mall next to St James's Park had cleared his head and put him in a good mood. The astronauts must definitely be affected by their confinement, he'd decided as he strolled through Green Park and past Buckingham Palace.

The waitress led him through the large room, still quiet before the lunchtime rush, until they arrived at a table occupied by a man in his early sixties. Tanned and good looking despite the receding hairline, Blake noted he was exceptionally well-dressed too, suspecting the man's suit cost more than his own car.

Lomax looked up and smiled, standing to shake Blake's

hand. He exuded confidence and had an easygoing charm that Blake imagined would captivate a room. He could see immediately how the man's force of personality had brought the other space organisations on board and had driven the project through to fruition.

'Inspector Blake? Chase Lomax. It's great to meet you.'

'Likewise, sir.' Blake glanced around as they took their seats. He was getting a feel for the other customers, wondering out of mild curiosity if any were Lomax's bodyguards but also, almost subconsciously, appraising the layout, making sure he knew where the exits were and what obstacles might be in his way. He suddenly realised Lomax had been watching him.

'Sorry,' he smiled. 'Habit.'

'It's reassuring,' Lomax replied. 'This is the first time I've met a real detective, it's fascinating.'

The waitress, Amy according to the little badge on her shirt, handed them each a menu and placed a wine list on the table.

'Can I get you anything to start with, gentlemen?' she asked.

'Just a water for me, please,' said Blake. 'Still,' he added, pre-empting her next question.

'Make that two,' said Lomax. 'It's four in the morning where I just came from, my body doesn't know if it wants an espresso or a double whiskey.'

Blake smiled. 'Came in on the red eye?' he asked. 'Actually, while I think of it, I have to say thank-you for the use of your plane. I could get used to that sort of treatment.'

'My pleasure. I hope Freya and Nick looked after you.'

'Best flight I've ever been on.'

Lomax grinned. 'I appreciate you taking the time to meet me. I know you've got a lot on your plate.'

'Not a problem,' Blake replied. 'You're one of many people I was hoping to talk to and your call came at a good time. Yesterday's whirlwind trip to Kazakhstan was a bit of an eye-opener, and helped me get a better feel for the two cosmonauts and the Russian side of the operation. I was hoping you might be able to give me a similar overview from the Lunarsol perspective.'

'Absolutely. Where would you like to start?'

Just then Amy returned with two glasses of ice and a large bottle of still water. 'Have you chosen or would you like a little more time?' she asked.

Lomax glanced at the menu. 'I'll have the foie gras then the halibut,' he told her.

Blake, suddenly put on the spot, quickly picked up the menu. £250 for beluga jumped out at him from the top of the page. He hoped he wasn't expected to pick up the tab.

'Uh, could I have the snails then, er, the ox cheek.' He handed back the menu, pleased with himself for making some adventurous sounding choices.

'Why don't you surprise us with a couple of sides to go with those mains too, Amy,' Lomax said. 'I'll trust your judgement.'

She smiled at him. 'No problem, sir, leave it with me. Just give me a wave if you need anything else.'

'I guess we should begin with the astronauts themselves,' Blake said after Amy had left. 'How did you identify each of them as suitable candidates for this project, and how did you ultimately select the final crew? Do you mind if I take a couple of notes while we talk by the way? I don't want to get things muddled up and have to ask you again later.'

'You go for it,' Lomax replied, waving his hand dismissively and relaxing back into his chair. 'It was a lengthy process. For a long time the whole thing was kept secret. We had the idea for the solar farm on the lunar surface but you wouldn't believe the number of hoops we had to jump through to get the whole thing off the ground.'

'I can imagine. Even a minor change where I work takes months. Your project sounds impossible.'

'It did feel it at times. We initially had a project team working on the feasibility of the venture. That started about six or seven years ago. Gradually the team grew as we started discussions with NASA. It soon became clear that space exploration is a team game these days so pretty quickly we also had Roscosmos and ESA involved. Around that time, as it was starting to look like this could become a very real possibility, I engaged our Human Resources Talent team to start looking for suitable candidates.'

'And all the astronauts you chose came from internally?' Blake asked.

'Not at that point, no,' Lomax replied. 'We narrowed it down to a shortlist of around fifty people, some internal, some not. We knew we'd need to recruit for different skill sets, from mining the raw materials through to production of the solar panels. That's our core business anyway and we already have the best in the business, so the majority of the names on the shortlist were our own people. We approached them directly to sound them out – a two year placement on the moon isn't everyone's cup of tea as you Brits might say. One or two declined but most were interested. A lot were already used to long periods away from home, it goes with the territory. The chance to go to the moon was too much to pass up. Kind of wish I had the skills to make the grade myself.'

Blake grinned. 'Me too. So, from there you whittled it down to the final five?'

'Pretty much, although at that point we hadn't settled on the final number. We put all the remaining candidates through a variety of assessment centres to make sure they were up to the challenge physically, and also that they'd get along with each other. At the time, you have to remember, we were still defining the mission and from our side of things it was all about the Lunarsol objectives. We weren't planning for additional external personnel. However, this was, and still is, a small operation and is really only intended to prove the concept. The overheads are huge and the expected returns from this initial foray won't meet them. That's a problem for my shareholders. To make it work, NASA, Roscosmos and ESA picked up a share of the costs and each had their demands for a seat on the plane. In the end we had to scale back our plans a little and reduce the team to only five, the bare minimum we'd need to make it work.'

They paused as a waiter arrived with their starters. Blake looked at his snails wondering what had possessed him to choose them. Spreading his napkin over his lap, he took a sip of water and waited for the two of them to be left alone again.

'Was that frustrating? Losing overall control of the operation?' Blake asked, tentatively forking a snail and putting it in his mouth. They were surprisingly tasty and he hoped his relief wasn't too obvious.

'No, it was a godsend!' Lomax laughed. 'We'd already spent a fair chunk on the feasibility and it was starting to look like the whole thing would be a financial disaster for us. I put a lot of effort into wooing the other organisations and, between you and me, was extremely grateful when they all signed up. It brought a whole new level of bureaucracy, sure, but it meant the whole thing was definitely now possible. The logistics of sending up pre-supply ships, the launch itself and lunar landing, the construction of the base – all of that could be handled by the others and we could focus on the Lunarsol operations. It's a perfect set-up for us.'

'Tell me about your guys then,' Blake prompted.

'Well, first we've got Jon Daley, project manager of our on-site operations. He's been with us for around fifteen years now. A good man, Jon. He's installed more solar farms around the globe than anyone else on Earth. He's a good problem solver and is used to difficult conditions – deserts and suchlike. He was an obvious choice to lead the team up there.'

'Any family?'

'No, not something he's got round to yet. There've been girlfriends I'm told, but he's never around in one place long enough for them to last. Hazard of the job I'm afraid. We do what we can, even offering positions to partners when our employees are posted away, but it's often simply not what they want to do. Realistically we don't expect men like Jon to do this job for ever. The pay's very good, then they can settle down once they've earned enough to retire. He got to that stage some time ago, but then the moon opportunity came up and he was attracted to the challenge. It wouldn't surprise me if he semi-retired once he gets back. I'd like to think he'd stay with us, perhaps helping to train future astronaut hopefuls, but that's up to him.'

'Have you ever had any doubts about Mr Daley? Not so much with his ability to do the job, rather how he gets on with other people?'

'Honestly, no. He's a hard worker, and expects his teams to do the same, but he's fair and will always back up his crew. If anything, it's more of a problem for me as he'll defend them rather than tow the corporate line, but I like that in him and it's never been an issue.'

'Ok, how about Sying Cheng?' Blake asked, finishing the last of his snails. He made a note to pick up some mints on his way back to the office. The garlic would not endear him to the rest of his team.

'Ah, now, he is slightly different. Of the five who made the final cut, he's the only one we recruited externally. He's brilliant, has worked in the industry for years and is personally responsible for several ground-breaking advances in solar technology. We've tried to poach him before but he always stayed loyal to his previous employer. Can't knock him for that. The chance to go to the moon was too much for him to resist though. You know, his name actually means Star in Chinese. 'Accomplished Star' I think, something like that. Maybe he was destined to get up to the heavens.'

'I understand he's doing some PR with Chinese state media?' Blake said as their empty plates were cleared away.

'Yeah, that's a bit of a bonus,' Lomax admitted. 'The Chinese have their own project in the pipeline, very similar to our own. They've been working on it for several years, round about the same as us. At one point, in my narrow world at least, it became the new space race. Who would get there first. We won, but politically it helps them save face that we have a guy of Chinese descent who's largely responsible for the technical side of things. He does a lot of video blogs for schools, both in the States and in China, showing the kids how everything works.'

'Aren't you worried he'll pass on your technology to the Chinese?' Blake asked.

Lomax waved the suggestion away dismissively. 'You'd think so, wouldn't you? I'm not in this game to make money though. The Chinese are the biggest polluters on the planet. Nearly a third of the world's carbon dioxide production comes from them. Not that the US is much better. Still, if they can get their own lunar solar farm up and running they'll be able to drastically cut back on their emissions and we'll all be better off. It wouldn't surprise me if they offered Sying the job of leading their mission once they're ready to proceed.'

'That's very magnanimous of you I'm sure, but I have to say I'm surprised. Aren't your shareholders concerned about the potential conflict of interest?'

'Not especially,' Lomax replied. 'At the moment we're alone up there, so we're the only ones with a chance of making a profit. The Chinese are years away from getting their operation off the ground, by which point the technology Cheng is dealing with will have been surpassed anyway. Sure, there are lessons to be learned from his work currently, and who knows, in twenty or thirty years maybe there'll be a bidding war over the price of solar energy, but the moon is a big place with plenty of room for all of us. If competition means that cheap, renewable electricity is the end result then who's to argue. Not our investors, who tend to be ethical funds and environmentally conscious organisations anyway.'

Lomax paused as the main courses appeared, along with some Dauphinoise potatoes and a portion of sautéed spinach. Blake looked at them, impressed. 'Better than my usual sandwich, that's for sure.'

'You're in for a treat,' Lomax said as he scooped some of the spinach onto his plate. 'They love all their pretentious presentation in these places but the good news here is it tastes even better than it looks.'

'Okay,' Blake said, helping himself to some of the potatoes. 'So what about Cheng personally? If he's new to the company has he had time to gel with the rest of the crew?'

'Well, I say he's new,' Lomax replied, taking a bite of his fish, 'but that's relatively speaking. He came on board around three years ago as the plan was really starting to gain some traction. His work was a combination of solar production in our existing operations as well as his astronaut training, so he's had the chance to get to know the workings of the company while at the same time going through plenty of team building exercises with the rest of the guys.'

'And again, no personal issues you're aware of with the other astronauts?'

Lomax shook his head as he put another forkful of food into his mouth. 'No, nothing. He's quiet, compared to the others. Tends to keep himself to himself. But then, a lot of his work is solitary and he's the kind of personality who likes to just get on with things.'

'So he was on friendly terms with Doctor Nash?'

'As far as I know. They wouldn't have crossed paths all that much but I've no reason to believe there was anything other than professional courtesy between them. I know it's a small group up there but Nash would have been largely tucked away in the ESA lab, while Cheng has been busy with the solar plant. I don't know the details of what kind of experiments Nash was conducting and frankly I don't particularly care. I doubt they're of much interest to anyone outside of ESA and perhaps one or two specialists in whatever obscure fields he was studying.'

'Maybe,' Blake conceded. 'Although I think it's probably a few more than that. NASA, Roscosmos, maybe even the people on the Chinese space programme that Cheng has been talking to would have been following his progress.'

'I guess,' Lomax said. 'Didn't interest me, that's for sure. You might feel differently. I hear you're a bit of a technical genius yourself.'

'Hardly,' Blake commented. 'I scraped through uni but a lot of this stuff would have been way over my head even back then.'

'You're too modest. A First from Exeter University in Aeronautical Engineering, then the fastest rise through the ranks at Scotland Yard in twenty years, becoming the youngest detective inspector they've ever had, before you upped sticks and moved to Bristol? I'd say you're not the kind of guy who scrapes through. I'm curious about why you relocated though.'

Blake gave a small smile, clearly ill at ease. 'Quality of life,' he answered vaguely. 'Been checking up on me?'

'Had to,' Lomax replied. 'Don't take it personally. When this kicked off four days ago there were crisis meetings going on all over the shop. We were all involved in the decision to pick you as the lead investigator. I was sent your file, among others, and did a background check of my own. I wanted to make sure you were the right man for the job. Everything I have is tied up in this venture Mr Blake. I need this resolved as much as you and had to be sure we had someone competent running the investigation. Relax,' he added. 'So far I'm pleased with the progress you're making. How's your ox?'

'Delicious,' Blake said, thrown slightly by the compliment then abrupt change of subject. 'Haven't had this since my gran used to cook it when I was a boy. It's making me slightly nostalgic.'

Lomax smiled. 'Ah, the good old days.' He took a sip of water then continued his summary of the remaining Lunarsol astronauts. 'So, what can I tell you about the others. All of them have been with me for a while. Eric Wrycroft originally ran one of my mines in Western Australia. He was already starting to make a name for himself, but was ready to move on and when I set up the solar side of the business he was ideally placed to make the transition. What he did there revolutionised the way we manufacture the panels in situ and meant we could expand exponentially. Our HR guys flagged him because he ticked several boxes – air force pilot, geology PhD, a good problem solver and so on. I like him because he gets results. Women, my daughter included, like him because he's handsome. Sending him to the moon for two years gives the rest of mankind a chance!'

'Your daughter? And Wrycroft?'

'Hell no, nothing like that. She accompanied me once on a tour of some sites we control. It was the off-season – she's on the US winter Olympic team. She teased me later that I hadn't told her how good looking some of my staff were. Daughters, they know how to get to you. You've got all that to look forward to.'

Lomax winked, subtly reminding Blake he'd done his research and knew all about him. Blake wasn't used to the people he was questioning knowing anything about his personal life, but managed to hide his irritation. 'Feels like I'm already there sometimes. My eldest is seven going on seventeen. Says she already has a boyfriend. What about Lonnen?' he asked, keen to change the subject.

'Another good man. Been with us for fourteen years, again, with a background on the mining side of things. He used to work with Daley setting up new sites for Solarcorp but when he got to Australia he ended up staying on. He and Wrycroft make a good team so it worked well for everyone. Chris is the only one of the five who has a family by the way. That's one of the reasons he settled in Australia. He'd met this girl on a previous job in the States, then she went with him on the Oz trip. They're a good example of our 'take your partner to work' policy. We found her a role out there so she could accompany him, and they settled in the area. They have a small baby now. It's tough being away for so long but he made the call that it's an age where he can get away with it, plus he's earning so much he'll be able to make it up to the lad when he's back. He'll be the coolest kid at school anyway, who wouldn't want to say their dad's an astronaut.'

'Must be hard, missing out on those early years.'

'Maybe,' Lomax said, 'but everyone's different. A lot of families have one or even two parents missing for a time. Military service, work, prison even. Two years can pass quickly. If they even make it that far. Depending on how this investigation pans out he might be back sooner than planned.'

'Would that cause you a problem?'

Lomax finished his last mouthful of food and put his knife and fork back down on his plate. 'I could have done without it, sure. It's not cheap sending people to the moon and back. But we can handle it. It's always been in plan to change crew periodically. If we need to bring that forward then so be it.'

Blake looked at him, trying to gauge how much truth was behind his words. Lomax held his gaze, almost as if he was daring the detective to challenge him. 'Fair enough,' said Blake eventually. 'That just leaves Velasquez. Anything I need to know about him?'

'Interesting guy,' continued Lomax amiably. 'From what I gather he had a tough childhood. His parents moved from Argentina to the States in the early Eighties. He was born a couple of months later, but times were tough and his father was, shall we say, difficult. From what I gather there was no love lost between them. Gabriel was a smart kid though, and managed to hide his bruises.'

Blake raised an eyebrow. 'Yeah,' Lomax continued. 'Not a nice guy, his old man. At fourteen he ran away from home. Quit school and got a job on a construction site. Lied about his age, took cash in hand, lived one day at a time. He moved around from job to job until he ended up at a small family firm in the mid-West. That's when things suddenly started to look up for him. The owner recognised something in Gabe, encouraged him to take some courses, continue his education. He did well, working for the business in the day and going to evening classes. He'd probably still be there now if we hadn't taken over the firm.'

'You took them over? How did he take that?'

'Hard, at first. The old man running it didn't have the fight in him to resist us. There was a big project going on. Can't even remember what it was now. I didn't have much exposure in the area and, rather than compete with a local firm it was easier to swallow them up. Hey, what can I say, I'm a businessman. Given time I think the original owner, Glenn something, would've liked Velasquez to take over the business. It was small fry though. Once Gabe joined us he really had his eyes opened and could see what might be possible. We nurtured him, of course. Feelings can be a little raw in that sort of situation, but he soon got over it and did well for us. We got him away from the mid-West as soon as we could, showed him a bit more of the world. Then when the lunar project came along his was one of the names that kept coming up. Those evening classes paid off, he made the final cut.'

Blake tapped his pen thoughtfully on his notepad as their plates were cleared away. Amy reappeared, asking if they'd like dessert. Lomax looked at Blake enquiringly.

'Not for me thanks. I'll fall asleep this afternoon if I have too much,' Blake said in reply.

'Same here. Could I have a coffee though please Amy. A double espresso. Can you charge all this to my room? And put a hundred on for yourself.'

Amy's eyes lit up. 'Thank you, sir, that's very kind. Can I get you a coffee too?' she asked, turning back to Blake who was relieved to hear he wouldn't have to submit an expenses claim after all.

'An Americano, please,' he said. 'Thank-you,' he added, turning back to Lomax. 'So, with all five of them, none had a history with Nash?'

'No, they would have only met him a year or so ago when the final line-ups were confirmed. Look, I know you have to investigate all of them, but I have to say it's highly unlikely any of my guys had anything to do with it. They'd no reason to. The others – Yuridov, Medvelev, Ellis – they'd all known Nash, and each other, for years. They've all done astronaut training together, they've all had previous trips to the ISS, there's a lot of history there. Don't get me wrong. I'm an open book, available any time you need me and you have all my resources at your disposal, but I'd say the odds are it's one of those three who's your culprit. And of course, it might not even be a personal issue. I'm sure you're already looking into all angles, but the possibility of a Russian agenda is definitely one which can't be ignored.'

Blake, midway through making a note on his pad, looked up at Lomax. 'Ok, you've got my attention now, Mr Lomax. Is there something I should know?'

'Nothing specific, inspector,' Lomax replied. 'I'm just interested in every possible scenario for what might have brought this about. I appreciate you're used to dealing with people. I'm used to dealing with corporations. When you've spent the last five years trying to bang European, American and Russian heads together, the first thing that went through my head was, ok, someone's pissed off with ESA. Which of them is more likely? And I'd have to say it's the Russians. All the way through this they were the ones with a chip on their shoulder.'

He paused as their coffees arrived, then continued. 'When I first had the idea for this venture, it soon became obvious that NASA weren't going to be able to get us there. Not for a while. They're ten years off the pace. The private space entrepreneurs are closer, but aren't quite there yet. So I spoke to the Russians, and for a while it was looking like being their show. A joint venture between Roscosmos and Lunarsol. Then it turned out that although they could get us there, they didn't have the right design for the base itself. Only ESA had that. Of course, NASA were never going to let a lunar mission happen without their involvement. Politically it was too sensitive. But they do have deep pockets, so before long we had all three agencies signed up. The Russians accepted the arrangement and on we went, but it hasn't been easy. Maybe things have escalated that I'm not aware of and someone in the Kremlin has decided to take things further. Forgetting the space project for a minute, things are a little tense out there in the real world right now.'

'I'd noticed,' said Blake. 'Still, I can't see what the Russians would have to gain from killing Nash. The moon is a world away from international politics. My impression was it's one arena that seems to be above the usual squabbles.'

'True. But don't forget, a single death triggered the first World War. Who's to know what the agenda is this time round? One astronaut dies, tensions run high, someone crosses a border somewhere they shouldn't and before you know it a whole shitstorm has descended. It's unlikely, maybe, but not inconceivable. Good luck looking into that one.'

'Feels like we're heading way above my pay grade now,' Blake said grimly, downing the last of his coffee. 'I think that's nearly everything I need for now, Mr Lomax. There's just one more question though before I leave you in peace. You mentioned Jon Daley has travelled all over the world for you. Has he ever been to Botswana?'

Lomax coolly considered the question. 'I don't think so, but can't be sure. I'll have to get Human Resources to check the records. Why?'

'I heard there was some kind of incident he might have been involved in.'

'Oh, that. Not our finest hour. Yes, there was a terrible accident. People died. A couple of locals plus an American on our team, Harry Pepper. At the inquest they found out he'd been stressed, over-worked, made a mistake. Simple as that. Shouldn't have happened, and we've put procedures in place to ensure it doesn't happen again, but ultimately it was human error. Nothing to do with Daley though, he wasn't on that particular operation.'

'I must have been mistaken. Well, I don't think I have anything else for now. Thank-you very much for your time. And for lunch.' He picked up his notepad and stood, reaching out to shake Lomax's hand.

'Not at all,' replied Lomax, standing to return the handshake. 'Best of luck with the investigation, detective, and if there's anything you need at all, just let me know.'

'Oh, I think the private jet is enough for now,' smiled Blake. He turned and left the restaurant, heading out onto the busy street. He looked at his phone and saw two missed calls from DCS Whiteley, and a text saying "Call me". Uh-oh, he thought as he dialled her number.

'We've a problem,' she said, skipping any preamble.

'What's happened?' Blake asked, ducking into a side street to get away from the noise of the traffic.

'Someone's tweeted ESA, asking why Nash hasn't sent any updates lately. People are starting to notice something's up. You'd better stop off in Didcot on your way back to see Higgins and Maddix. I'll meet you there. They're deciding whether to put out a statement.'

'Shit,' was all Blake could think to say.

10

'No one's told them yet?' Blake asked incredulously. He was at the ESA offices where DCS Whiteley and Kathryn Bennett had travelled up to join him for the meeting with Higgins and Maddix. It transpired no one had broken the news to Nash's parents yet about his death.

'It wasn't for lack of trying,' said Maddix. 'They're both retired and had gone away on a walking holiday in Scotland. Turns out there was no mobile coverage so the emergency contact number we had wasn't getting through. We didn't know where they were, and you'll appreciate our enquiries to friends and old work acquaintances had to be discreet. We only managed to track them down this morning when their cleaner arrived. She confirmed they're due back this evening.'

'Christ,' said Blake. 'He died four days ago. How are you going to break it to them?'

'Actually, inspector,' answered Maddix, 'we rather thought it might be better coming from you. With my support, obviously, since I know the family.'

Blake looked at Maddix and thought about arguing but could see the scientist was already struggling enough with his conscience at the delay. 'Okay, I'll speak to them,' he said finally. 'It will help having you there, I'm sure Nash's parents will appreciate your presence. We can have a police bereavement officer on hand as well. So,' he paused, 'what am I going to say? We have to tell them the truth about the date it happened, try to get through the inevitable anger and shock, then make sure we keep them fully appraised from this point on.'

'Yes, we came to pretty much the same conclusion,' Higgins said. 'Do you think we should disclose we suspect he was murdered, or just confirm we're exploring all possibilities at this time?'

'We'll tell them,' Blake said firmly. 'They need to know. Besides, I'll have lots of questions for them which won't make sense if we've led them to believe it was an accident. What about the wider issue of the public? How long do you think we can hold them off?'

'Not long,' said Higgins. 'A day maybe. Two at most. You've got time to speak to the Nashes but after that it's going to get out sooner rather than later. The investigation will get a lot harder I'm afraid.'

'It was always inevitable. Is Mary lined up?' Blake asked, turning to Whiteley.

'Yes, she's ready. She doesn't know the details yet, only that a high profile murder has occurred and she's going to be running interference with the press. You'll need to bring her up to speed.'

'No problem. Can you ask her to come to Bristol tomorrow morning, say elevenish, and I'll fill her in? I'll have a better feel regarding what message to give out once I've seen Nash's folks. Is there anything else I should know?'

'Not that I can think of right now,' said Higgins. 'We'll leave you to get on with things. You're welcome to stay and work in this room this afternoon if that's easier. Thanks inspector.'

'Nash's parents live near Kemble in the Cotswolds,' added Maddix before he left. 'It's just under an hour from here, I'll have a car meet us outside at six, ok?'

Blake nodded then waited until the two ESA directors had gone. 'Okay, looks like I'm here for the next few hours. I need to have a look round Doctor Nash's office anyway. Let's get the others on the phone for a catch up first.'

A few minutes later they'd all dialled into a conference call, with Blake, Whiteley and Bennett listening on a speakerphone. 'Thank God this thing's clearer than the ones we usually have to put up with,' said Blake. 'How's everyone getting on?'

'Phil and I had an interesting conversation with Velasquez while you were out,' replied Hamilton. 'We got a message that he was available for interview so the two of us went ahead, hope that was the right thing to do?'

'Absolutely. What did he have to say?'

'Well, he's feeling pretty low actually. He and Nash had their argument the night before Nash died, which everyone saw. Remember Yuridov mentioned it? Velasquez claims the two of them made up. He went to see Nash later in the evening to apologise. It had been a long day, he'd snapped, he knew he was in the wrong. They chatted for five minutes or so and parted amicably. No witnesses to that effect, all we have is his word. Velasquez says he's glad he did, given the circumstances. He would've felt even worse if this had happened before he'd had the chance to clear the air, but still, the timing's odd. He's convinced he's being set up. Whoever wanted to kill Nash waited until there was an opportunity to frame someone else. Their public falling out the previous evening was, in his view, the cocking of the trigger.'

'Interesting theory,' said Whiteley. 'Or he could have gone to see Nash later that night, the argument continued and escalated, which in turn led to him killing him, perhaps unintentionally. Now he's playing the victim card to deflect attention.'

'Maybe,' said Blake. 'Doesn't feel right though. That suggests there would have been a struggle and there was no sign of any disruption, either to Nash's quarters or the lab he was found in. Plus no one else heard anything. This doesn't strike me as a spur of the moment thing. Whoever did this meticulously planned it and was waiting for the right opportunity. The night of the argument provided that. It gave them a possible motive and meant everyone would be focussed on Velasquez. Could still have been him of course, no reason to suggest he didn't orchestrate the whole thing himself so I'm not ruling him out, but the scenario plays out.'

'Plus,' Palmer added, 'if Velasquez saw Nash in his quarters as he claims, how did Nash's body get from there to the lab? I know the moon's gravity has made him lighter but still, it's a risky move.'

'Nash could have gone back to finish off something in the lab after dinner,' Blake suggested. 'Velasquez would've looked for him in his room first then gone on from there. No, I think we can assume the good doctor was killed in that laboratory. It's not a very large base. Like Phil says, the chance of being caught moving the body is way too high. It would've been an unnecessary risk.'

'Maybe Nash was lured back to his lab?' said Bennett. 'Something to do with that gunge on the table. The killer would have known the fish tank was in there so could have planned to force him face down into it?'

'Again, you'd expect some sign of a struggle though. There's something about that which doesn't add up either. I think we have to take a gamble and get the astronauts to perform a post-mortem.'

'It's risky,' said Whiteley.

'I know. But if we pick two of the astronauts so they have to work closely together, supervising each other, that risk is minimised. One from the scientist group, one from Lunarsol. The obvious choices are Yuridov, Medvelev and Ellis. They're the ones with the most medical training, which means I'm reluctant to pick any of them. We can't have just two Lunarsol people doing it though.'

'Do any of the Lunarsol crew know how to do an autopsy?' asked Whiteley.

'Not according to their records,' Hamilton replied. 'Wrycroft was in the Aussie Air Force and has a reasonable level of medical training. The others have basic first aid skills from their pre-moon lives, plus additional courses from their astronaut training. We can't have Ellis and Velasquez doing it together obviously, the link between them is too close. I'm leaning towards Yuridov, as Base Commander with medical knowledge and experience, supervised by Wrycroft.'

'Makes sense,' agreed Blake. He looked at Whiteley. 'We'll need your authorisation to proceed.'

Whiteley considered the options. 'Let's hold off on a full post-mortem at this stage. Get Yuridov and Wrycroft to take blood samples for analysis and to perform a visual inspection of the body for any other signs of trauma which might have a bearing on the case. Once they're done, Doctor Ellis can repeat the exercise, backed up by Mr Daley.'

'Will do. Anything else from Velasquez, Jim? Did you discuss his relationship with Ellis?'

'We did, yes,' Hamilton replied. 'He was fairly dismissive of it, but I guess he would be. The less attention he draws to it the better as far as he's concerned. Yes, he's been seeing her for a few weeks. No, it hasn't caused any problems with the rest of the crew. No, he doesn't see why it would have any connection to Doctor Nash's death.'

'We did go through the timeline in detail with him though,' chipped in Palmer. 'He went to see Nash to make amends shortly before retiring for the evening at around 11pm. From there he went directly to Doctor Ellis' quarters. The beds aren't built for two though and although they dozed off he woke during the night and went back to his room. He managed to do that without disturbing her, he thinks, and he didn't notice anything unusual on the way back to his quarters. We couldn't get anything more useful on that one.'

'Lomax said something interesting,' said Blake. 'Velasquez had a pretty tough childhood but was taken in by a family firm who looked after him, helped him develop. Sounds like the first time anyone had ever done something positive in his life. Then Lomax took over the company and Velasquez lost that. He mentioned there was some ill-will between them to begin with. Lomax said it passed, that they took care of Gabriel and he soon came round, but maybe there's more to it.'

'You think he still holds a grudge against Lomax?' asked Hamilton. 'He destroyed his new-found family's business so now Velasquez wants to scupper Lunarsol?'

'It's worth looking into. I'd certainly be interested to know how Velasquez feels about the whole thing now, see if that feeling of moving on is reciprocated.'

'Well, it didn't come up today. The rest of our conversation was just shop talk for the most part,' Hamilton added. 'He told us lots of stuff about the crater, angles of sunlight and the problems of moon dust. He even started talking about a second solar site at one point on the far side of the crater to cover the periods when the first is in shadow, guaranteeing continual power. All very interesting, and it was clear he loves his job, but nothing we could connect to Nash.'

'Doesn't sound like someone who'd commit murder,' mused Blake. 'Already planning big things for the future. Again, could be an act. Ok, good work, both of you. Anything else?'

Bennett was the first to answer. 'I have a call scheduled this evening with the NASA psychoanalyst people. They have a whole team of counsellors to monitor Doctor Ellis' state of mind, more so since Nash died. I'm hoping to find out a bit more about her that isn't in the official files. I was going to see if you wanted to join me but you're tied up with the Nashes now. Jim, Phil, either of you planning to still be there when I get back? It's at eight pm.'

'Sorry,' said Palmer. 'That clashes with a video conference I've got scheduled with Cheng.'

'You might have to shuffle things round a bit,' interrupted Whiteley. 'No point delaying the superficial post-mortem exercise. See if you can get them to expedite that this evening. Get comms set up so you can listen in. You'd better still go and see the Nashes, Tom, we can't delay telling them any longer, but the rest of you try to be there. I'll go and speak to Mary Phillips and will get a bereavement officer ready to support you this evening. Let me know if you need anything else. Sergeant Bennett, I need to make a few calls and speak to Director Higgins, but I can give you a lift back to Bristol in about half an hour if that suits?'

Bennett looked to Blake for approval, who nodded.

'So, come on then, sir,' teased Bennett after Whiteley had left. 'How was the caviar?'

'Expensive,' Blake replied. 'But at least I wasn't paying.'

'Find out anything useful?'

'Yes, some good background, although it feels like there are now more questions than answers. He tried to come across as the heroic philanthropist, ostensibly in this for the good of the planet. He even said he's not in this to make money. I don't buy it though. His businesses have expanded quickly, aggressively even if you consider the way they've taken over smaller companies on the way. He has his charitable foundation and appears at plenty of fundraisers, but I'd be curious to see how much he actually contributes himself. Wouldn't surprise me if it was all largely a self-promotion exercise.'

'That's not necessarily a bad thing,' came Hamilton's voice over the speakerphone. 'He's good on the publicity front and if it makes him successful at getting backers on board for his projects then good luck to him.'

'Yes, but there were other things he said which didn't ring true either. Like the backup crew for the Lunar base. He's got another team in training, preparing to replace the ones who are up there. He made light of the effort to do that but I'm sure it's a bigger problem than he's making out.'

'Probably him putting on his public face again,' said Bennett. 'Always appear in control otherwise it makes your investors nervous.'

'Anything on the astronauts themselves?' Palmer asked.

Blake filled them in on the conversation he'd had with Lomax, going through each of the five Lunarsol crewmembers in turn.

'This is getting way out of our league,' Palmer commented. 'Russian conspiracies, Chinese espionage, African cover-ups, South American domestic abuse. Do they seriously expect us to make sense of all this?'

'Yeah, I came away from the meeting feeling a bit beaten up,' Blake admitted. 'Maybe that was his intention. We'll do what we can. You're looking into Cheng. See if you can find anything in this suggestion of him leading a future Chinese mission. I'm curious about whether any of Nash's experiments might have been of particular interest to them too. Lomax kind of changed the subject when they came up. Kathryn, it might be a good idea to check out the family angle before you speak to Lonnen. See if there's anything which might make him desperate to get back to Earth. It's an unlikely motive for murder, granted. I know he can't exactly jump on the next flight out but there must be easier ways to instigate a transfer home.'

'Anything in particular you want me to focus on?' asked Hamilton.

'Velasquez. I'm curious about his childhood. Why did his parents move to America, and find out what you can about his construction job being taken over. See if you can track down an expert in Russian affairs as well. On the quiet. Would they have anything to gain from a collapse in relations over the lunar colony, or any other outcome of that sort.'

Blake ended the call and turned to Bennett. 'You'd better go and meet DCS Whiteley, don't want you missing your lift home and not making it to the autopsy broadcast in time.'

Bennett reached into her bag and handed Blake some extra strong mints. 'Here,' she said, smiling. 'You might want to have some of these before you meet Nash's parents.'

*

Blake spent the rest of the afternoon in Nash's office at ESA, reading up on the diverse assortment of experiments he was running. Maddix found him there just before six o'clock, deep in concentration.

'Find anything useful?' he asked.

Blake held up the ring binder he'd been reading. 'Not unless you think Nash's experiments on intermetallic alloys and crystallisation of semiconductors in a vacuum had anything to do with his death.'

Maddix smiled sympathetically. 'Wait until you get to the one on the behaviour of liquid metal alloys in microgravity, it's a real page turner.'

Blake followed the older man out of the office and down to the foyer. As they stepped into the bitter autumn air they saw two cars waiting, their exhausts already emitting clouds of smoke. A uniformed policeman and a lady in a smart suit were standing beside the second vehicle, and as they approached Blake realised it was PC Morgan. Was that armed robbery case only four days ago, thought Blake to himself. Feels like a lifetime already.

'Evening Constable. Shouldn't you be staking out the parks of East Bristol?'

'No need, sir,' Morgan replied. 'That was a good call on the dog bins. We found the cash safely wrapped up in one in Gaunts Ham Park that first night. Chappell confessed to everything when we dropped it on the table in the interview room. Wouldn't shut up after that, claimed he was reluctantly forced into it and gave up the rest of the gang without any qualms. We're still collecting evidence and filling out the reports but DCS Whiteley said I could be spared to support you this evening. Thanks for your help on it though, sir.'

'Don't thank me. Olivia can take the credit for that one.'

'Yes, sir,' smiled Morgan.

Blake turned to the lady beside him. 'Inspector,' she said as they shook hands. 'I'm Stephanie Pugh, bereavement counsellor with the Avon and Somerset Constabulary.'

'Thanks for coming. This is Doctor Maddix, Flight Director for the mission. Have you been brought up to speed on the situation?'

'Yes, sir,' replied Pugh. 'DCS Whiteley briefed us this afternoon. Constable Morgan and I will wait outside while you speak to Mr and Mrs Nash, then we'll take over once you're ready. Please call us in at any time if you feel they need support. This will be a terrible shock to them and people react in different ways.'

'Understood.' He got into the front car with Maddix and the others followed behind. The driver told them there'd been an accident on the A34 so he'd take the cross country route instead. It was slow going but it gave Blake the chance to learn more about the Helioselene project from his travel companion. As they passed Swindon the conversation moved more towards Maddix's history with the Nashes.

'I joined ESA in '78, soon after it was formed,' Maddix said. 'William, although only in his twenties back then, had already taken over the running of the family business.'

'That's young. I barely even knew what I wanted to do when I grew up when I was that age.'

'Yes, he was thrown in at the deep end. He made mistakes, of course. Bad ones. Desperate to prove himself. Corners were cut, projects were rushed. It was too much too soon.'

'What did the company do?' asked Blake.

'All sorts,' said Maddix. 'They make a lot of machinery and have contracts all over the world. Shipping, oil rigs, mines, factories, you name it. He wanted to take things in a new direction though and started going for military contracts. Not an easy world to break into but he managed it, not least because he was always competitive on price. The more established suppliers had got lazy, were used to charging what they liked, then William came in with good products at a fraction of the cost. It wasn't just down to money of course, he made sure the quality was always high and delivery dates were met. He recognised even then that if he got it right and managed to get a toehold in the military market he'd make a fortune. And so he did.'

'And that was his route into the space industry as well?'

'Yes. We were tendering for several contracts at the time. Satellites, high orbit telescopes, various probes. The moon landings may have ended but the appetite for space exploration was as strong as ever. It was a busy time. Astronauts weren't on the agenda but there was a huge amount of scientific research and unmanned exploration going on. William became one of our main suppliers of equipment, and was often at events over the next couple of decades. He hosted a fair few of them. That's when I met Richard too of course. He was a lovely boy, always curious and not afraid to ask questions. Intelligent ones too, you knew you had to be on form when you saw Richard approaching.' Maddix smiled as he remembered the old days with an obvious fondness.

'Is Mr Nash still involved in the industry?' Blake asked.

'Not directly,' Maddix replied. 'Although men like

William never really give up their babies. He stepped down a few years ago but the company's still in the family which probably helps him stay close to it all. Richard's brother and sister are on the board now, and Richard himself holds a non-executive position. Well, he did anyway. Still can't quite get used to speaking about him in the past tense.'

'I know, especially given all the secrecy around what's happened,' Blake said. 'Once this is out in the open it will get easier.'

'Yes, of course. I hope you manage to find out what happened, inspector. It's the not knowing that makes it so much worse.'

They travelled in silence for a while, until the car turned off the main road and took them down a country lane, stopping when they reached a set of wrought iron gates. Their driver paused briefly to speak into an intercom, after which the gates opened automatically and they passed through. Morgan and Pugh followed them but pulled over just inside the entrance, where they'd wait until needed. Blake peered into the darkness as they swept up the tree-lined driveway. They passed a large pond and several outbuildings, one of which appeared to house a motorbike showroom, before they pulled up outside the main house.

As they stepped out of the car the front door opened and a white haired man dressed in bright yellow trousers and a navy cardigan skipped down the couple of steps to greet them. Behind him, a lady stood in the doorway wearing dark trousers and an autumnal knitted shawl, coloured in large brown, deep orange and mustard yellow squares.

'Frank! What a tremendous surprise. Come on in out of this cold,' said the man, reaching out his hand to Maddix.

'William, it's good to see you. Good evening Deborah,' Maddix added, looking past him at the woman on the doorstep.

'You're fortunate to catch us, we've not been back long.' He glanced over as Blake came round from the other side of the car.

'This is Detective Inspector Blake from the Avon and Somerset Police,' Maddix said. 'I think we'd better go inside.'

At the sound of Blake's employer the atmosphere changed instantly. Deborah Nash's hand involuntarily rose to her shoulder and a worried look appeared on her face. Her husband's smile faded just as rapidly.

'What is it?' he asked. 'What's happened?'

Maddix had steeled himself for this moment but when he opened his mouth no words came. Blake moved alongside him. 'It's Richard, sir,' he said. 'I'm very sorry to tell you this, but I'm afraid he's dead.'

Nash stared back at him, his mouth open in shock. Deborah let out a gasp and put her hand to her mouth, hugging herself with her other arm. Nash looked round at her, then back at Blake and Maddix, then turned and went to his wife without saying a word. She collapsed into his arms, looking at Maddix through her tears as she quietly mouthed the word 'How?'

'We don't have all the details yet, Mrs Nash,' Blake replied. 'There's rather a lot to fill you in on though. Might we go inside?'

She nodded and composed herself, wiping her face and leading them into the house. Blake noted the house was very modern, with a large, marble entrance hall leading to several rooms. A curved glass balustrade looked down on them from the first floor, and he could see an enormous kitchen through one of the open doors. Deborah Nash took them into a slightly more cosy drawing room, with dark wooden flooring and a grand piano in the corner. The feature fireplace was already lit, the flames adding a dramatic edge to the already taut atmosphere.

They took their seats and William Nash, having recovered from the initial shock, was the first to speak.

'Please, tell us what happened. Was there an accident?'

'We're still trying to establish the details, sir,' Blake

replied, 'and don't have a confirmed cause of death yet, but so far the indication is this was not an accident. We believe your son may have been murdered.'

'Murdered?' Nash exclaimed. Again, his wife's hand moved to her mouth in a subconscious gesture. 'That's impossible,' he added. 'Who would want to murder Richard?'

'We don't know, sir. I wondered if you might have any idea?'

'Me? No, none whatsoever.' It suddenly occurred to him what Blake was saying. 'Are you telling me it was one of the other astronauts?'

'Yes, sir, we believe so. As yet we've not been able to establish a motive. In fact there are a lot of things we don't know, but it seems fairly certain that one of the other inhabitants of the lunar colony is responsible.'

'My God,' said Nash. The words hung in the air as the news sunk in.

'There's some more you need to know. Richard's body was discovered on Monday –'

'Monday!' cut in Mrs Nash. 'You mean he's been dead all this time and we didn't know?'

'I'm afraid so, ma'am,' Blake replied. 'We had a little difficulty locating you and only discovered your whereabouts earlier today. I'm very sorry.'

Her husband reached over and held her hand for support. 'I understand,' she said pragmatically. 'We've been walking in Scotland for the last week. Off the grid I think they say.' Blake had seen this before. Shock had set in and she was operating on autopilot for the moment. 'People think we're mad for going there at this time of year but I love it. The fresh air, no distractions –.' Her voice tailed off as she realised what she'd said and she burst into tears again.

'Deborah thinks I spend too much time on my phone,' Nash said, by way of an explanation. 'We make an effort to step away from it all now and again, spend time together. I never expected, I mean. Well, we knew there were risks with Richard going up there. He was always quite calm about it, even the launches which terrified us. Even with my experience, working with Frank and the others, it's different when it's your own child going through it. Worried us to death. Not Richard though, he was always undefeatable. Said his training had prepared him, the risks were all known, that he'd be as safe up there as he would be here.' He paused, before adding 'This is the first time I've ever known him be wrong.'

'We don't know that yet, sir,' Blake said. 'Whoever did this to Richard may have tried to do the same here too.'

Nash didn't hear him. He carried on talking, almost to himself. 'The worst bit was over though. When they got through the launch and made it to space we all celebrated. We even had a party here a few nights later when they touched down on the surface. I was a young man the last time that happened, still a teenager dreaming of going up there myself.'

'Like we all did, back then,' Maddix said thoughtfully.

'Yes,' smiled Nash. 'That feeling when man first stepped on the moon, like we could conquer anything. Then it all went away, until Richard went there. It was like discovering it for the first time all over again. The whole world watching as if it had never happened before. Did you know, inspector, only twelve men walked on the moon during the Apollo missions. Twelve! Then none for nearly fifty years. Richard was the third to step out of the landing module. Number fifteen. We were so proud, so proud.' He shook his head sadly.

'I'm forgetting my manners,' said Mrs Nash abruptly, wiping her eyes with her free hand. She let go of William's and placed both hands on the tops of her legs and sat up straight. 'Can I get you gentlemen a drink. Tea, coffee?'

'A black coffee would be lovely, thanks Deborah,' Maddix replied. 'I'll give you a hand,' he added, standing up. She looked at Blake. 'Thanks,' he said. 'With milk though, please, if you have any.'

'Oh yes, Rachel came earlier, our cleaner. She knew we were back today, she always makes sure we're stocked with the essentials. William, dear?'

He looked up at her absently, then nodded when he realised she was waiting for some kind of response. He watched her walk out of the room, then suddenly seemed to snap out of his trance and looked sharply at Blake. 'How did it happen?'

'It appears he drowned, sir. We don't believe it was an accident though.'

'Oh God. Drowned? What an awful thing to do to him. My poor boy.' He shook his head again, trying to process it. 'Drowned?' he asked again.

'Yes, sir. They have fish tanks in their laboratory you see.'

'Yes, I like to keep track of the experiments Richard's doing up there,' Nash said absent-mindedly. 'It's all on the ESA website. I was never all that interested in scientific studies before, always preferred taking things apart and fixing them rather than looking through a microscope, but I've rather become quite fascinated by some of his work. I've even emailed him questions a couple of times. He must have despaired.'

'I doubt that, sir. I'm sure he was happy his father was taking such an interest in his work.'

'Suddenly doesn't seem very important now.'

'And you can think of no reason why anyone would want to harm him?' asked Blake.

'Like I said, none at all. Richard's always been so closeted away with his work, he never had any enemies. I could understand if it was me, God knows I've made a few in my time. But not Richard.'

Deborah Nash and Maddix reappeared, the latter carrying a tray of cups which he placed on a glass coffee table.

'What will happen now?' asked Mrs Nash as she sat

down next to William. 'To Richard, I mean.'

'Well, the location of his body does make this a particularly unusual situation,' Blake said. 'We haven't established the exact circumstances surrounding his death, and a full post-mortem hasn't been conducted yet.'

'Do you need our consent for that?' asked her husband.

'It's not necessary, sir. Formally speaking, the coroner will decide if and when a post-mortem is required. In Richard's case it's more a question of when, and how, not if. We are going to run a couple of tests in the hope they'll provide a clue but that's all for now. What happens after hasn't been decided yet. I imagine it will depend largely on how the case develops and whether they decide to bring the rest of the astronauts home early.'

'I see,' said Deborah. 'So there's a possibility Richard could be left up there?'

William reached over and took hold of her hand again as Blake replied. 'I'm told that is the official protocol, Mrs Nash, yes. Richard knew that and agreed to it before he left, although I believe it's not set in stone.'

'I don't like the thought of him being left up there,' said William. He turned to Maddix. 'Call me sentimental, but do what you can Frank, please? For old time's sake? Bring our boy home.'

Blake realised now wasn't the time to push the Nashes on any further questions. 'There's a bereavement officer waiting outside. I think perhaps it would help if she joined us.'

He took out his phone and called Morgan, asking him to bring Ms Pugh up to the house. 'I'll go and let them in,' he offered.

Blake stood and walked into the hallway. As he waited for the sound of the car to pull up outside, he noticed a small dresser with some photos on. There was one of Richard as a boy standing with both of his parents and siblings, taken on holiday somewhere with perfect blue skies in the background. Next to it was another, this time of him as a young man standing with his father.

'He was always fascinated by everything he came across,' said a voice behind him. Deborah Nash had left the others to come and wait with Blake. 'That was taken in America, in 1993 or 94 I think. William had some problems with a steel supplier, there was some sort of crisis going on with production at the time. Richard was living over by then, doing his doctorate in the States, and managed to get some time off to join us. I wouldn't normally go on William's business trips, but seeing as Richard was free I tagged along. We had a wonderful time exploring. I remember us going on a tour of a factory that automatically packed tea bags. It all seemed highly futuristic back then.'

She smiled ruefully as she reminisced, and fought the tears welling up in her eyes. Blake was relieved to hear Pugh and Morgan's car pull up outside. He put his hand on Deborah Nash's shoulder and gave it a small squeeze as he opened the door to let them in. He introduced them as Maddix and Nash came through to join them.

'We haven't gone public with the news of Richard's death yet,' Blake said, 'but it'll have to be announced soon. I'll keep you fully up to date with progress in the meantime, and if you want to talk to me about anything here's my number.' He handed them a card, then along with Maddix said their goodbyes and escaped to the cars.

'That's the worst bit over,' Blake said once they were inside. 'But now I'm more determined than ever to find out who did this.'

11

The astronauts gathered round the table in the common room. Wrycroft and Velasquez, the two biggest men, both plonked themselves heavily in their chairs. Lonnen, more thoughtful with his movements, sat down carefully. 'What's this all about then,' he asked wearily. It had been another exhausting shift. They were still trying to make up the time they'd lost on the day after Nash's body had been found, but the extra two hours they were putting in each day was taking its toll.

'We've had the go-ahead to proceed with an external post-mortem,' Yuridov announced. 'Obviously there's a certain lack of trust so we're going to double up. Myself and Mr Wrycroft will perform the first pass, with me leading, supervised by Eric.'

'Why me?' asked Wrycroft.

'They didn't say,' Yuridov replied. 'Maybe they pulled names out of a hat. This is a bloods workup and visual inspection of the body only at this stage. Once we've completed our analysis Doctor Ellis and Mr Daley will repeat the process.'

'You're not doing a full autopsy?' Velasquez asked.

'Not yet, no,' replied Yuridov. 'I think they're hoping we'll find something without resorting to that. If not then I guess we'll be asked to complete the full workup. I imagine they'll shuffle the pairings so you're not off the hook yet Gabriel.'

The Argentinean grimaced. 'I'm no doctor.'

'Nyet,' Yuridov agreed. 'If asked you'll be paired with one of us. Plus for that we'd need a live feed with ESA and direction from a pathologist.'

'They must have beefed up the encryption then,' commented Daley. 'Last I heard live feeds were off limits for the time being due to the possibility of hackers.'

'That is still a consideration,' said Yuridov. 'Hence why we're not doing one this time round. We'll have voice comms with Capcom but no video. A full post-mortem is different though. They'll want eyes on for that so the risk has been deemed worth it.'

'How will this work then?' asked Wrycroft. 'You do the work and I stand leaning over your shoulder?'

'They'll direct us once we're in there. All I know at this stage is that we're collecting blood samples then proceeding directly to the visual examination. We can both perform that, working down a side of the body each then swapping positions.'

'And testing the blood?' asked the Australian. 'I've had some medical training but I'm no pathologist. I wouldn't know what I'm looking at.'

'On this round Doctor Ellis and Mr Daley will test the blood we extract. We will check the blood samples they take. As you know this base is a fully equipped laboratory designed for all sorts of medical tests. For the most part our role will simply be to feed the samples into the analysis machines, and sitting back while the computer runs the tests. We can also take photographs through the digital microscopes and send those to the forensics team at ESA.'

Wrycroft nodded. 'Ok,' he said. 'When do we get started?'

'Right away,' Yuridov replied. 'Once you're cleaned up anyway,' he added, alluding to Wrycroft's appearance. After a day stuck in the lunar rover and two sweaty EVAs in his spacesuit he was looking grimy and dishevelled.

'I'll go take a shower,' he said, getting up and leaving the room.

Twenty minutes later Yuridov and Wrycroft entered the maintenance pod. Nash's body lay under a blanket on a table to one side.

'Houston, this is Lunar Base, are you receiving?' Yuridov said once they'd closed the door behind them.

'Loud and clear, Commander' came the voice of Henry Heffer over the intercom. While Wrycroft had been in the shower Yuridov had opened up comms with NASA and set up the feed to go through to their makeshift autopsy room.

'Doctor Nash is currently on a table against the north external wall. We're going to move him so we have access from all sides.'

'Copy,' came the voice over the intercom. Heffer could just make out a light scraping noise as the two astronauts shifted the table. The conversation was being relayed to the team in Bristol where Bennett, Hamilton and Palmer were all listening in. They'd been joined by Doctor Luan Cowlishaw, senior forensic pathologist for the Avon and Somerset Police.

'Will they be able to move him ok?' asked Bennett.

'Shouldn't be a problem,' Heffer said. 'Don't forget everything weighs less up there.'

'Of course,' she replied. 'I keep forgetting. Must be weird.'

'Ok, the body is in position and we have clear access on all sides,' came Yuridov's voice.

'Can you ask him to describe what he can see, please,'

Bennett said into the speakerphone.

'Commander Yuridov,' Heffer relayed to the astronauts. 'Please can you describe the status of the body.'

'Da. We are removing the sheet now.' There was a pause before Yuridov continued. 'Doctor Nash is dressed in a long sleeved navy blue t-shirt, black boxer shorts and slip on shoes. No jewellery. He's lying on his back. It appears decomposition has been minimal, as expected due to conditions on the lunar surface. Temperature in here has been maintained at four degrees centigrade in order to delay the onset of putrefaction and algor mortis. For the purposes of this investigation I've raised it and we are now showing –,' again, a pause while Yuridov confirmed the reading '– nine degrees centigrade.'

'Very good, commander,' Heffer said. 'Please take photographs for the record.'

Yuridov proceeded to take pictures from all angles. The digital camera he was using was synchronised with the computer on the lunar base, and a few seconds after taking them the photos appeared in the command centre in Houston and at the ESA investigation room.

'All done,' Yuridov said when he'd taken all the images he could think of. He looked at Wrycroft who shrugged agreement.

'You can proceed with taking blood samples now,' Heffer said.

'Proceeding with blood samples,' acknowledged Yuridov, placing the camera back on a side table. 'I'll do the right forearm first.'

Wrycroft filled in a label with the date, a 1 to indicate this was the first sample, and 'Right forearm' to remind them where the sample had been taken. He then handed Yuridov a syringe and stood watching as the Russian drew back the plunger and filled the small vial, then returned the syringe to Wrycroft who attached the label.

'First sample collected,' confirmed Wrycroft as he placed the vial upright in a stand. He picked up an empty syringe and handed it to Yuridov. They repeated the process three more times, describing as they went which part of the body each sample was being extracted from.

'Fourth vial labelled and stored,' Wrycroft said.

'Ok, please swap positions,' came Heffer's voice. 'Four more vials to be extracted by Eric, with Andrei in support.'

'This is tenser than I expected,' commented Wrycroft as he unzipped his jacket and placed it on the floor below the table. He accepted the first syringe from Yuridov and began extracting his first sample. Ten minutes later the eight vials of blood were labelled and securely stored in the sample container.

'Thank-you gentlemen,' said Heffer. 'Let's proceed to the visual inspection. We'll start with the head then move to the hands. You'll then need to very carefully cut off his clothing to check the rest of his body.'

'Who the hell did I piss off to get this gig,' Wrycroft muttered to himself as he stepped forward. He looked down at Nash, whose lifeless eyes stared straight back. 'Henry, give me a clue here will ya,' he said. 'What am I looking for?'

'Anything out of the ordinary, Eric,' came the voice from Houston.

'Ok, well, his face is out of the ordinary,' Wrycroft said. 'He's all puffy from being in the water. Hanging around in here for the last few days hasn't improved things.'

'We'll get you to check his mouth and nasal passages later,' Heffer said. 'For now it's a hands-off visual check only. Commander Yuridov, please take a close up photograph under Nash's fingernails. Any signs of a struggle?'

'Nyet, they're clean,' replied the Russian. In Bristol the pathologist and the three detectives all leaned closer to the screen, but had to agree with Yuridov. From what they could see Nash's fingernails were spotless.

'Can you run the ultraviolet light over his hands please in case anything shows up which isn't visible to the naked eye,' Heffer asked.

Yuridov did as instructed but no fluids or fibres fluoresced under the scope. 'All clean,' he reported.

'Ok, proceed with removal of the clothes. Please try to disturb the body as little as possible.'

Yuridov and Wrycroft looked at each other, then the Russian turned and picked up a sharp pair of scissors from the side table. Carefully he lifted Nash's shirt and cut straight up from the waist to the neck, pulling the two sides apart to expose the chest.

'I see a red welt running in a straight line from shoulder to shoulder,' said Yuridov.

'That's consistent with the pressure of having lain against the edge of the fish tank,' Cowlishaw confirmed to the detectives alongside her.

'Noted,' said Heffer. 'Please continue.'

Yuridov resumed cutting through to the right shoulder and down the length of Nash's arm. He passed the scissors to Wrycroft who slowly repeated the same cuts on the other side.

'What the hell is that?' Wrycroft asked as he peeled back the left sleeve of Nash's shirt.

'Photograph the area, please,' Heffer said over the intercom. A slight sense of urgency could be detected in his voice.

Yuridov obliged and seconds later they were all looking at a deep purple bruise on the outside of his arm just below the shoulder.

'We're seeing clear bruising on his upper left deltoid muscle,' Yuridov said.

'We see it too,' confirmed Heffer. 'Had Nash reported any incident which might have caused it?'

'No, he did not,' Yuridov replied.

'He never said anything to me, either,' said Wrycroft.

Yuridov leaned in closer. 'I can see a needle mark. It looks like he might have been injected with something. Did any of his experiments require him to self-medicate?'

'Bear with us,' said Heffer. 'Just bringing up his roster now.' There was a delay while the team at NASA checked through everything Nash had been doing in the days leading up to his death. 'That's a negative. We'll get ESA to validate this but we can't see anything in here which would have required any injections. It certainly looks suspicious. We'll have to see if the toxicology tests reveal anything.'

'Ask him to check the clothing for any sign of a hole from the needle,' said Dr Cowlishaw to Bennett. She relayed the message to Heffer who passed it on to the astronauts. Yuridov lifted the cut sleeve back into position on Nash's arm to check the position against the bruise, then slowly lifted it away to let light through.

'Yes, Houston. I can see a clear pinhole in the fabric in the same location.'

'Thank-you, commander. Please continue with the rest of the visual examination.'

'Mr Heffer,' Hamilton said, leaning towards the intercom. 'I know there's already been a check of the laboratory where Doctor Nash's body was found, and also that several days have passed so any evidence could have been taken, but please could you ask two of the other astronauts to go and check the lab thoroughly for any sign of a needle. There are a lot of experiments going on in there so I imagine there are plenty of potential hiding places.'

'Will do,' Heffer replied. He patched his call through to the common room and asked Cheng and Medvelev to perform the search.

'If that comes up empty we'll have to get them to search each other's quarters and all the communal areas,' Bennett commented.

'Can you get them to take an inventory of all chemicals and medical supplies too,' said Doctor Cowlishaw. 'Many toxins are hard to trace in blood samples, particularly after a certain amount of time has passed. You might have more luck identifying the source by finding out what's missing.'

'It won't be easy,' Heffer replied. 'There are tons of different elements in that base. The labs each have a lot, but the Lunarsol manufacturing plant does too, plus the first aid kit. We'll get it done but it could take some time.'

'Understood,' said Bennett. 'It might be worth starting with the areas more people have access to. You can probably leave the solar plant until the end, so I'd suggest the medical items first then Lab Two where Doctor Nash was discovered. We can expand the search from there if nothing's found.'

'Copy,' said Heffer. They went back to listening to Yuridov and Wrycroft describing Nash's body. They carefully examined his eyes, nose, lips and ears then moved on to the neck and torso. Nothing untoward was forthcoming. They continued their checks of the rest of the body but the needle mark on Nash's arm was the only obvious sign of foul play.

'I think we're complete,' Yuridov announced finally.

'Okay, thanks Andrei,' said Heffer. 'We're happy you've covered all you can for now. Please can you and Mr Wrycroft transport the blood samples to Laboratory One for Doctor Ellis and Mr Daley to perform the tests.'

The astronauts left Nash's body in the centre of the room but covered it again with the sheet. Wrycroft retrieved his jacket while Yuridov set the temperature back to four degrees and picked up the blood samples. He handed them to the Australian then collected the camera and other items they'd brought with them. As they left he turned to take one last look at the scene before shaking his head sadly and sealing the door behind him.

12

The car dropped Maddix off at his home in Lechlade then took Blake back to the office on the outskirts of Bristol, arriving just before ten pm. He contemplated heading straight home but decided on a whim to pop into the investigation room to see if there had been any developments. He was surprised to bump into Palmer in the corridor.

'Evening Phil. What are you still doing here?'

'Oh, hi, sir,' Palmer replied. 'I was about to head next door. My interview with Cheng got delayed because of the post-mortem. Are you able to join me? Wouldn't mind the support, especially if he goes all technical on me.'

'Yes, of course.' A small part of him fleetingly wished he'd headed straight home after all but it was too late now. As they stepped into the video room and settled themselves in front of the camera Palmer gave him a quick summary of the autopsy and the discovery of an injection.

'So was he drowned or poisoned?' Blake asked.

'Doctor Cowlishaw thinks drowning is still the most likely cause,' Palmer replied. 'Based on the statements from the astronauts who tried to resuscitate him, and their description of water being expelled from the lungs. That wouldn't have been there if he was already dead when he was placed in the tank.'

'Then why the –' he stopped talking as a red light appeared on the camera facing them and the large screen came to life. The chair facing them in the moon base was empty. Reluctant to discuss any aspect of the case while the line was open, Blake changed the subject.

'How's your training going? For the marathon.'

Palmer pulled a face. 'Non-existent at the moment, sir. It's still five months away though so plenty of time.'

'It'll go fast. Tell you what, it's Saturday tomorrow. Why don't we meet for the Pomphrey Hill Parkrun. It's close to here and is only 5k, I should be able to manage that. It'll do us good to get out of this place.'

'Sounds good, sir. Thanks. I'll text Kathryn and let her know.'

The door on the screen in front of them suddenly opened and Cheng hurried into the room.

'So sorry I'm late,' he said, sitting down in front of the camera. 'It's been a crazy evening. I only just got out of the search of Lab Two.'

'No problem Mr Cheng, we appreciate your time. I'm Detective Inspector Tom Blake, this is my colleague Detective Sergeant Phil Palmer. Did you have any success with your search?'

'No joy I'm afraid. There are hundreds of experiments set up in there, mostly tucked away in drawers. Lots of syringes too. It's going to take a while to tally them up with the stock register. It probably all made sense to Richard but it was a minefield to me. Fortunately Commander Medvelev was with me and he was able to determine which ones were more relevant or not.'

'More relevant? Surely all of them are?'

'Well, that was my first thought too,' Cheng replied. 'But Sergey was dismissive of some needles because of their size, and told me off when I started rummaging through the first drawer. I think he felt Richard would have been upset if his experiments were spoiled.'

'Interesting. Were Doctor Nash and Commander Medvelev close?'

'Yeah, they were. I'd say Sergey was closer to Richard than any of us. These scientist types stick together. Don't get me wrong, I'm curious about a lot of this stuff myself. I'm probably nearer to their way of thinking than I am to any of my Lunarsol colleagues, but I'm no way near the level of those two. Plus they've known each other a long time, through all the astronaut training and their ISS trip.'

'So in your opinion Commander Medvelev is the least likely suspect in Doctor Nash's murder?'

'Apart from myself, obviously,' Cheng replied with a small smile. 'Probably, yes. I find it hard to picture him doing it.'

'And who do you think is most likely?'

Cheng put his hands in the air. 'Well, that's the million dollar question isn't it. I don't know. It could have been any of them. Sergey included. Richard wasn't always the most popular person up here. He could be a little tetchy at times. Clearly he rubbed someone up the wrong way.'

'But not you?' pushed Blake.

Cheng smiled again. 'No, not me. I tend to stay hidden away in the production line most of the time. I don't really mix with the other astronauts other than pleasantries at mealtimes. Beyond that the only thing I'm interested in at the moment is the assembly of the solar cells. I've no reason to have wanted to harm Richard.'

Blake looked at Cheng and his surroundings. The room was familiar enough to him now, having performed a couple of interviews. Greys and whites filled the screen, projecting the image of a sterile environment. Cheng was dressed in a vivid red jumpsuit though, contrasting enormously with everything else on view.

'I'm curious. Does your red uniform signify anything?'

Cheng glanced down and smiled. 'No. Not to me anyway. The psychoanalysts were worried everything would look a bit bland up here so we were all given a selection of outfits. I just happened to put this one on today. It probably sounds silly but I think they're right, it's good to have a bit of colour about the place.'

'Fair enough. Tell me more about the solar farm,' Blake said. 'It feels like a lot of effort to go to for solar energy. Do you think it'll work?'

'Most definitely. I don't know how much you know about what we're trying to achieve here Mr Blake. The moon receives 13000 terawatts of power from the sun. To put it in perspective, current forecasts show that by the year 2050 the population on Earth will require only twenty terawatts. We're no way near that capacity of course. We're a small operation and it'll take thirty or forty bases, larger than this, to achieve those numbers, but the potential is huge. Done right we could conceivably meet the entire planet's energy needs. Ultimately, of course, the moon will also become the first step for launching further missions to the other planets in our solar system. It's a very exciting time in space exploration.'

'And so far, how's it looking?' Blake asked. 'Is the technology holding up?'

'It's too soon to tell for sure but there's no reason to think it won't,' replied Cheng. 'We're very close to getting our first array up and running. The first batch of cells are almost ready, and now the build has just completed on Lab Three I finally have a second 3D printer robot working on the casings to hold them. We're on track to have our first completed solar panel up and running in a couple of days.'

'Really? So soon? That must be exciting.'

'Yes. Well, it should have been. Richard's death has dampened the mood somewhat. But still, it's a huge milestone for us. This first panel will prove the whole concept, and although the bulk of our initial phase will go towards powering the base we will be able to send some back home. Gabriel has done a great job of preparing the site, so once the array is in place the energy it collects will be transmitted through wires he's already buried below the surface and fed into our microwave generators. They'll in turn bounce the energy down to Earth.'

'And most of this is being produced from resources you're finding up there? Amazing.'

'Yeah, well, we brought a lot of it with us this time round. The microwave generators for one thing. But the solar cells themselves are all home grown and they're what needs the bulk of the materials, especially as we expand. The guys have been collecting lunar soil which we then melt down using concentrated sunlight to form the glass sheets and other components of the solar cells. We also have an abundance of silicon, aluminium and iron up here which can all be extracted and used. It's pretty neat.'

'So what happens next Mr Cheng? Assuming everything works, and you get to stay there for the full two years as planned, what will you do after that?'

Cheng smiled. 'You're talking about the rumours of my move to CNSA? The Chinese National Space Administration? I don't know. Right now my only thoughts are on the current project. If this is the success we hope it'll be then I can think about my options. I'm enjoying being here but it's hard on the body. Ask me again in eighteen months and I might have reached the stage where I never want to come anywhere near this place again.'

'Wouldn't blame you,' Blake said. He looked at Palmer. 'Phil, any questions?'

'Er, yes, hello Mr Cheng. Could you please tell us about the last time you saw Doctor Nash alive?'

'Sure. It was the day before he was found.' His eyes dropped slightly and the easy smile faded as he thought back to that moment. 'I guess you've already heard about the altercation between Richard and Gabe?'

'Why don't you tell us,' said Blake.

Cheng shifted in his seat, evidently uncomfortable at being asked to potentially incriminate a colleague. 'It was nothing really,' he said. 'They were both tired after a long day and took it out on each other. It was silly of them but these things happen, especially in a close environment like this.'

'Has it happened before?'

'Once or twice,' Cheng admitted. 'Not just with Gabe either. It's the only time I've seen Commander Yuridov come close to losing his temper. He's always ice cold, you know. In control, emotionally. Nash had complained one too many times about something or other and Andrei was a bit short with him. It was hard though, we were all getting on edge caged up in the landing module while the base was being built. It would've been nice to have been able to send the robots on ahead to get that done, but it needed human input to scout the ideal location and to control elements of the build. Our forced captivity was unavoidable. In time we'll get slicker. We've learned an awful lot and future missions to new sites will hopefully have it easier.'

'So you saw the disagreement between Mr Velasquez and Doctor Nash on the evening prior,' said Palmer, bringing the conversation back to the murder. 'What next?'

'Not much to say really. Richard left after the argument. I hung around in the common room for a bit, made one final check of the machinery operating in Lunarpod Three, then called it a night.'

'And the next day?'

'Let me think. I got up, worked out for a bit, grabbed a bite to eat, then got to work.'

'Did you see anyone else at breakfast?' pressed Palmer.

Cheng drummed his fingers on the table in front of him and looked up as he thought. 'Uh, yeah, Commander Yuridov was there.'

'Are you sure?' Palmer asked. 'Just him?'

'Pretty sure, yes,' Cheng replied. 'We're often the first ones up. I don't remember anything particularly unusual about that day. Not until the evening anyway, when Lydia discovered Richard's body. I'm not going to forget that in a hurry.'

'Quite,' said Blake. 'So, apart from that, nothing stood out for you as being odd. No one behaving differently?'

'No. Like I said, I was on my own in the manufacturing plant all day. I didn't see any of the others until the evening, other than a brief visit from Jon Daley who came to bring me a coffee and see how things were going.'

'So Mr Daley would have come directly from the common room then gone straight back?'

'I presume so.' Cheng thought about it for a second. 'Although now you mention it, he did take the alternative route back so he could have a look at Lunarpod Four.'

'The alternative route? Oh, yes, down the access passageway?'

'Yes. It's a safety thing really. Gives me an escape route if anything catastrophic happens in one of the other pods. It leads to the laboratory wing then from there back to the main hub.'

'Okay, well, thank-you Mr Cheng. I don't have any more questions for now. If you think of anything which might be relevant please let us know.'

'Will do, inspector,' Cheng said, ending the call. Blake and Palmer returned next door to the investigation room.

'Thoughts?' asked Blake.

'It's like Velasquez all over again,' Palmer said. 'He spent more time talking about his work than the murder. I can't tell if that's their way of coping or if they're being deliberately talkative to distract us from the crime scene.'

'That's partly my fault,' Blake admitted. 'I find the whole thing fascinating, couldn't help asking him about it. You're right though, he was certainly more keen to chat about that side of things than he was about Nash.'

'The breakfast thing is the biggest anomaly. Ellis says Cheng wasn't there. Cheng says he was but she wasn't. Yuridov thinks they both were but can't be sure what time. It could be they just missed each other but something doesn't feel right about it.'

'Daley's movements are interesting too,' Blake added. 'His stroll around the base to bring Cheng his coffee would have taken him right past our Lab Two.'

'Before or after Nash was murdered though?' Palmer asked.

Blake sighed. 'That's the question, isn't it? Someone's not telling the truth. Let's sleep on it. See you at Pomphrey tomorrow morning.'

13

'Can we run Dad? Can we? Pleeease,' asked Sophie and Olivia as they walked towards the crowd of runners gathering by the cricket pavilion.

Blake looked at the girls, then at Emily. 'I can do the first lap with them and see how they're doing,' she suggested.

'Sound ok, girls?' said Blake. 'If you like we might be able to do the junior one at Victoria Park tomorrow morning as well.'

'Yay!' they screamed in unison as they ran ahead.

Blake spotted Palmer and Bennett amongst the throng. 'Who's idea was this?' he asked in a mock grumpy voice as he walked up to them.

'I believe that would be you, sir,' Palmer replied, smiling.

Blake put one hand on his wife's back and gestured to the other two. 'Emily, this is Phil Palmer and Kathryn Bennett, don't think you've met before have you?'

'Nope. Heard all about you both though,' Emily replied as she shook their hands. 'Tom won't tell me much about the case. How's it all going?'

'Well, we're stuck in a windowless office while the boss gets to go for high powered lunches at the Savoy and on private jets to space ports,' said Palmer, 'so I'd say it's going better for some than for others.'

Blake laughed. 'I'll take you on the next trip, promise.'

They went quiet as a safety briefing was announced, then they made their way towards the starting point. 'Be good, girls,' Blake said to his daughters, 'and see you at the end.'

The throng of people suddenly started moving forward and the three detectives eased into a steady jog as they made their way back up the slope and past the pavilion. Several spectators were enjoying bacon sandwiches and Blake looked at them longingly as he passed.

They reached the top of the path after another short but steep slope then turned to follow it down and along the edge of the field. Palmer had already filled Bennett in on the call with Cheng the previous evening, so once the crowd thinned out Blake asked her what she thought of it all.

'Phil's right. There must be something in the discrepancy between his story and Ellis' version of events. From what I gather speaking to NASA yesterday there's a definite divide between the Lunarsol astronauts and the other crewmembers.'

Blake glanced at her. 'Apart from Velasquez, you mean?'

'That was the strange thing,' said Bennett as they passed a large pond. 'They don't know anything about it. I didn't mention it obviously,' she added quickly. 'But they were concerned about the group dynamic, particularly now that Nash's death has skewed the numbers even further in Lunarsol's favour.'

'How did they think she's holding up in general?'

'Coping, is the best way of describing it. She's upset, obviously, but has worked so hard to get up there she doesn't want to give it up. It sounds like her and Nash were quite close, and had worked together quite a bit pre-launch on preparation for the experiments they're doing. It's hit her hard, but she's a scientist and has a job to do so has thrown herself into her work.' Bennett stopped talking as they moved into a single file while the path climbed through a narrow stretch flanked by bushes.

'They're worried she's overdoing it now,' she continued, once they were on the flat again. 'Trying to do her tasks and Nash's, but she won't stop. According to one of them she won't be able to sustain it and they're hoping she realises before she exhausts herself.'

Blake nearly commented that he knew the feeling, but stopped himself just in time. He didn't want to appear weak in front of his younger colleagues, and hoped he was giving them the impression he was silent because he was thinking rather than because he was finding it harder to speak with each step. He realised with relief they were starting the second lap. Two more to go, he thought to himself, I'll be ok.

'Doesn't sound good,' Palmer commented. 'I wouldn't want a worn out colleague in a place like that.'

'No, and you're not the only one,' agreed Bennett. 'Ellis doesn't know this, but apparently they've restricted her access to essential parts of the system. Commander Yuridov is keeping an eye on her, as even the tiniest mistake up there could prove fatal, not just for her. For now though she's buried herself away in the NASA lab so isn't a danger to anyone, and they can monitor what she's up to easily enough. I get the impression they're playing it by ear on a daily basis on how best to handle it.'

How are they finding this so easy, was all Blake could think. He was starting to get out of breath, and was annoyed with himself for getting so out of shape. A five kilometre run never used to be this hard.

'I've been thinking about Cheng,' said Palmer, for which Blake was immediately grateful. 'Is there any way we can get hold of their email logs? Maybe there'd be something in there which could validate his whereabouts while Doctor Ellis was getting her breakfast. It might not prove anything, but it could help clear up the confusion over their whereabouts. Didn't she say she took her breakfast back to her room to send some mails? That would give us the time she got back, which we can cross check against Cheng's. And the rest of them I guess, although I'm not sure what it would tell us.'

'Good call,' Blake managed, hoping he sounded better than he felt. At that moment, his phone, zipped inside a running belt around his waist, started ringing. He took it out as they were still jogging and saw it was Whiteley. He held up his hand to indicate to the others to stop, as he pulled over to the side of the track and answered.

'Where are you?' asked Whiteley.

'With Bennett and Palmer, ma'am. Discussing the case.'

'You sound out of breath. Are you ok? Never mind. It was just to let you know Jonathan Daley is available any time today for an interview. No rush, whenever you get here.'

'On our way, ma'am.' He hung up and looked at the others. 'We need to go, sorry.' He moved a few steps against the flow then took a shortcut that led them back to the starting line. Emily and the girls were just finishing their first lap as they got there. Blake let her know he might be late home then turned to leave.

'Probably just as well,' Palmer said to Emily with a glint in his eye. 'I was starting to get worried he wouldn't make it.'

*

'Glad we packed those overnight bags now,' Bennett said as she drove them round the ring road on the way to the office in Emerson's Green. She looked down at her luminous patterned running tights. 'I'd feel pretty self-conscious in these things all day.'

None of them had their passes on them when they arrived ten minutes later. Brown struggled to keep a straight face as he printed out replacements. 'Would you like me to take new photos for you, sir?' he asked. 'Those outfits are rather fetching.'

'The old ones will do, thank-you,' Blake replied, picking up the cards. He had enough time to get a cup of tea before confirmation came through that Daley was already in the video room.

'Morning,' Daley called out as the three detectives entered. He took a sip of coffee as they settled into their seats. 'Didn't realise I'd been away that long. I see fashions have moved on a bit.'

'Sorry, you caught us going out for a run,' Blake replied.

'Ah, now that is something I do miss,' said Daley. 'The treadmill we have up here gets very monotonous.'

'I understand you're the project manager up there, in charge of getting the solar plant up and running?'

'That's right, yes. And, more importantly, responsible for my crew. It's not hugely different to my job back home, except for the obvious. Mostly sitting at a laptop looking at spreadsheets and project plans while everyone else does the real work.'

'You don't get out much then?'

'Oh, I wouldn't say that. Can't come all this way and miss out on the interesting stuff. I try to find an excuse to join Gabriel or the others some days. It helps to see the conditions they're working under. That's what I tell them anyway. Really it just makes me feel more like Buck Rogers than an accountant.'

Blake smiled. 'How about Nash and the other non-Lunarsol crew?'

'Same as me I'd say. Most of their work keeps them

here at the base but you'd go mad if you stayed inside the whole time. Everyone finds a reason to go out now and again. Except Cheng I guess. He seems happy enough in his factory.'

'He's a bit of a loner?'

'He's quiet, yeah, but you could say the same about several of the people up here. We can't all be big personalities. I try to visit his area at least once a day, partly to see how things are progressing but also to see how he is, make sure he has some human contact. The rest of my crew would speak up if something was bothering them but Cheng's the sort who would keep things bottled up.'

'And you saw him on the day Doctor Nash died?' asked Blake.

'Yeah. Andrei and I had our regular call with Capcom, then I took a coffee over to Cheng's pod.'

'And where was everyone else at that point?'

'Well, Gabe was out preparing the site of the array. Chris and Eric were off digging up materials. Lydia and Sergey were in their labs. I assumed Richard was too.'

'And Commander Yuridov was in the main hub?'

'Yeah. He said he was going to go and have a word with Richard about the argument the night before. Come to think of it, he never mentioned if he got round to that. When I got back he was sitting alone in the control room. I left him to get on with his work and I took care of mine.'

'Yes, we heard about the argument. Tell me about it from a Lunarsol perspective. Do the others ever get in the way of your operations? I'm interested in the dynamics of how everyone fits together in such a confined space. It must be easier to manage if everyone was on the same project.'

'Not really. Like I said, it's similar to home. There are always other people around. It's actually a lot easier up here. They're professionals with their own jobs and respect that we have to do ours. Plus we have fewer protesters here blockading the entrances to the quarries,' he added drily. 'In truth their knowledge and experience is definitely a bonus, we'd struggle without them. No, the biggest distraction here is dealing with the media and the bosses back home. It's such a high profile project with a lot riding on it, they're on my back a lot more than they –'

Daley stopped talking as an alarm went off and the lights started repeatedly dimming off and on.

'What's happening?' Blake asked.

'That's the fire alarm,' Daley replied. 'It's probably a drill, NASA springs them on us sometimes. I'd better go take a look. Want to see for yourself? I can carry this camera with me.'

'Sure, thanks, if you don't mind.'

'No bother. Come on then,' Daley said, standing up and reaching for the camera. The image flickered a couple of times, and was disorientating as it moved around, but Blake and the others could see Daley's other arm reach out and open the door. Immediately they saw Medvelev running past, quickly followed by Ellis carrying a fire extinguisher.

'Maint——d Two,' they just about heard her say. Daley glanced into the common room and Blake caught a quick glimpse of Yuridov furiously working away at two consoles in the command centre.

'Maintenance Pod Two?' Bennett suggested. 'Nash's body?'

The image disappeared for a couple of seconds then came back as Daley ran after the other two astronauts. His long, loping strides in the low gravity made the picture smoother than it might otherwise have been. The image flickered again as Daley reached them. Blake could see Medvelev now holding an extinguisher of his own. The image kept cutting out briefly, with the sound of the alarm coming and going and the lights continuing to switch on and off. The three detectives watched as Medvelev and Ellis looked at each other, before the Russian opened the door. A burst of flame shot out into the corridor. The picture went black but they could still make out the sound of the alarm. 'Go go go.' Ellis's voice. There was a loud hiss then silence for a couple of seconds before the alarm and hissing noise re-emerged. Blake heard Daley mutter 'Jesus' before the sound cut out again.

'What is it Mr Daley?' Blake asked. 'Daley?' But it remained silent. They waited helplessly for the sound or picture to come back. Ten seconds passed. Twenty seconds.

'What the hell just happened?' Blake asked as they continued to stare at the blank screen.

'Nothing good, I can tell you that much,' Palmer replied, shaking his head slowly.

14

Half an hour later Blake and his team found themselves sat round a table on a conference call with DCS Whiteley and Henry Heffer at NASA. Janet Higgins joined from a car on her way to Whitehall just as they were starting. Heffer brought everyone up to date on the latest development.

'Ok, first things first. The fire has been extinguished and the crew are all safe. They're running through diagnostics now but initial indications are that the base is stable and there is no need to evacuate.'

'How far did the fire spread?' asked Blake.

'It was contained to Maintenance Pod Two which as you're aware is where Doctor Nash's body is being stored. The automatic safety procedures kicked in when the base computer detected the rise in temperature. It automatically started withdrawing oxygen from the atmosphere in that room in order to starve the fire. Unfortunately when Commander Medvelev opened the door it provided the flames with a fresh source of fuel, causing the flare up that I understand you witnessed. The sudden burst of heat played havoc with the comms which is why you lost your connection.'

'Have to admit they had us worried,' Blake commented.

'I'm not surprised,' Heffer replied. 'A fire is one of the most dangerous scenarios we have on the base, but the good news is that means we're prepared. There's nothing flammable in there. Even the blanket covering Doctor Nash's body is fireproof. The computer sensed the threat and reacted, and Commander Medvelev and Doctor Ellis were able to get it under control quickly once they were in. That said, it happened despite all our precautions, and even appears to have been quite a large one.'

Blake glanced up at the large printout of the base that someone had stuck to the wall. 'Is there any way this could have been coincidence? That it happened in that particular room I mean. An electrical fault perhaps?'

'We think it's unlikely. All the equipment in there has come through reasonably unscathed. So far as we can tell there's no serious damage. Scorch marks on the surfaces and a few melted wires but nothing that can't be easily repaired. No, the blaze itself was concentrated in a single area.'

'Nash's body,' cut in Palmer.

'Exactly,' confirmed Heffer. 'It looks like someone has attempted to cover their tracks. Commander Yuridov and Mr Daley are currently taking fresh photos and video footage of Doctor Nash which will be placed on your secure drive. His body is in a bad way as you'll see when you look at the pictures. I'm afraid any further post-mortem examination may be limited.'

Blake pondered the situation for a moment. 'This is good,' he said at last.

'I'm sorry?' said Higgins. 'I don't understand.'

'Our killer is getting nervous,' Blake answered. 'This feels like a desperate attempt to me. It's possible he or she has made a mistake.'

'Who had access to that room?' asked Bennett.

'Only Commander Yuridov, Commander Medvelev and Mr Daley,' Heffer replied. 'That's in their capacity as Base Commander, First Officer and Lunarcorp Project Leader.'

Blake looked at Palmer then turned back to the speakerphone. 'Medvelev is First Officer?'

'He is now. The position was actually held by Nash, until his death. It then passed to Doctor Ellis until Commander Yuridov raised concerns regarding her mental state. Her access was restricted and Commander Medvelev was promoted. It's standard procedure. Those astronauts are all far more experienced than any of the Lunarsol crew so the hierarchy favours them.'

'So, just to clarify, we now have the two Russian cosmonauts in charge of the base,' Blake said. 'Both with access to Doctor Nash's body.'

'And Mr Daley, yes,' Heffer replied.

'Well,' said Bennett. 'We were interviewing Mr Daley when the fire started so that gives him a pretty cast iron alibi.'

'Not necessarily,' Blake commented. 'It's tight but he could have set it going just before we spoke to him. I don't suppose anyone's installed video cameras in the last few days?' he added, directing his question to Heffer.

'Afraid not, inspector.'

Blake looked down at his notepad. He realised he'd been absent-mindedly doodling a picture of a flame. 'Do we know what actually caused the fire?' Blake asked, crossing out his drawing. 'Did any of the astronauts report hearing an explosion?'

'No, the first any of them knew about it was when the alarm went off,' Heffer replied. 'We don't know how it started yet. Commander Medvelev and Doctor Ellis were the first on the scene, and were able to extinguish the flames very quickly. None of the other astronauts were in the vicinity at the time. Wrycroft, Lonnen and Velasquez weren't even on the base as they were all out on EVAs.'

'Where are the blood samples that were taken yesterday?' Blake asked suddenly.

'They're safe. They had already been taken to Lab One. Lydia and Mr Daley started running the tests last night. Nothing out of the ordinary has shown up yet but they'll run further tests today.'

'Can we verify those samples haven't been tampered with?' Blake pressed. 'Whoever started the fire may have wanted to destroy those too.'

'We've checked,' confirmed Higgins. 'Two of the vials were loaded into the haematology diagnostics machine yesterday evening. Two others have already been analysed under microscope by Doctor Ellis. The results of both, including high definition photographs from the latter, have been saved to our servers and are available on your drive. The remaining four vials were locked in a secure store which can only be overridden by Control here in Houston. None of the astronauts can gain access without entering their clearance codes first.'

'So what was the point of the fire?' Blake asked, almost to himself. 'We have samples of Nash's blood, and have already seen the evidence suggesting a needle which administered a substance of some kind. Chances are we don't need his body any more. Why risk it?'

'Like you say, desperation?' Whiteley suggested.

'It could be the drug has already left his system,' Bennett said. 'Didn't Doctor Cowlishaw say a lot of substances have a shelf life once they've been administered? The killer might know the blood samples will be clean so they're not a threat. Doctor Nash's body itself may still contain the bigger clues.'

'Get back to the pathologist,' Blake said. 'Find out more about what drugs might have been used to sedate Doctor Nash. They'd have to be fast acting or he'd have been able to raise the alarm. At the very least I'd expect some signs of a struggle. Ask her if any are untraceable after a certain amount of time has passed. Then cross check that list against the inventory of drugs on the lunar base.'

Bennett stepped away from table to sit at her own desk. 'Thanks for the update Mr Heffer,' continued Blake. 'Appreciate you're busy. We'll let you escape, please keep us updated with any developments.'

'I'll leave you to it as well, inspector,' came Higgins' voice. 'I have enough information to brief Downing Street. We can catch up later to discuss the plans for going public with the news in the next few days.'

Blake ended the call then sat pondering the next move. 'Phil,' he said eventually. 'There's still something which doesn't add up on Cheng's movements. Seems a bit unnatural to me, from what Daley was saying, that he stays hidden away in his factory. You'd think he'd want to get out like the rest of them. Do a bit more digging will you? Check his whereabouts during the fire. And see if you can find out whether any of the chemicals in his production line could have been used to start it.'

He looked at his watch. 'It's ten forty. Mary will be here in twenty minutes. If you don't mind, I'm going to put some proper clothes on.'

15

Blake stood under the hot shower for as long as he dared. Reluctantly he dragged himself out, dressed and got back just as Mary Phillips was being escorted in by Jim Hamilton who had also just arrived.

'Mary, good to see you,' Blake said, giving her a hug.

'Morning Tom. Just got up?'

Blake ruffled his damp hair playfully. 'I wish. Thanks for coming all the way down here on a weekend. Am I right in thinking you're still in the dark about this case?'

'Totally blind,' Phillips replied, smiling. She and Blake had worked together many times before in his old life at the Met Police and he knew he could rely on her to put on a good show for the cameras. In her late thirties, her easy-going yet professional manner was ideal for dealing with the press. She wore minimal make-up and her dark brown hair was tied in a ponytail, helping to present a no-nonsense image that would be needed on this case.

'You'd better sit down, there's a lot to catch up on,'

said Blake. Bennett, on the phone, gave her a little wave and Palmer came over to say hello.

'Don't envy you on this one, ma'am,' he said. 'It's a doozey. Can I get you a brew while the boss fills you in? Sir?'

They both asked for tea and Palmer went to put the kettle on. He looked out of place, still dressed in his running kit, but other than a raised eyebrow and a quizzical expression thrown in Blake's direction Phillips didn't pursue it.

'Hope you don't mind,' started Blake. 'This is going to be a major public relations exercise. It's a high profile murder investigation and you're gonna get thrown right in front of the wolves. Still interested?'

'Stop teasing me Tom,' Phillips replied. 'How bad can it be?'

Blake pursed his lips. 'Pretty bad. You might have noticed this is a European Space Agency building. Our victim is the lunar astronaut Richard Nash, found dead on Monday evening. All indications point to this being a premeditated killing. Cause of death is unconfirmed but drowning is the most likely. He was found with his head submerged in a small fish tank in one of the laboratories. There's a recent complication though. It's looks like he may have been injected with something prior to his death which may or may not be related.'

As he was talking Phillips' eyes widened. 'Wow,' was all she could think to respond when Blake finished his summary.

Palmer appeared with their drinks and Blake gestured for him to sit down and join them. 'It's an unusual one, that's for sure. There are some things working in our favour. Primarily our finite list of suspects. There are eight other astronauts up there so our murderer has to be one of those. Also, so far, we've been able to keep a lid on it and do a lot of the legwork without outside pressure influencing anything. On the downside, we haven't been able to access the crime scene or the body, our suspects are all four hundred thousand kilometres away, and more pertinently from your perspective, this is a political minefield, what with the various organisations and nationalities involved.'

Phillips turned to look at Palmer. 'A doozey, right?' Palmer grinned at her.

'The press will be all over this once the news breaks,' said Blake. 'It's going to be carnage. Sorry. Honestly, I feel bad landing you in it. We just don't have the manpower to deal with them and run the investigation. It'll be a godsend that you're able to run interference.'

'Are you sure you don't want the publicity Tom?' asked Phillips. 'This case will make you famous.'

'Ha, no thanks. Fame's not really my thing,' Blake replied. 'Especially if we don't manage to solve it.'

'You'd better. If I'm being paraded in front of the world's cameras I want to know there's a good chance I won't be left hanging.'

'I'll make sure that doesn't happen. We've a lot of leads and haven't really narrowed it down yet, but we will. For Nash's parents' sake if nothing else. I met them last night and broke the news to them. We'll introduce you to them too, sooner rather than later. They'll be hounded by the media no doubt so will need your support to navigate that. You can discuss directly with them whether they want to appear alongside you at any of the press conferences. There are a few people here at ESA who will be able to assist you on that front too. It'd be useful if you went to their offices near Didcot and met with Janet Higgins, the Programme Director, and Frank Maddix, Flight Director of the Helioselene Mission.'

'The what?'

'Helioselene,' Blake repeated. 'Something to do with the Greek gods of the sun and moon. They're using the moon to harvest solar energy you see. Five of the astronauts are employees of Lunarsol Incorporated. The other three are your more traditional Neil Armstrong, Yuri Gagarin types. Doctor Nash was in that camp. Like I said, there's a lot of politics.'

'Eight astronauts, eight suspects. Ok,' said Phillips as she scribbled frantically on her notepad.

'Yeah, there are four of us so we initially took two of them each to do the background research,' Blake explained. 'There's a lot of overlap though so you can probably ask any of us if you have specific questions. I'll give you a brief rundown now but you've got a lot of reading ahead of you.'

Blake stood and walked over to the wall with the photos stuck to it. Four days into the investigation, the space below each was now covered with notes. Phillips and Palmer followed him.

'Okay, first we've got Commander Andrei Yuridov from the Russian space administration, or Roscosmos for short.' The photo staring back at them showed a handsome but deathly pale face, serious yet with a twinkle in his eye that suggested a certain hidden warmth. His brown hair was slightly dishevelled adding to his good-natured appearance, but that was contrasted by his unsmiling expression. 'I know what you're thinking. He looks a bit contradictory. Solemn but somehow fun at the same time. I'm putting it down to a consequence of his military training and the Russian approach to formal photography. From what I can make out he's a decent guy, well liked by his colleagues and popular back home. He's a veteran astronaut with several previous flights, and an experienced leader. Having said that, there are questions to be asked about the way he's handled some of the conflicts which have occurred amongst the other members of his crew.'

Blake moved along the wall to the next photo. 'Here we have his Roscosmos colleague Sergey Medvelev.' Younger than his superior officer, Medvelev had the same white skin, but with close cropped hair and a humourless air he lacked the amiability of Yuridov. 'Co-pilot, scientist, hero of the Russian Federation, etcetera, etcetera. You can read his cv for yourself. What you won't find in there are references to occasional lapses in his temper. From what we gather though, he was good friends with Doctor Nash.'

'So neither of the Russians are high on your list of suspects?' asked Phillips.

Blake considered the question for a moment. 'My initial thought was no, they're unlikely to have done it. But, a slightly unusual consequence is that these two are now numbers one and two in the chain of command up there.' Blake shrugged. 'Maybe there's some hidden political agenda we haven't stumbled onto yet. Bear in mind they're both military so could simply be following orders.'

He tapped his finger on the next picture. 'Doctor Lydia Ellis from NASA. Our third and final scientist. She's been hardest hit by Nash's death, which might be genuine or could be an act to deflect suspicion. She doesn't look strong enough to have forced Nash into the tank to drown him, so I had moved her down my list of suspects too, but the recent discovery that Nash might have been drugged first means we can discount that. An unresponsive victim, coupled with the moon's low gravity means she would, in theory, have been physically capable of carrying this out.'

Phillips looked at the photo smiling back at her. 'She doesn't look like a killer.'

'No,' Blake agreed. 'But you know as well as I do that means nothing. She is currently in a relationship with this guy,' he said, taking a couple of steps back and rapping his knuckles on the photo of a tanned, strong looking man with dark brown hair and a day or two of stubble. 'Gabriel Velasquez. Our first Lunarsol employee. American, of Argentinean descent. He's responsible for setting up the solar farm on the moon's surface, and it sounds like he spends a lot of his day alone out in the field. We can't be sure, but it's possible Nash had feelings for Doctor Ellis and was jealous of Velasquez. That's pure speculation though. What we do know is the two of them didn't get on particularly well, and they had a very public quarrel the evening before Doctor Nash was murdered. Velasquez is also the last known person to see him alive.'

'Doesn't look good for him then,' commented Phillips.

'No, it doesn't,' Blake agreed. 'But then again, it's not great for this guy either. Sying Cheng, responsible for building the solar panels. He's also a bit of a loner, and there are some questions surrounding his whereabouts on the morning of Nash's death. He's a little on the short side but don't let that fool you. When we interviewed him his biceps looked bigger than Jim's stomach and that's saying something.'

'I heard that,' called Hamilton from his desk.

'Next we've got Eric Wrycroft, an Australian geologist and miner,' continued Blake.

'Another big lad,' observed Phillips.

'Yes, there's no doubt he has the physical strength to have done it. We're interviewing him later this afternoon which you're welcome to sit in on. Might be useful for you to get a feel for how we've been doing things in case you get asked by a reporter.'

Phillips made a note on her pad. 'Anything in particular I need to know about him?'

'He's a bit of a rags to riches story, although the same could be said for several of the others. Particularly Velasquez who really did start with nothing. In Wrycroft's case, he grew up in an outback mining town in Queensland. Did well at school, then joined the Aussie Air Force after uni. After he left them he followed the family tradition of mining, except Eric based himself in Western Australia rather than his home state. Turns out it's sunny there, and it wasn't long before he'd moved on from fossil fuels to renewables instead.'

'And one giant leap later he was on the moon,' Phillips finished.

'You've got it. That leaves us with these two,' he said,

pointing at the next photo. 'Chris Lonnen. Working alongside Wrycroft on the mining side of things. They're up there sourcing the raw materials needed to produce everything.'

'Everything?'

'Pretty much. The solar cells, the casings, the structural arrays used to hold it all together. Even the base itself. All of it can be made from resources found on the moon. There are some fascinating clips on YouTube if you need to find out more. I found a great video showing how the robotic 3D printers build the pods they're living in. Fairly cool actually.'

Phillips smiled. 'That sort of thing will help with the media. They love a good graphic.'

Blake looked back at the picture of Lonnen. Slim, with a tanned face and deep crinkles around his eyes, you could tell he was used to working outdoors. 'I feel sorry for the seven innocent suspects in all this. The press are going to be all over them. Lonnen here is the only one with a family so I guess they'll be the most vulnerable. They might need some support through all this. They're in Australia though so I don't think we're the ones to give it. I'll drop Chase Lomax a line, see if there's some way Lunarsol can step in to protect them.'

'Lomax? Who's he?'

'Oh, wait 'til you meet him,' said Blake. 'He's the head of Lunarsol, and is the man who put this whole thing together. He's full of contradictions too, but at least he knows how to lay on a good lunch.'

'I see,' Phillips replied, clearly not really seeing what Blake was referring to.

'And last but not least, Jonathan Daley,' Blake continued, looking at the photo of the African American team leader of the Lunarsol crew. 'Project Manager, site foreman, whatever you want to call him. His background was originally on oil rigs but by the time he joined Lomax's enterprise he was more into the design and build of new sites. He's travelled all over the world setting up solar farms. Apparently he was seen as the best man to lead the project up there. No obvious motive yet, although there's a bit of a question mark over a possible incident in his past. We're still looking into that one.'

'Right,' said Phillips. 'One victim, eight suspects, some with motives but nothing concrete yet.'

'That's the gist of it,' Blake concluded. 'It's a lot to take in. We'll try to hold off making any announcement for another day or two. It'll give you a fighting chance of getting to grips with everything, and gives us more time to crack it. If you need any extra support for producing briefing packs and so on then you'll need to run it past DCS Whiteley. Any questions?'

'Hundreds,' replied Phillips. 'But I think it would help if I could sit and read through some of your notes so far and maybe meet with those ESA people you mentioned.'

'There's some video footage too,' Palmer said. 'We've interviewed several of the astronauts now, I'll show you where the recordings are on the server.'

'Speaking of interviews,' Bennett said, walking over to join them, 'I've just been told Chris Lonnen is available now. I'm about to head into the video room if anyone wants to join me?'

'Perfect,' said Blake. He turned back to Phillips and grinned at her. 'Bet you didn't think you'd be chatting to an astronaut when you woke up this morning.'

16

The three officers sat in front of the camera and waited for the screen to flicker to life. Two minutes later Chris Lonnen's face came into view. Wearing a thin bottle green v-necked jumper over a white t-shirt, he was lying casually back in his chair as if he didn't have a care in the world.

'Mr Lonnen?' said Bennett. 'Thanks for taking time out to speak to us. I'm Detective Sergeant Kathryn Bennett. I'm here with Detective Inspectors Tom Blake and Mary Phillips.'

Lonnen gave a small wave. 'Nice to meet y'all,' he replied in a slow Texan accent that complemented his mannerisms. Blake immediately thought he wouldn't look out of place with a ten gallon hat on.

'I wondered if we could start with the events of last Monday when Doctor Nash's body was discovered,' said Bennett. 'It helps to get a picture of what everyone was doing. Could you describe your day to us?'

'Sure. Ah spent most of the day with Eric out in the

rover digging for al-oo-minum, or alumin-ee-um as you Brits say.' Lonnen drew the pronunciation of each word out slowly. 'Took us about half an hour to get out to the site. We lucked out and found the mother lode, collected enough for two whole arrays. We were on site for around six hours, then had the same half hour drive back to base.'

'What time did you leave that morning?' asked Bennett.

'Around seven thirty, maybe just after. There wasn't much point setting off any earlier as our rover has a limited range.'

'So you got back at around two thirty?'

'Closer to three ah think. By the time we'd loaded the goods and run through a few checks of the rover we were slightly over our time slot. There was so much to collect we got a bit carried away and stayed longer than originally planned. Still well within tolerance though.'

'You do those safety checks every time you set off do you?' chipped in Blake.

'Yes, sir,' replied Lonnen. 'Don't want to risk getting stranded out there.'

'And did you do those or Mr Wrycroft?'

'Either of us can do it. Ah think on that day Eric had got to the rover early and had run through them all before ah got there. I did 'em for the way back while he was securing the load.'

Blake nodded for Bennett to continue. 'So, when you got back, you unloaded?'

'That's right ma'am. We can depressurise a holding bay at the end of Pod One. We dropped the materials directly from the rover into there, then repressurised and spent the next couple of hours moving it to the relevant stores. We were mostly aluminum but did have a few other elements which we managed to separate. Only in a rough sense mind you. Sying's machines do the real job of splitting it all out. We just try to give them a head start.'

'So that was still just the two of you?' asked Bennett.

'To start with, but Gabe came and helped out for the

last hour or so.'

'And afterwards?'

'Sying had finished up his work so came and found us in Pod One on his way back to the main hub. We chatted for a bit about the site we'd been to and the likelihood of it being a reliable source for the duration of our time up here. Then we called it a day and all went to grab some food.'

'So you all went straight to the common room?'

'That's right ma'am. Mr Daley was already there, as well as Commanders Yuridov and Medvelev.' He paused then chuckled. 'It looked like Jon was struggling to stay awake listening to those two.' He patted his open mouth to mime a yawn, then sat forward and put his hands on the table. 'Doctor Ellis arrived shortly afterwards. She'd just had a shower. I can spot these things.' He tapped just below his right eye a couple of times with his index finger. Probably took on the role of the class joker among the astronauts, thought Blake.

'And did you see anything out of the ordinary?' suggested Bennett casually.

Lonnen smiled. 'What, like someone holding a dagger? No, nothing unusual ah can think of.'

'You don't seem particularly disturbed by Doctor Nash's death,' Blake commented. 'I can spot these things,' he added, tapping his finger below his eye.

'Touché,' said Lonnen, grinning. 'Truth is ah'm very disturbed by it. Just tryin' to put on a brave face, that's all.' He looked downcast for the first time. 'That first night after we found him ah didn't get any sleep. As the days have gone on it has got easier but between you and me I don't really want to be here anymore.'

'I thought you all voted to stay?' asked Bennett.

'We did, we did,' Lonnen said thoughtfully. 'Ah thought about saying somethin' then but didn't want to be the only one to bail.'

'Why not? No one would think any less of you surely.'

'You think? Ah'm not so sure. These guys, my colleagues particularly, are all tough. Outwardly at least. Men's men you might say. We're used to hard, dangerous work and have all seen deaths.' He considered that for second. 'Well, maybe not Sying, he's more of a lab rat, but the others definitely. Accidents happen, Ms Bennett, particularly when you're working in countries where the words health and safety are not in the vocab-u-lary.' Blake had to suppress a grin at Lonnen's languid delivery of the word. 'Fatalities are rare, thankfully,' continued the Texan, 'but we've been around long enough to have seen our fair share. You can't show weakness in this business, it would be the end of your career. Ah had to put on an act on that first day to show I was okay. Ah take it back, what I said just now. It's not bravery, it's simply survival. Ah've been playing the part ever since.'

Lonnen suddenly looked very tired. He rubbed his face with both hands, shook his head to steady himself, then looked imploringly at the camera. 'Ah just want to get home to see ma boy,' he said quietly.

'Tell me about him,' said Bennett gently.

'Otis? He's amazing,' Lonnen replied, his eyes lighting up. 'He'll be one next week. His mum tells me he's crawling now and is proving to be quite a handful.'

'Two years is a long time to be away,' Bennett said. 'Has it been harder than you expected?'

'Sometimes,' admitted Lonnen. 'Ah was already on the team and going through training when Helen told me she was pregnant. Ah wouldn't have said I was the paternal sort before then. Ah've never been broody or anything, but when he arrived my whole world changed. We sat down and talked about it, and in the end decided together this job was too much of an opportunity to pass up. We figured it'd go quickly enough and Otis would be too young to remember me being away. Ah sure do miss 'em though.'

'So if the chance comes up again to vote on whether to

leave, what will you say?' asked Blake.

Lonnen looked at him. 'Ah'm not a quitter Mr Blake. Ah want to leave, true, but ah'm here now and have a job to do. Ah'll see this through.'

Blake tapped his pen on his notepad. 'Tell me about the fire,' he said, changing the subject.

'Ooee, yes sir, sounds like the guys had an adrenaline rush there, that's for sure. Ah was out on the surface when the alarm went off, missed the whole thing.'

'Any idea what could have caused it?' asked Bennett.

Lonnen shook his head. 'It's a strange one. It shouldn't be possible to have a fire up here. The one we had was very localised, just on Richard's head and upper body according to Andrei. You're going to think ah'm crazy but it's almost like he spontaneously combusted.'

'So the rest of the room was unharmed?' Blake asked.

'Looks that way. It must have been intense as we have some fried wiring but that's about it.'

'Like you say, it's a strange one,' agreed Blake. He gestured an apology to Bennett for interrupting and held his palm out to indicate she should continue.

'Okay, let's go back to the day prior to Doctor Nash's death,' she said. 'Can you please talk us through the last time you saw him alive?'

'Doubt ah'll be able to tell you very much you haven't heard already,' said Lonnen. 'We'd had a long day and as soon as we got in Richard hit us with a grumble about where we'd been digging. It was probably justified although I thought he was overreacting. It's not as if we flattened any of his experiments. Not like Gabe nearly did the other week,' he added, smiling.

'Was Doctor Nash prone to be argumentative?' asked Bennett.

'Not really. He was a bit annoyed when Gabe drove straight through his sensor arrangement but he didn't kick up as much of a fuss as he could have. He was still trying to remain tolerant and be a team-player at that point. He actually came and asked me about some of the terrain we were seeing further afield shortly afterwards so ah took it that he was over it. Ah guess our little transgression with the mining near his patch must have got him worked up all over again.'

'So Doctor Nash had a go at you personally?'

'Yeah, but it wasn't anything serious. We could have diffused it easily enough but unfortunately Gabe's Latin temper got the better of him and he reacted. It wasn't even anything to do with him but, well, these things happen. Richard walked out and that's the last time ah saw him until Lydia discovered his body the following evening.'

'Just for completeness, can you fill in the gap between Doctor Nash leaving the room and you heading off for the following day's expedition?'

'Not much to say, ma'am. Ah had some food with the others. Lydia disappeared to speak to Richard for ten or fifteen minutes but she reappeared and sat chatting quietly with Gabe for a bit.' He stopped and looked at the detectives. 'You know about those two, right?'

Bennett and Blake nodded, so Lonnen continued. 'They got up and left not long after, then gradually the rest of us drifted off. Ah hung out for a bit, ah prefer the space of the common room than my own quarters, but ah had my headphones in and was reading a thriller so wasn't paying attention to any of the others.'

'You have books up there?' asked Bennett. 'What were you reading?'

Lonnen grinned again. 'Ah brought my Kindle, yeah. We have a lot of downtime here, it's not all work, and there aren't many opportunities for a stroll in the park. Ah'm on 'The Man Who Ran' at the moment by Tom Phillips. It's good, you should read it. We sometimes have the music on for everyone, it's good to have a bit of atmosphere up here although ah've not been able to convert Sergey to Country and Western yet. He'll come round.'

'Sorry,' said Bennett. 'I suddenly pictured shelves full of books and thought it sounded like an extravagance for your trip, what with the weight and all. So, you stayed in the common room until what time?'

'It's not a bad idea,' Lonnen said. 'This place could do with feeling a bit more homely but hey, needs must. Ah must have called it a night at around eleven. Sergey was the only one still up then. Ah read in bed for a bit then had a good night's sleep, the last one ah had come to think of it, then woke at seven the next morning. Some of the others have to fit an exercise routine into their day but Eric and I were going to be out doing physical work so we're usually spared that. Ah just got dressed, had a breakfast ration, brushed my teeth, made a flask of coffee then spent the day in the lunar rover.'

'How has Doctor Nash's death affected your plans?' Blake asked. 'Is everything still on track?'

'Yeah, we're good. We lost a day on Tuesday but we were already ahead of schedule. The timing could have been a bit better, as we're in the two week sun cycle at the moment and it's more pleasant working outdoors in daylight. One more week of this then we're back into darkness again, although it depends a lot on the crater wall and where we're working. We generally try to get more done during the lunar day but it's no biggie, we can make it up.'

Bennett gave Blake a shake of her head to say she had nothing else to ask. 'One last thing,' said Blake. 'Open question. Any ideas who might have done this, or why?'

Lonnen shook his head slowly. 'Been asking myself the same thing every day. And night. Ah have nooo idea. Initially I was nervous, like would ah be next kind a thing, but it doesn't feel like that now. Ah could be wrong, but I think this is something personal between Doctor Nash and one of the others. What was worth killing him for though ah can't imagine.'

17

'It's Sux,' said Palmer when they returned to the investigation room.

'What sucks?' asked Blake.

'No. S-U-X,' he spelt out. He looked at his notes and read slowly. 'Short for Sux-a-meth-onium chloride. Or succinylcholine. Not sure I've pronounced it right but anyway, it's used by anaesthetists. Fast acting, and I mean really fast. In seconds the patient experiences total muscle relaxation. Can't move, can't breathe, can't even blink. Get this though. You're still awake. Fully conscious and aware of what's happening.'

'That's what killed him?'

'No. I've spoken to Doctor Cowlishaw and she says it can definitely kill, and has been used to do so in some high profile cases. It's not guaranteed though. The effects are short term, so it's just about possible a healthy person could hold their breath long enough to survive. Especially a strong swimmer like Doctor Nash. He would have known that. As soon as he recognised the threat he would have taken a deep breath and attempted to sit it out. The moon base maintains a slightly higher than normal oxygen ratio too so he would have had a good chance of making it. If he hadn't been placed in the tank.'

'So are you saying he was paralysed but awake?' asked Blake. 'If he couldn't breathe then how did he drown?'

'He wouldn't have immediately regained all muscle control. Gradually his breathing would have come back, and slight movement in his fingers. The larger muscles would've taken longer. Too long for him to have pulled himself out of the tank though.'

'Oh God,' said Bennett. 'He was fully alert as he was lowered face first into the tank. He must have known what was coming when the effects of the drug started to wear off. Either he would die of suffocation before then, or he'd be powerless to fight off the urge to breathe when he started to regain control. He had to kneel there for his last couple of minutes waiting to drown. That's horrible. Who would do that to someone?'

'Someone that really, really didn't like him,' said Blake. 'Sounds like Nash didn't stand a chance. It takes some skill to mask that level of hatred through all their training together and the last four months of the mission. How sure are we this Sux is what was used?'

'Pretty confident,' Palmer replied. 'They have a fairly extensive medical kit up there and are trained to deal with all sorts of traumas. If an accident happened to one of the crew and they needed to intubate then the sux would've been used to relax the muscles to get the tube in. They've been auditing their supplies and there's some missing.'

'We need to find out who had access,' said Blake.

'All of them apparently. No one ever predicted medical supplies being abused. If something went wrong they'd all potentially need to get to them in a hurry. It's no good if the nearest person can't save someone because the pharmacy's locked and the only one with a key is out on an

EVA. A couple of them are qualified medics so if one of the crew got appendicitis or something they'd be the ones to operate, but they've all had training in this sort of thing. Administering drugs for an urgent intubation is par for the course for these guys. Any one of them could have done it.'

'Shit,' said Blake.

'Shit indeed,' said Palmer. 'There's one other thing. The missing drug is damning but we'll struggle to prove it was used on Doctor Nash. It's pretty much undetectable so it's unlikely to show up on any of the blood samples. Now we know what to look for we can get them to focus on that but it's still doubtful. The best chance is apparently to take fresh samples from the victim's brain tissues as they're more likely to show elevated levels of succinic acid. But what with the fire –'

'– any samples we take will have been contaminated,' finished Blake. 'So our killer wasn't panicking. They haven't made a mistake. It was all calculated, done to cover their tracks.' He sighed and sat on the end of his desk. Rubbing his face with both hands he realised he felt exhausted. Palmer wandered over to look at the layout of the base pinned on one of the walls.

'Something else on your mind Phil?' asked Blake.

'Just looking at the lab where Nash was found.' He ran his finger from the wing housing the laboratories along an access passage to the Lunarsol solar plant. 'This tunnel bypasses the central area. It would have been possible to get from here to Nash's lab and back without being seen. Just a thought.'

Blake and the others wandered over to join him. 'Good point. Cheng said Daley went back that way after coming to see him, but there's no reason Cheng himself couldn't have done the same. He was in there on his own all day, it wouldn't have taken him long to sneak out, kill Nash, and get back before anyone realised.'

'And if he had been seen he could have said he was just

taking the alternative route to the common room,' added Bennett.

They all stood in silence for a moment looking at the plan. 'Okay,' said Blake. 'Something else to think about. Let's get back to work.' He turned to Phillips. 'Hopefully you're starting to get a small idea of what we're up against. You're welcome to sit in on any of our other interviews but for now I'll let you get settled. It seems Brown's been as efficient as ever,' he said, pointing to a new laptop set up on one of the spare desks. 'Phil can show you where our files are. If you need anything just shout but otherwise make yourself at home.'

Phillips thanked him and Palmer accompanied her to her desk. Blake turned to Bennett. 'You ok?' he asked.

'Yeah, just can't get the image out of my head of Nash being helpless as he was left to drown,' she replied. 'Why do it like that? There must be a hundred easier ways to kill him up there.'

'You'd think so wouldn't you,' replied Blake. 'Not that there's a good way to go but this does seem particularly vicious.'

Bennett shuddered involuntarily. 'Someone's going to have to tell his parents. It's bound to come out eventually.'

'And about the fire,' Blake added. He shook his head. 'Poor people. I'll do it. Hopefully Pugh can join me.'

They were interrupted by Blake's phone ringing.

'Inspector Blake? It's Chase Lomax. Wanted to give you a call as I've been sent Jon Daley's HR files. No history of any assignments in Botswana. You were asking yesterday? I'll send them over to you, just thought you'd want to know.'

'Much appreciated Mr Lomax, thank-you,' replied Blake, not bothering to point out he already had the employment records for all of the Lunarsol crew.

'How's it all going, if you don't mind me asking?'

'Very well, sir. We've lots of leads to follow up.'

'Good, good. Listen, I don't want you to think I'm

interfering, but as you know I want this sorted just as much as you. I've had my guys doing some background checks on all the astronauts.'

'All of them?'

'Well, yeah. We know most of what there is to know about our guys already so the focus has been on the others, but we will be giving everyone our full attention.'

'Well, please keep me posted with anything you find Mr Lomax.'

'That's just it. We have found something. It might be nothing but then again, it may not. It's about Doctor Ellis. I can't talk right now but I'll get it sent over to you right away.'

'Okay Mr Lomax. I'll take a look. Thank-you.'

'What was all that about?' Bennett asked as Blake put his phone back in his pocket.

'Lomax. Trying to dig up dirt on the other astronauts to throw the scent off his guys. Possibly. Could be more to it, we'll have to see. Says he has something on Ellis. I had tentatively ruled her out because she's not strong enough to have overpowered Nash, but this paralysis drug means she's back in the picture. He's sending something over so let's worry about it when it turns up. I've got other things to worry about right now. Our interview with Wrycroft is in an hour, but more importantly, my mug's empty,' he said, turning and heading towards the kettle.

*

'Good afternoon Mr Wrycroft,' said Blake when the screen flickered on. 'Sorry it's taken us a few days to speak to you.'

'No worries,' Wrycroft replied. 'And call me Eric.'

'Can you tell us a bit about the work you're doing up there?'

'Sure. I guess you've been told about the solar panels we're setting up. My job is to find the materials they need to make them. We have detailed satellite images of the area but until you're up close you're never quite sure what you're gonna find. Sometimes it's readily available near the surface, sometimes we have to dig a little deeper. Depends what they're after.'

'By they you mean Mr Cheng?'

Wrycroft grinned. 'Up here yeah, but telling him what to do are a whole gang of managers, project controllers, risk officers, chief engineers, assistant engineers, assistants to the deputy engineers. You name it, the whole kit and caboodle.'

'Does that get annoying?' Blake asked, smiling back.

'Nah, we mostly ignore them.'

'How was your relationship with Doctor Nash?'

'Didn't have much to do with him really. He seemed ok. Kept to himself mostly. He did like his cricket, I'd been looking forward to giving him a bit of stick when the Ashes is on next month. Other than that I rarely spoke to him.'

'Can you think of any reason why one of the other crew members might have wanted to kill him?'

'Nah, doesn't make sense. He wasn't always the most popular but I didn't see anything that would've deserved what happened to him. It's fucked up, that's what it is.'

'Yeah,' said Blake, sighing. 'Ok, just for the record, can you please describe your movements, starting from the previous evening when Doctor Nash and Gabriel Velasquez had their little argument.'

'That was unfortunate. Gabe feels bad about it, although he said they made up later. That's the last time I saw Nash. He left, the rest of us stuck around. I had my dinner, but the tension in the room was unpleasant so I had an early night. The next morning I suited up, did the safety checks on the rover, then when Chris arrived we set off for the centre of the crater.'

'Any idea why Lonnen was late getting to you?' asked Blake.

'He didn't mention anything to me. You'd have to ask him.'

'Okay, so the two of you spent the day in the field. What then?'

'We unloaded. Took a while as we'd had a good day. Gabe came to help us. Cheng was there too towards the end although he takes more of a hands-off approach to the dirty work. When everything was cleared we all made our way to the dining room. Lydia went to check on Nash's whereabouts and, well, you know the rest.'

'What happened after his body was discovered?'

'Everyone was in a state of shock,' replied Wrycroft. 'Commander Yuridov sealed the lab and we all went back to the common room. I had to get away from it though, couldn't stand being in there. I was still filthy from unloading the minerals so had a good excuse to leave and take a shower. When I got back, Jon had been in calls with Lunarsol HQ, and the Commander was speaking to Houston and the other agencies. The rest of us weren't sure what to do, just kept running over what had happened. We stayed up til the early hours but eventually the adrenaline of the moment wore off and I couldn't keep my eyes open any longer. Don't forget Chris and I had been on our feet all day. I was shattered so went to bed.'

'And you slept ok?'

'Passed out the minute my head hit the pillow.'

Blake tapped his pen on his notepad. 'Tell me, Mr Wrycroft, Eric, what made you go into the mining industry? You were a fighter pilot, seems an unusual move.'

'Not really. I grew up in a mining family, it's what I know. The air force was fun for a few years but all that military stuff can get a bit wearing after a while. I never was great at polishing my shoes or marching, couldn't see the point. I'd signed up to a twelve year contract when I was at uni, and when that came to an end I needed a job.'

'You didn't head back home though?'

'Nah. Deep mining didn't appeal. Especially after what happened to my old man. I know geology though, and an open cast mine out west gave me a chance. When they expanded into solar energy I took a punt and made the move. Next thing you know I'm up here. Funny how things work out.'

'Tell me about what happened to your father,' said Blake.

'Is that relevant?'

'I'm just trying to get an understanding of each of the crew,' replied Blake. 'I'm curious about what drives someone to become an astronaut.'

'Oh, I didn't ask to be an astronaut,' said Wrycroft. 'Lomax talked me into it. Offered me a lot of dough, plus the smooth talking bastard said I'd be a hero and would be fighting the women off when I got back. I agreed before I really knew what I was getting into.'

'Yeah, he can be a hard man to say no to,' Blake commented. 'So, your father?'

Wrycroft looked back at Blake for a moment before speaking. 'He was old school. Spent his life underground. He was a good story teller though, I'll give him that. When I was young he was full of tales about elves and goblins down there, made it sound like a fantasy land. As I got older the stories became more, ah, inappropriate. Him and his mates were typical Aussie blokes, you know? I loved hearing it all, always thought I'd end up joining them once I got out of uni.'

'But you didn't.'

'No, I didn't'. Wrycroft paused, looking past Blake into the distance. 'I knew something had gone wrong the second mum phoned. I was down in Sydney when it happened. Dad and his crew were three kilometres down, tunnelling deep beneath an underground lake. The supports gave way and the roof caved in.' He snapped out of it and looked back at Blake. 'It happens, they all knew the risks. At least it was over fairly quickly, so they told me.

I couldn't do deep mining after that though. Never thought I'd join the air force either, but they came to the campus recruiting not long after the old man died. I couldn't face the thought of going back home so when they said they'd sponsor my PhD if I signed up I jumped at the chance. It was just what I needed too, apart from the shoe polish obviously. Had a great time. When it was time to leave them the mining was still in my blood but I couldn't go back to Moura. So I ended up in Western Australia, which, as it happens, is a good place for solar harvesting.'

'Sorry to hear how it came about though,' said Blake genuinely.

'Ah, don't sweat it. Ancient history. And like I said, funny how things work out. Without that I wouldn't be here. Which despite my initial reservations has been a hell of an adventure.'

18

'You need to see this,' said Palmer when Blake walked back into the investigation room.

Blake pulled a chair over to Palmer's desk. 'What've you got?'

'Lomax has sent over what he claims are details of Lydia Ellis' bank account. Not her main accounts. This is a separate savings account that appears to have been withheld from NASA. Have a look at this.' Palmer pointed to the transactions. 'The account was opened eight months ago. Four months before they left. The first payment was made into it two weeks ago. $125,000. Then on Wednesday this week there's a second payment. Another $125,000.'

Blake whistled. 'How did he get this?' he wondered out loud.

'I don't want to know. I'm checking to see if it's genuine but if it turns out to be true then it's not looking good for Doctor Ellis.'

'Where's the account based?'

'Bermuda. Which being a British overseas territory gives us a bit more leeway than we might have otherwise. I don't think we should mention this to NASA yet. There could be an innocent explanation.'

'Not likely,' commented Blake. 'Stay on it.'

He pushed his chair away and rolled back to his desk just as Jim Hamilton came in.

'Fancy another trip chief?' he asked, walking over to Blake.

'To Bermuda? Hell yes.'

'What? No, Mar del Plata. Near Buenos Aires. What's happened in Bermuda?'

'Never mind. I'm guessing Velasquez?'

Hamilton nodded. 'That's a long flight,' said Blake. 'I doubt Lomax's plane can make it in one go. What have you got?'

'I've been looking into his past. You know Lomax told you his parents moved from Argentina to the States in the early eighties? Does that date set any alarm bells ringing?'

'Fuck me. The Falklands?'

'Si. Las Islas Malvinas. It was just a hunch but the timing made me curious. I tracked down Velasquez's father, gave him a call. Said I was a reporter for an astronomy magazine doing a feature on the Lunar project, wondered if I could ask a few questions. He wasn't interested and was about to hang up, until I said we'd pay for the interview. $200, hope that's okay.'

'We'll square it somehow. What did you find out?'

'Well, I can see why young Gabe ran away. Señor Velasquez is a lowlife. Spent two years in jail for assault after repeatedly beating Gabriel's mother. Doesn't think much of his son either. Want to know why?'

'Humour me.'

'He's not his son.'

Blake raised an eyebrow. 'Well, he is,' continued Hamilton. 'But he's not his biological father. Gabriel's mother was already pregnant when they got together. Mr Velasquez never took to his adopted son, hence the difficult childhood.'

'Do we know what happened to his biological father?'

'He died.' Hamilton paused. 'In the early eighties.'

'Ah ha,' said Blake, seeing it all fall into place. 'So, Mr–'

'–Gutierrez,' said Hamilton.

'Mr Gutierrez gets killed during the conflict. His girlfriend panics. She's pregnant and unmarried in a devoutly Catholic country. She goes with the first guy that'll take her. Señor Velasquez. For some reason they have to hot tail it out of Argentina. Maybe he's avoiding getting drafted into the war. Gabe's born a few months later.'

'Pretty close,' said Hamilton. 'He wasn't avoiding the war, just running away. Velasquez was, is, simply a petty crook. He stole from the wrong guy and found himself in a lot of trouble. Gabriel's mother gave him a way out. She wanted to get away too. The stigma of having an illegitimate child would have never left her. They decided on a fresh start in a new country so had a quick wedding, flew to the States for their honeymoon and never left. Immigration enforcement was a bit more relaxed in those days.'

'What do we know about Gutierrez's death?' asked Blake.

'Ah, well, that's where it gets interesting. Velasquez knew nothing about it, just the guy's name, but I've been looking into it and there was a bit of a scandal at the time. Before the war started actually, but linked to it. The Argentines had all sorts of economic problems at the time, and were in the middle of moving from one military junta to another. They were building up their naval forces. There was an accident at a shipyard and three men drowned. Gutierrez was one of them. Seems the incident was brushed under the carpet.'

Blake sat upright. 'So you think Velasquez blames the

Falklands crisis for leading to the death of his father? Would he have gone as far as murdering Nash in revenge though? It seems unlikely.'

'Why not?' said Palmer. 'If your father had died at the hands of the Argentineans you might want some sort of vengeance too. His mother ended up with a bully who made his childhood a misery. Velasquez suffered for years. If he blames us for all his troubles then who knows how far he'd go. To do it by drowning, imitating the way his father died, would send a clear message to the British. You ruined my life, I'll ruin one of yours. That's normal enough in the gangs where I grew up, grudges aren't easily forgiven.'

'We're going to have to tread very carefully on this,' said Blake. 'If we accuse an innocent Argentine hero of murdering a British national then we're in danger of triggering a major international incident. Besides, there's a good chance Velasquez knows nothing of all this. Ok, Jim, it's definitely worth a closer look. Can you set up another call with Velasquez. Let's confront him with it and see how he reacts. In the meantime find out all you can about the accident at the shipyard.'

'Will do. I already have an interview lined up with Sergey Medvelev later, I'll see if we can squeeze Velasquez in before that.'

*

'Good afternoon Mr Velasquez, thank you for seeing us at such short notice,' opened Blake as he and Hamilton settled themselves in front of the camera.

Velasquez leaned back in his chair, seemingly quite relaxed about the interruption to his day. 'What can I do to help, officers?'

'Tell us again about your childhood,' said Blake.

Velasquez looked back at him curiously. 'I can't pretend it was a particularly happy one,' he replied. 'My old man was a piece of shit, beat me regularly. Wasn't too good to my mom either. He ended up in prison after hitting her one too many times. I'd already left by then. Escaped that world and never looked back.'

'This might sound a little strange but please bear with me. How much do you know about your parents' lives before they came to America?'

Velasquez looked back at Blake coldly. He shook his head slowly before continuing. 'Oh,' he said finally. 'That.'

'Go on,' coaxed Blake.

'Mom didn't have a lot of luck with men,' he began. 'I guess you've found out how she got pregnant with me but before they could marry he was killed in an accident. I'm not even sure they would have got married. She wanted to but from what she told me once he wasn't all that sold on the idea. He was still young, reckless. Why tie yourself down to a girl who was stupid enough to get knocked up, right? Anyway, it's academic. He broke into a shipyard with a couple of his mates one night. I'm not gonna judge. Times were hard, they were desperate. She never got the full story on what happened but reading between the lines they managed to sneak into the dock without being seen. They were only after tools or anything they might be able to sell. They tried to escape in a small boat but were too heavy and capsized still in the boatyard. I guess they were weighed down by the goods they stole and didn't make it.'

'Was foul play ever suspected?' asked Blake.

'No, not that I heard. Maybe they were caught and someone decided to make an example of them, who knows. From what I gather he was always getting into trouble. If he hadn't got himself killed when he did then something else would have got him sooner or later. I would've had a crappy childhood in Buenos Aires instead of a crappy childhood in Phoenix.'

'Have you ever tried to find out more? About what happened?'

'What's the point? Chances are I wouldn't find out

anything, but honestly, I don't care. My childhood isn't something I give a lot of thought to. For a while I lived in the moment, surviving day to day, but since going back to school and finding work I actually enjoy life's got better and better. I can make plans now, think about my future. I don't dwell on the past other than knowing I don't want to make the same mistakes my mom made.'

'Like you?' asked Blake with a slight grin.

Velasquez smiled for the first time. 'Yeah, like me. She didn't do too badly though did she, I turned out ok.'

'What do you think?' Blake asked five minutes later when they returned to the investigation room.

'Came across as genuine enough,' Hamilton replied. 'If he's faking it then he deserves an Oscar.'

'Yeah, that's the impression I got. But if he doesn't connect Gutierrez's death with anything to do with the conflict, and doesn't bear the British any ill will, then we've lost our motive.'

19

It felt like they'd barely had a chance to sit down before Blake and Hamilton were making their way back to the interview room.

'Okay, Sergey Medvelev,' said Hamilton as they sat down in front of the blank screen. 'Thirty-four years old, making him the youngest on the crew. But, he does have six months under his belt on the International Space Station making him the third most experienced astronaut up there after Yuridov and Nash.'

'Good friends with Nash too, according to Cheng,' added Blake. 'Let's see what he has to say about that.'

They stopped talking as the camera switched on and the large screen flickered into life, showing Medvelev just sitting down in his chair.

'Good afternoon, commander,' said Blake. 'Thanks for joining us, I appreciate you're busy.'

'It has all gone little crazy,' replied the Russian in a thick accent.

'I understand you've had to pick up a lot of Doctor Nash's experiments?'

'Yes, is full workload, for certain. My original rota was already one hundred percent utilisation. I have now stopped, or postponed, some of my work and have picked up selected areas of Doctor Nash's instead.' Medvelev paused before adding. 'I don't mind. He would do same for me.'

'You were friends then?'

'Da, of course. I have known Richard for many years. He spent lot of time with us in Star City, learning Russian among other things. That's what we call Yuri Gagarin Cosmonaut Training Centre near Moscow. Rolls off tongue better Richard used to say.'

'And I'm told the arrangement was reciprocated?' prompted Blake.

'That is correct. I had several trips to UK and US working on my English. I'm not perfect still, sorry.'

'Don't worry,' said Blake. 'You're better than a lot of teenagers I overhear. I can barely understand a word they say these days.'

Medvelev smiled. 'Da, is same all over world.'

'So tell me, do you have any suspicions regarding who might have killed Doctor Nash?'

Medvelev sat back in his chair and steepled his fingers by his lips as he considered his reply. His closely cropped hair and dark eyes gave him a slightly sinister look, but Blake knew from experience that appearances didn't mean much.

'I have my suspicions, yes, although they may be –' he struggled to find the right word. 'Do you say unfounded?'

'Yes, that's right,' Blake replied. 'That may turn out to be true, but I'd be interested to hear them all the same.'

'I find Mr Cheng's behaviour has been a little –' again, he paused as he tried to think how best to describe it. '– unusual.'

'In what way?'

'Like when we asked to search Laboratory Two yesterday. It is like he is looking for something, but not for what we were meant to be looking. Is right? He was quickly going through Richard's drawers, but I felt his approach was, how you say, haphazard? I like this word. Yes, haphazard. I had to tell him to be more careful. He did not like that.'

'I see,' said Blake. 'Is your relationship with Mr Cheng usually on more friendly terms?'

'It was, in early days,' said Medvelev. 'But then I catch him coming out of Richard's laboratory once. He was surprised to bump into me. He said he was just passing and had gone in to speak to Richard, but he was not there. Said he touch nothing in lab. It seemed genuine at time, so I let it go. Since then he keep distance from me.'

'Interesting. When was this?'

Medvelev looked to the ceiling as he worked it out. 'Must have been around ten days ago. Two weeks at most.'

'And have you seen him in Laboratory Two since then?'

'No, but –' Medvelev stopped, clearly torn whether to go on.

'It's ok,' Blake reassured him. 'Anything you say is completely confidential, and if we find out later it's irrelevant I don't mind. However, it might also be that a tiny detail you have dismissed could end up being crucial. It would be better if you told me.'

'Da. Well, it is probably nothing but on morning of day we found Richard's body I wanted to speak to Mr Cheng about the utilization of the 3D printer robots. I could not find him though. I try his quarters but he is not there, then I try common room, but Commander Yuridov say he has not seen him. I decide to look for him in Lunarsol pods but again, no sign. When I finally get back there he was getting some food, and we speak for maybe ten minutes. But it has been at back of my mind, do you say, since then.'

'Where was he,' stated Blake for him.

'Exactly,' agreed Medvelev.

'Had you looked in the lab area?'

'Nyet. There was no reason for him to have been there so I never considered it.'

'Well, as you say,' said Blake making a note. 'There's probably an innocent explanation. Tell me,' he added, 'what's your impression of the Lunarsol crew in general?'

Medvelev snorted. 'They are not cosmonauts,' he said simply.

'Meaning?'

'There is no discipline. Being in space is dangerous. You must follow protocols. It concerns me sometimes they are too relaxed. Too, how you say, cavalier? No discipline,' he repeated. 'Except perhaps Mr Wrycroft. But of course, he is pilot. He understands risk and consequence better than the others. We are trained to evaluate a situation and make judgement on how to react. We learn how to maintain control of our emotions. That is why I think it cannot have been a true astronaut who killed Richard. It is one of the Lunarsol team.'

'You say you are always in control of your emotions,' said Blake. 'But what about the incident in the training pool at Boscombe?'

Medvelev looked momentarily embarrassed but recovered quickly. 'Yes. Well, nobody is perfect,' he said sheepishly. 'That was long day and several things go wrong. I make mistake, and technician supporting me not spot it. Richard could have been seriously hurt. At the time I was cross with assistant, but on reflection I could, and should, have prevented it. It was good lesson for me.'

'And a lucky escape for Doctor Nash,' Blake mused. 'On that occasion.'

'Yes, he was excellent,' said Medvelev. 'Thoroughly professional. Did not get angry, but evaluated situation and helped put in steps to make sure it never happen again. As a good astronaut should. Again, another important lesson for me. I learned a lot from Richard, he was good man. I will miss him.'

20

Blake stepped out of the ESA building following the interview with Medvelev and walked over to the small pond around the corner. He often found it easier to think away from the confines of an office. Something about fresh air helped him gather his thoughts.

It was a clear evening and as he lowered himself onto a bench he realised he was being presented with a picture-perfect view of his crime scene. There wasn't a cloud to be seen, but the stars weren't bright enough to compete with the nearby streetlights. The only thing in the night sky was the moon, unusually big and, Blake realised the more he looked, visible in extraordinary detail. The contrast between the dark patches and lighter areas was mesmerising, and he became lost in thought as his eye travelled down towards the southern tip where he knew the astronauts were now living. All such a long way away, he reflected. It was strange to think of them all up there, carrying on with their work while sat here, a world away from everything they were experiencing.

After staring at the scene for a few minutes he shook his head and reached for his phone.

'Good evening, inspector,' answered Janet Higgins. 'Dare I ask, how's it going?'

'Still more questions than answers at the moment I'm afraid.'

'Anything I can help you with?'

'There is one thing I was wondering,' said Blake. 'Would it be unusual for another astronaut to go into the ESA laboratory? Without Doctor Nash accompanying them?'

'Not necessarily,' Higgins replied. 'A lot of equipment isn't duplicated in all the labs so it could easily be the case that, for example, Doctor Ellis might have needed to use something. The astronauts support each other a lot too, so Richard might have asked one of them to check on part of his research if he was out in the field or busy with something else. They're all familiar with one another's work.'

'What about the others?' asked Blake. 'The Lunarsol crew.'

'Ah. That would be less likely. I can't immediately think of a reason why any of them would go near the labs. In fact I'd be quite concerned if they did. Not for any malicious reasons, but there's no reason for them to and they could end up inadvertently messing something up.' There was a pause where neither spoke for a few seconds. 'Why?' she asked slowly.

'Off the record? It's one person's word against another and is completely unverified at this stage. I don't want to accuse someone of anything untoward if there's an innocent explanation.'

'Off the record,' Higgins agreed.

'Sying Cheng was seen coming out of Doctor Nash's lab a couple of weeks ago. Claims he was just passing.'

'That does sound odd. She thought for a moment. 'It is

possible for Cheng to walk via the laboratory wing to get back to the main communal area, so the 'just passing' comment stacks up. Curious.' She considered it then, almost to herself, muttered 'I wonder,' before her voice trailed off. Blake looked at his phone, wondering if they'd been cut off, but then heard the tapping of a keyboard in the background.

'Richard sent a message sometime last week,' she said as she typed. 'He had a feeling someone had been in the lab. Here it is. There's a bit about one of his experiments, then he ends by saying "I can't explain why, it's just a sense that something's not quite right. I think one of the others has been in here. Probably nothing, but I'll keep an eye on it and let you know if it happens again." That's all he said.'

'And no more was said on the matter?'

'No. Richard died a few days later. I'm so sorry, I didn't realise the implications at the time. It was only just now that you reminded me. God, could we have prevented this?'

'We don't know if it's related yet,' said Blake. 'Like you said, one of the other astronauts might simply have been borrowing some piece of equipment, and Nash himself didn't seem overly concerned. Still, if Cheng has been snooping around that does make it more interesting. Would you mind giving me access to all of Doctor Nash's emails? There could be something else in there.'

'Of course,' replied Higgins. 'I'll get IT to set you up with proxy access.'

'Thank you.' Blake was about to end the call, but looked again at the moon, still incredibly clear in the early evening sky. 'Photos never really do it justice do they?' he said. 'I keep catching myself looking up, seeing the moon floating there. There's a magic to it I'd never appreciated before.'

'You know, without it we probably wouldn't be here,' said Higgins. 'The Earth happens to exist in the habitable zone around our sun, but people underestimate how important a role the moon has also played in helping life to flourish. There's still so much more for us to learn. I agree though, it's not just the scientific aspects. It is beautiful.'

'Beautiful,' echoed Blake. 'But deadly.'

*

As Blake sat there he realised he was starting to get very cold, but it was good to be outside after a day of interviews with the astronauts. Was it really only four days since he'd sat here and texted McHugh? It felt like a month.

Prompted by the memory, Blake dialled his old friend's number.

'Tom,' came the jovial voice on the other end. 'Good to hear from you so soon. How's the case going?'

'Getting more complicated by the minute,' Blake replied. 'Listen, sorry to bother you on a Saturday night, do you have a minute?'

'Of course. What do you need?'

'I'm just curious about the five Lunarsol astronauts. In particular Cheng. Did he or any of the others ever come to you for training?'

'No, sorry,' said McHugh. 'They've got their own facilities. We're more geared up for zero gravity spacewalk training and some of the more intricate low gravity external maintenance manoeuvres on the base itself. We worked closely with all the other astronauts, and ISS crews, but I can't tell you much about the rest. Just rumours really. Can I ask what this is all about yet?'

'Soon,' Blake promised. 'It's likely there will be some kind of announcement tomorrow. Monday at the latest. Once that happens give me a call and I'll fill you in.'

'Exciting. I'm starting to understand why you became a policeman instead of following the rest of us into the aerospace industry.'

'I dunno,' said Blake. 'I might be looking for a new job if this case doesn't work out.'

'Anything in particular you're looking for with Cheng? I've not met him but I know a bit about the work he does if that helps.'

'No, it's not so much his solar work I'm concerned with. More any interest he might have in Doctor Nash's work for ESA. Is there any link you're aware of?'

Blake heard the sound of McHugh blowing out as he thought about it. 'Well, Nash is working on a hundred different studies. I don't know about most of them. If you're able to drop him a line directly then he's the best person to ask, although his time's limited and he's not always the quickest to respond to questions. Still, he probably has a better idea than anyone which of his experiments might relate to Cheng.'

'And if I can't get hold of Nash, who else might know?'

'There are plenty of people at ESA who will be able to tell you about Nash's work. You might want to approach this from the other angle though. Look for someone at the China National Space Administration. I know Cheng's American, and is employed by a US company, but it's no secret he's also working with the Chinese. He does social media events and so on as a publicity exercise, but rumour is he's also being touted as a future CNSA expedition leader.'

'So I've heard,' said Blake. 'I don't suppose there's any chance some of these Chinese space guys are based in London?'

'Ha, you are optimistic. No, they're all out in the Haidian District near Beijing. You'll have to speak to someone there, but I won't lie to you, that won't be easy. They're not thrilled to have been beaten to the moon, which is mainly why Cheng has been thrust so much into the limelight over there. You'll need some friends in higher places than me to get anywhere near them.'

*

Blake thanked his friend then called Higgins back. Without naming McHugh, he broached the subject of speaking directly to the Chinese. Higgins promised to call him back as soon as possible.

Five minutes later his phone rang. 'That was quick.'

'Okay, you've got your interview,' said Higgins. 'Mr Bo Tse has agreed to it.' She pronounced his surname Chay, then spelled it out for Blake to avoid any confusion on his arrival. 'He won't do it over the phone though, insists you go to visit him.'

'To China?' asked Blake, looking at his watch. It was nearly nine in the evening. Higgins must have woken Tse to set up the meeting.

'I'm afraid so. Bo is a senior director in the CNSA. He works on their lunar programme and has dealt directly with Cheng a number of times. On the few occasions I've met him he came across as one of the good guys, but don't necessarily take my word for it.'

'Okay. If Lomax's plane is still available then I'd better get going. Thank-you.'

Blake hurried back to the investigation room to find the whole team, including Mary Phillips, were still there. Palmer had done the initial background work on Cheng and Blake was relieved to see him still at his desk. 'You know I promised you could come with me on the next trip?' he asked. 'Well, be careful what you wish for, because we're off to Beijing. Right now. Gather all the files we might need, we can review them on the plane.' He turned to Bennett. 'Sorry Kathryn, would you mind checking how soon we can get the jet in the air? We need to get going tonight if possible.'

While Bennett was checking on the logistics of the flight Blake went over to Phillips. 'Sorry to abandon you. Are you all set to go if they decide to break the news before I'm back?'

'I think so, yes,' Phillips replied. 'I've pulled together a press release with the basics of the mission and a profile of Doctor Nash. The media outlets will scurry off to do their own research anyway. Doctor Maddix is taking me to meet Nash's parents tomorrow morning, and I'd like to involve them in the press conference if they feel up to it. The Twitter speculation hasn't really got any worse so I'm hoping we can hold off until Monday, but I'll keep you posted.'

'Good. I'd let Janet Higgins give you a steer on how much to release. That there's been an accident is a given. That Nash has died is, I suspect, inevitable. The opening of a murder enquiry is one for her and DCS Whiteley to decide. Check how they want to play it.'

She nodded as Bennett put down her phone. 'I've just spoken to Nick Meyer, the co-pilot. The plane is always kept fuelled and ready to go. Captain Berry and he will meet you at Bristol airport. They'll have the flight plan filed and will be ready to leave as soon as you get there. They aren't meant to take off after ten pm on a weekend so you need to hurry. It'll be close but at this time of night you should just make it.'

Fifty one minutes later Blake and Palmer were running across the tarmac and onto the plane. Meyer quickly closed up behind them and ran through the safety briefing while Phillips taxied to the runway. The wheels lifted off the ground with a minute to spare.

'End the day as we started,' commented Blake once he got his breath back. 'We should've kept our running gear on.' Five minutes later Meyer came back to join them.

'We need to stop and refuel en route. We'll do that in Baikonur as we already know the guys there and they can fast track us. All being well we'll arrive in Beijing early evening local time, then it's a forty-five minute transfer to the CNSA headquarters. I assume you'll be wanting to fly home later that night if you're able to get what you need?

At a push we could get back to the UK in the early hours, but Bristol has a quota on the number of night flights they're allowed. We can play it by ear but it might be easier all round if we spend a couple of hours at the stopover in Kazakhstan to time our arrival for the minute Bristol opens at 06:00 on Monday morning.'

'Sounds perfect, thanks Nick,' said Blake. 'Sorry to have dragged you away on a weekend.'

'Don't worry, we're used to it. Most of the time there's a lot of waiting around so it's good to get some air time. Plus we haven't been to China since Cheng left for the moon. It's a big one. Three runways and a lot of air traffic, but hopefully we'll get a clear run in. They've nearly finished building a new airport a bit further out to the south east of the city which will ease things. Until then we'll have to take our chances.'

'You've taken Cheng out there?' Blake asked.

'A few times, yes. We've flown all the astronauts at one time or another. The ones up there who you know already and those who are still in training. They often have to move around from one training centre to another so if we can we give them a ride.'

'What are they like?'

'The astronauts? They're good guys. Mostly they take the opportunity to get some sleep when they're with us so can't say I know them all that well, but they've always been friendly enough. Cheng had some meetings with the Chinese media we took him to. He had to do photo shoots for magazines and interviews and so on. He joked a bit about it on the way back. Velasquez had similar attention in Buenos Aires. These guys are all celebrities now of course.'

'And Lomax doesn't mind giving up his plane for them?'

'No, he's very generous when it comes to his chosen ones. He keeps us busy enough with just his trips but if the schedules work out he's happy to share. The only exception is Wrycroft as we struggle to make it all the way to Australia without making several refuelling stops on the way, and Mr Lomax doesn't like us to be out of action from his perspective for that length of time. Eric doesn't mind though, he still gets to fly first class on the commercial carriers.'

'I'm curious,' said Blake. 'When Cheng was over there, was it just for media reasons or did you ever take him to their space agency as well?'

Meyer shrugged. 'I never asked. We're just a taxi service really. Once he's left the airport I couldn't say where he went, although he never mentioned anything to me. Not that I'd expect him to of course.'

On the other side of the world Lomax and Brent, his chief security officer, were listening to the conversation.

'This Blake character is more interested in our guys than I'd like,' said Brent. 'I guess he didn't buy the Ellis transfer.'

'He needs to investigate everyone,' said Lomax. 'Ellis will still be on his radar.'

'You think Cheng did it?'

'I hope not, but the important thing isn't who did it, it's how soon it's resolved. We need to prepare damage limitation in case it does turn out to be one of our guys. Starting with delaying Blake. Talk me through extraction and replacement timescales again.'

'The Helioselene 2 crew have moved to a fast path schedule. Don't get your hopes up, it only knocks a couple of weeks off their training so they're still almost six months off being ready. If this thing is wrapped up any time soon then the astronauts will either be made to abort, in which case we're screwed, or an agreement will have to be made to lock the culprit up. That's the angle we need to work on. The closer it is to Crew Two being ready the more of a case we have. Of course, if the murderer is one of ours then the ideal scenario is some kind of arrangement for them to continue working while they're there. Call it community service, whatever.'

'Community service? You're joking.'

'It won't be popular but it is pragmatic. It's not as if they could run off anywhere. That's just an interim measure until they're back on Earth, then they can face trial like any other person accused of a crime.'

'Good. Ok, we can work with that. I don't know how well it would play with the rest of the crew but it's definitely worth looking into. What other options are there?'

'Well, in theory Greschenko could launch the rescue rocket. Options then are to bring them all back and abort the entire mission, or the rest of the crew can stay on site and just the guilty party is flown home. That doesn't work for two reasons. First, the operation would be down one astronaut. If it's Ellis or one of the Russians they could be replaced as their reserves are fully trained already. If it's one of ours, like I said, we're screwed. Second reason is cost. Hundreds of millions of dollars to bring back one guy who will be coming back a few months later anyway. It doesn't make sense so I can't see it happening. Best case? Either this Blake guy doesn't solve it for six months, then we can legitimately do a full crew swap. Or, if it's solved sooner, we push for temporary incarceration up there. Whether that's locked in a cell or given some leeway to keep working is down to you to negotiate.'

'Alright. We'll work up the case for no extraction. That leaves us with Blake and his team.' Lomax thought for a minute. 'At the moment it doesn't feel like he's getting anywhere so we might not need to do anything. Then again, he could find something in Beijing and the whole thing's over this time tomorrow. We need to buy ourselves some time.'

'Did you get the file on Blake? Why he left London?'

Lomax spun a pen round on his desk, deep in thought. 'Yeah. I got it. Let's keep that one on the backburner for now. We might need it as leverage later. Any other ideas?'

'You could bring the plane back? Leave him stranded over there.'

Lomax smiled. 'That'll only save us a few hours, seems a bit churlish. Mind you, it won't hurt to make his life a little more uncomfortable and it'll give us time to think of something else. Why not.'

21

'Inspector Blake?'

Blake slowly opened his eyes, momentarily confused about his surroundings. 'Morning Nick,' he replied. Or at least, that's what he'd tried to say but his mouth was so dry the words were barely intelligible.

'Sorry to wake you, sir,' said Meyer, handing Blake a glass of water with one hand and a phone with the other. 'There's a call for you. Director Higgins from ESA. If you want it to come through on the speakerphone just push this button over here.' Meyer pointed towards a switch on the side of the cabin. 'Can I get you some tea or coffee?'

'You're a lifesaver. A tea would be wonderful, thank-you,' Blake replied. 'Where are we? Is it much further to Kazakhstan?'

Meyer smiled. 'We've already landed, refuelled and taken off again. You slept through the whole thing. We're about two hours out of Beijing. Local time there is currently half past three in the afternoon, although it's still seven thirty in the morning in London. I'll get your tea.'

Meyer moved towards the rear of the aircraft. Taking a sip of water, Blake lifted the phone to his ear. 'Tom Blake,' he said formally into the receiver.

'Inspector, it's Janet Higgins. Sorry to disturb you but I'm afraid rather a lot has happened since you left. It's been a long night here.'

'Oh dear. Should I ask them to turn the plane around?'

'No, no. You're nearly there now, and I think it will be worthwhile meeting the Chinese. That's the good news. They're awaiting your arrival and will help you in any way they can. Sounds like you're going to get the full VIP treatment so enjoy it while it lasts.'

'Thank-you. What's the bad news?'

'Social media has kicked off. Some blogger posted something about Doctor Nash being awfully quiet at the moment. A few others picked up on it and tracked back to his last communication over a week ago. He'd been talking about one of his experiments and said he'd give an update in a few days. That raised suspicions as he hadn't come back when he said he would, then more people got involved. It escalated very quickly, and now appears to have gone viral. This all happened throughout the night. Apparently these people don't sleep.'

Blake sighed. 'We knew this would happen. I guess we should be grateful it took them this long. Have there been any decisions taken yet on what to do about it?'

'Yes. We've discussed it and decided the only option is to come clean. Full disclosure. We'd only be setting ourselves up for more recriminations down the line if we try to delay things any longer. So, we'll say Doctor Nash has died, and that it happened several days ago but we had to inform the next of kin first before making a public announcement.'

'And what about the murder inquiry?'

'The consensus is to say we're still trying to determine the exact cause of death, which is true, and that we haven't ruled out foul play at this stage. It's not an out and out admission that we've opened a full blown murder investigation but people will realise that's where things are heading.'

'When's this going to happen?'

'In an hour. I'll read out a statement, and Inspector Phillips will follow on with more information. I have to say I've been impressed with her so far, she's got up to speed very quickly and seems to have a sixth sense on what we should, or in some cases shouldn't say.'

'Yes, she's good,' Blake agreed. 'She'll give the media a few snippets to keep them happy but won't reveal anything we don't want them to know yet. What about Nash's parents?'

'They're being brought in as we speak. We have our reservations about parading them in front of the cameras, but it's either here in an environment we can control, or the reporters will be all over their front lawn. Mr Nash in particular was keen to be involved when we called so we decided to go ahead and have them at the press conference.'

'Okay,' said Blake. 'I'd probably keep them away from any direct questions from reporters if you can. It's still very raw for them, and I doubt they're quite as media-savvy as Mary. I agree though, it's good for them to be there.'

'I'd better go,' said Higgins. 'I just wanted to keep you in the loop. Wish us luck.'

'Good luck,' Blake replied, as the phone went dead.

Palmer dropped into the seat facing him and raised an eyebrow. 'Bollocks,' said Blake.

*

'I don't suppose this tv can pick up a live feed can it?' Palmer asked Meyer a little while later as he and Blake sat drinking their teas.

'Yes, of course. We have access to all the major

networks. What are you after?'

'Anything with the UK news will do I suspect.'

Meyer brought them over some sausages, mushrooms, tomatoes and toast then turned on the television and found BBC News. He handed Palmer a remote control then went back to the cockpit. They sat in silence and watched it for ten minutes while they ate. A scrolling banner at the bottom mentioned there was going to be an announcement from ESA at 8.30, but it came across as very low key and apart from that there was no other reference to anything to do with the moon base. Palmer muted the sound once the news started to repeat itself.

'What do we know about this Mr Tse then?' asked Palmer.

'Not a lot. This already feels like it could end up being a waste of time.' He doodled absent-mindedly on a notepad as he talked. 'Higgins said he's a good guy, but he'll probably just show us some magazine covers of Cheng being the golden boy of Lunarsol's operations, tell us a bit about the video blogs he does for Chinese kids, then deny any knowledge of the rumours of Cheng's involvement with their space programme. Like I said, a waste of time.'

He threw the notepad on the table so that it landed in front of Palmer and stood up. 'I need a piss before this press conference starts,' he said as he made his way to the back of the plane. Palmer glanced at the notepad and saw Blake had scribbled a message. 'Is this plane bugged? I don't trust Lomax. Say nothing.'

The last two words were underlined. Palmer didn't move, except for his eyes which darted around the cabin looking for some kind of listening device. He quickly realised how pointless it was so picked up a piece of toast and relaxed back in his chair instead.

'No news yet?' Blake asked as he settled back into his seat a couple of minutes later.

Palmer shook his head. 'Still a few minutes to go. How bad do you think it'll be once it's out?'

'The public? Christ knows. There'll be a feeding frenzy in the media for the next couple of days but you know what they're like, things'll calm down soon enough. There's only so many graphics of the moon base they can stick on the news. In a way it's probably no bad thing we're well away from it all.'

'Hope Inspector Phillips doesn't hold it against us though,' Palmer commented.

'Ah, but on the plus side when we do solve it she'll get all the good publicity too,' Blake said. 'Gotta stay positive.' He leaned over and picked up the remote control. 'Let's see how this goes first though,' he added as he turned the volume up.

The news had cut to a conference room where Janet Higgins and Mary Phillips, in her police uniform, were seated behind a plain table. The full room wasn't shown but Blake knew there would be several rows of chairs facing them. He felt a surge of relief that he wasn't the one sat there.

'Thank-you for coming here this morning,' began Higgins. 'My name is Janet Higgins and I'm the European Space Agency Programme Director for the Helioselene Mission. As you know we, along with our colleagues in NASA and Roscosmos, flew a crew to the moon just over four months ago. Working alongside the commercial Lunarsol team, the nine astronauts have established a base near the southern pole of the lunar surface.'

She glanced at her notes before continuing. 'One of our most experienced astronauts, Doctor Richard Nash, has been an integral part of the mission. However, it is with deep sorrow that I have to announce Doctor Nash has passed away. His body –'. She paused while the room erupted. Several camera flashes went off and it seemed to Blake that everyone was talking at once. 'Ladies and gentlemen. If you can please remain seated I'll tell you what we know so far, then I'll hand over to Detective Inspector Phillips who will be able to provide further details. We will take questions from the floor at the end.'

She waited while the noise in the room subsided. 'Doctor Nash's body was discovered earlier this week. The exact circumstances surrounding his death are not yet known but I can confirm a police investigation has been opened. Obviously, given the inaccessible location of the lunar base we are severely hampered and have not been able to formally appoint a coroner as would normally be the case. However, the other astronauts are cooperating fully with our investigation. I would also just like to take this opportunity to express my sincere condolences to Doctor Nash's family and would ask that they are given time and privacy to grieve. Thank-you. I'll now hand over to Detective Inspector Phillips.'

The camera moved across to Phillips who gave a small nod to Higgins then turned to the reporters. 'Good morning. My colleagues are currently handing round a press briefing pack with further information on Doctor Nash, the lunar base, and the type of work he's been doing over the last few months. You will also find details regarding Doctor Nash's death. Since this involves the death of a British citizen the investigation is being run by a UK task force. It is a nationwide investigation involving the Met Police in London as well as officers from Doctor Nash's home constituency covered by the Avon and Somerset Constabulary.'

Blake couldn't help giving a little smile. Phillips had deftly made their team sound larger than it was while at the same time deflecting attention away from his team being the central base of the investigation. The fewer reporters on his doorstep the better as far as he was concerned. He listened as Phillips continued.

'I can confirm we have not ruled out foul play at this stage.' Again, the noise level in the room rose as the implication of this sank in among the reporters. Phillips waited patiently until it went quiet. 'Perhaps it would be useful if we opened the floor to questions now.' The screen changed to take in a wider angle with around thirty reporters all clamouring to be noticed with their hands in the air. Blake watched as one of them lowered his hand slightly and started speaking after Phillips had presumably indicated for him to go first.

'Thank-you inspector. Dan Curtis, BBC. Can you tell us who found the body?'

'Doctor Lydia Ellis, the NASA representative, discovered Doctor Nash in his laboratory. She immediately raised the alarm, then her and base commander Andrei Yuridov attempted to resuscitate. They were not able to do so, and as a qualified medic Doctor Ellis formally pronounced him dead at eight thirty pm our time on Monday evening.'

'Monday?' asked the same reporter. 'Forgive me but it's now Sunday. Can I ask why an announcement hasn't happened earlier?'

'It's a fair question,' Phillips replied. 'There are several factors that had to be taken into account, not least of which has been informing Doctor Nash's next of kin. Also, we are dealing with an unprecedented situation where the death of a British national has occurred outside of British territory. Indeed, outside of any territory. And we have the safety of the other astronauts to consider. It was not appropriate to say anything before today.'

It was clear the people in the room weren't entirely satisfied with this answer but Phillips swiftly moved on by selecting a different reporter.

'Thank-you. Heather Brownlee, Sky News. Are there any plans to bring Doctor Nash's body or the remaining astronauts home?'

'Not at this stage, no,' answered Higgins, leaning towards the microphone. 'There are a number of reasons for that. Firstly, we don't know exactly what happened yet, and we don't want to react hastily or make a quick decision based on the wrong assumptions. Secondly, we felt the investigation itself might be compromised if all of them were to come back to Earth and return to their home countries. Finally, the astronauts themselves discussed it and unanimously agreed they wanted to persist with the mission. We are, however, constantly reviewing the situation, and depending on how the investigation develops that decision might change. We already have the existing lunar descent vehicle available on the moon, plus we are assessing contingencies such as replacing the existing team with a relief crew.'

Thirty hands were still in the air so Phillips pointed towards another reporter in the front row.

'Bob Macdonald, the Times. You say you haven't ruled out foul play. By that I take it the circumstances surrounding Doctor Nash's death are suspicious enough to warrant an investigation into the other astronauts. Have you ruled out any of them as suspects at this stage?'

Blake grimaced. Phillips would now be forced to admit publicly that all of them were being investigated.

'They know who did it!' came an angry shout before Phillips had a chance to reply. The camera panned round and Blake's eyes widened in horror as he saw William Nash on his feet pointing at the front table. 'You know! It was Velasquez, that Argentinean lowlife. He blames the British for his father and now he's killed my boy.' Pandemonium broke out as all the reporters near Nash tried speaking to him at once. It took Phillips a couple of minutes to get the room back under control, during which time Frank Maddix managed to tactfully usher William Nash outside.

'Ladies and gentlemen, please,' called Phillips. 'Mr Nash is understandably very upset about his son's death, and I'm afraid he may have jumped to certain conclusions. We are looking into many lines of enquiry currently and no one astronaut has been singled out. Thank-you for your time today. I'll end the briefing there and will provide you with updates as and when we have them. Thank-you.'

Phillips and Higgins stood up and quickly left the pack

of reporters calling after them.

'Shit,' Blake said as they continued to watch the story unfold. The news anchors were doing their best to repeat the information they'd just heard while no doubt a frenetic research team in the background were hastily pulling together anything they could to embellish the story.

'I think we just reignited tensions with Argentina,' said Palmer. Blake looked from the screen to Palmer, couldn't think of anything to say, then looked back at the tv. 'Shit,' he said again.

A few minutes later a call came through. 'Sir? It's Jim,' came the voice. Blake leaned over and pressed the button Meyer had shown him earlier to switch it to the speakerphone.

'Well that went well,' opened Blake.

'Saw it did you? Christ, what a clusterfuck. Mary's been dragged into a crisis meeting with DCS Whiteley, and Ms Higgins is on her way to Number 10. It's all a fucking mess here, you're well out of it.'

'How did it even happen? We barely even considered that as a possible motive in the first place. The link between Velasquez and the British was tenuous at best.'

'It was Frank Maddix. Apparently Mr Nash called him last night and while they were chatting he accidentally let it slip about the potential Velasquez angle. He says he didn't make a big deal of it, was just trying to give him some reassurances that progress was being made. It appears Nash spent the night stewing and, well, you saw the result.'

'Jesus, what was he thinking?' asked Blake. 'Okay, too late now, it's out there. We need to plan what happens next.'

'Well, Inspector Phillips looked pretty deflated immediately afterwards. Not her fault obviously but I think she's expecting to take a bollocking from Whiteley, and it's not exactly the first impression she'd been hoping to make with the media. Higgins looked shell-shocked too. It's like the chief said yesterday, if we handle this wrong it could trigger a major international incident.'

'And now we've handled it wrong,' Blake said. 'We'll let Higgins and the politicians worry about that side of it. Our priority has to be Velasquez. I got the impression he knew little about his father's death, in which case we'd better be the ones to break this latest development to him before the press work it all out. I don't want him finding out from someone else. Especially if it's an Argentinean news source that paints a very one-sided picture of the whole affair.'

'I'll try to set something up,' said Hamilton. 'Good luck with the Chinese, it'd be nice if you could wrap this all up before you leave.'

'Wouldn't it just,' said Blake. 'Let me know how it goes with Velasquez.'

22

A limousine was waiting when Blake and Palmer stepped down from the plane. The temperature, Meyer had told them, was a balmy eight degrees centigrade, the same as they'd left behind in Bristol, but the lone man standing beside the car was wearing just a simple suit with no overcoat. Must have only just got out of the car thought Blake as he walked towards him.

'Inspector Blake?' greeted the man as he bowed his head slightly and stepped forward to shake Blake's hand. 'My name is Bo Tse. It is an honour to meet you.'

'Likewise,' replied Blake, introducing Palmer.

'Please, let's get out of this cold,' Tse said, gesturing towards the car. A chauffeur had appeared from somewhere and stood holding the rear door open for the three men.

'I wanted to meet you personally,' said Tse once they were seated, 'as this is a rather delicate situation. My colleagues at the National Space Administration will meet us when we get to Haidian district. They will likely tell you a great deal about the Chinese space programme, and about the commendable work Sying Cheng is doing to promote the exploration of space. I regret to say I do not think you will hear anything to help your investigation.'

'That's disappointing to hear Mr Tse. I was led to believe we would be given full cooperation.'

'Yes. And outwardly that will appear to be the case. However, they will tell you nothing of importance. I on the other hand –'

'– will be able to speak more candidly?' Blake asked, his hopes rising. This whole trip had felt like a folly from the moment they'd left Bristol but he suddenly felt a surge of anticipation.

Tse bowed his head almost imperceptibly. 'I trust you can be discreet, inspector? As you may know we are also working on our own expedition to the moon. However, we are currently several years away from being ready. Our first launch of any kind wasn't until 2003, some way behind the other superpowers. We're fast learners though. We do now have the rocket technology to get there, and the resources to fund such a venture, but we still have a great deal of work to do on many other aspects of a successful lunar mission. Notably with regard to the establishment of a base itself.'

'So Cheng is helping you gain that knowledge?'

Tse hesitated. 'Yes. In many cases that has been done openly. He's made video blogs for school children showing them around the base, and during those he has been able to point out seemingly innocuous features which are of crucial importance to our development.'

Blake could see where Tse was leading. 'But not all cases?'

'I must admit that yes, in some instances Mr Cheng has perhaps overstepped his remit and has adopted a slightly more, shall we say, clandestine approach. In short, he has been paying closer attention to certain areas he perhaps would not have been expected to.'

'He's been spying,' said Blake. It was a statement rather than a question.

Tse nodded. 'I can assure you there is no malicious intent behind it. It has been purely from a fact gathering perspective. The more he can tell us about the base, the experiments that are being run, the surrounding terrain, and so on, the more it accelerates our progress.'

Blake turned to look at Tse more closely. 'Does he know something about Doctor Nash's death?'

Tse looked slightly uncomfortable. 'You would have to ask him.'

'I have.'

'Yes. I think perhaps it could be time to ask him again. Only this time you will know more about his activities. I tell you this in confidence of course. I would not want the other astronauts to discover what Cheng has been up to. It could make life difficult for all of them. I know what he's been doing is bordering on unethical, but it was done with good intentions. The advancement of space exploration is in the interest of all mankind.'

'Mr Tse, I appreciate your candour. For the purposes of expediency though, I believe you already know what Mr Cheng will tell me when I question him. Could we please dispense with politics and get straight to the point. What did Cheng do?'

Tse drummed his fingers on the window ledge as he looked out at the suburbs passing by. Palmer opened his mouth to say something but Blake subtly shook his head, wanting to give Tse time to decide for himself that he should talk.

'It's not what he did,' Tse said eventually. 'It's what he saw.'

'And what did he see?'

'Doctor Nash's body.'

'Go on.'

'Cheng had got up during the night to have a closer

look at some of the work going on in the laboratories. It was foolish, and something he decided to do of his own accord. He is genuinely interested in a lot of the experiments, but it was an unnecessary risk. If he'd been caught it would have raised questions. He let himself into Doctor Nash's laboratory and saw the body. He checked for any sign of life but Nash was already dead. Sying didn't know what to do. If he'd raised the alarm not only would he have had to explain what he was doing there, it would have made him a likely suspect. So, he left, careful not to touch anything, and went back to his quarters. He expected Nash to be discovered when the rest of the crew woke, and avoided joining them for breakfast for as long as he dared. But still there was no alarm. He couldn't say anything then of course, so hid away with his work all day waiting for someone else to discover the body. He thought Nash would have been found a lot quicker than he was.'

Blake shook his head. 'He could have told us this before. It would have helped to know more accurately what the time of death was. We now have a much shorter window on which to focus.'

'He knows. And he feels terrible about it. Not so much because of your investigation, but he's tearing himself up over whether anything could have been done to save Doctor Nash if he had raised the alarm sooner. The answer is no I'm sure, but that's not helping Sying accept it.'

'So,' Blake summarised. 'Cheng can confirm Nash was dead at some point during the night. Do you know the exact time?'

'I'm sorry, no,' replied Tse.

'Okay, we'll ask him. So the reason he wasn't at breakfast was because he was hiding in his room waiting for someone else to discover the body, but no one did and he had to spend the entire day waiting, presumably nervously, for that to happen. Is there anything else you can tell me?'

'I don't think so. Other than that I'm very sorry.'

'There doesn't seem to be much point in us continuing to meet your colleagues Mr Tse. Would you be able to drop us back at the airport?'

'I would prefer not, if you don't mind. I know it's a lot to ask, but if you don't show up then my colleagues will know I have spoken to you. It will also cause great offence. If you can spare two hours to take a tour it will mean we can avoid any unpleasant repercussions.'

'You mean you can avoid them,' said Blake. 'Okay, Mr Tse, I must admit you've been very open with us when there was no need to. You can have your two hours. Thank-you by the way.'

'You're welcome. I only wish I could do more.'

'I'll let you know if you can,' Blake said amiably.

'This is the National Space Agency just coming up,' Tse said, pointing out of the window. 'My colleagues will be waiting for us. It might not help your case, inspector, but you may still find some of what they tell you interesting.'

23

Blake looked up at the departures board for the thirtieth time. Still a 35 minute delay, still no word on the departure gate. Five hours earlier when they'd left the airport they'd assumed the executive jet would be waiting for them when they got back. After the useful meeting with Tse on the drive in, Blake and Palmer had had to endure an interminable display of plainly misdirected cooperation, before being driven back to the airport to discover they'd been abandoned.

Blake didn't bother trying to find out where the plane was. It seemed fairly obvious Lomax would have been furious at the way Velasquez had been incriminated, and who could blame him. He checked his phone and there was no word from anyone at Lunarsol, but he did manage a small smile when he saw a text from Shaun McHugh simply saying 'Wow.' Blake quickly tapped a reply to say he was out of the country at the moment but would give him a call when he got back.

A voicemail from DCS Whiteley explained the whole investigation team was in the doghouse for Nash's outburst at the press conference, and the world's media were whipping up Anglo-Argentine animosity in what she felt was a thinly disguised attempt to start another Falklands conflict. The two of them were to find a way to get back as quickly as possible.

They'd been fortunate. Turkish Airlines flight TK21 was due to depart just before one o'clock in the morning, and even accounting for a transfer in Istanbul the time difference meant they'd get back to London just after nine am UK time. So long as this delay meant they didn't miss their connection.

'The one major drawback of flying on that jet is we now know what we're missing,' Palmer observed.

Blake grunted agreement. He leaned back, stretching his arms above his head, arching his back and letting out a long, loud yawn. Several unimpressed faces looked his way. He glared back at them, not in the mood for their condescension.

'Sorry I got you into this Phil,' he said. Blake knew this monumental cock-up of a job could end up costing Palmer his career as well as Blake's. There was a chance the whole team would be expected to hand in their resignations. That's if they weren't prosecuted in some way, or sued for slander by Lunarcorp.

'Don't sweat it,' Palmer replied. 'The pay's crap and the hours are shit. We'll be rich this time next year when we've gone private.'

Blake smiled. He knew that'd be the last thing Palmer would want to do, but maybe it was the right move for him. He'd escaped the Met for reasons he'd managed to keep to himself, but then had played it safe by staying in the police in Bristol. This could be the prod he needed.

'Of course,' Palmer added, 'you'll need to change your name first.'

Blake's smile faded, then they looked at each other and

both started laughing.

'Might have to emigrate too,' Palmer went on. 'Not to South America obviously, you won't be very popular down there. Probably best to avoid Russia too. And China, Australia and America, just in case. Are there any countries we haven't offended?'

'I've heard Timbuktu's nice this time of year,' suggested Blake. 'Or –'. He was cut off by the tannoy announcing their flight was now boarding from Gate 36. 'Come on, let's go before they change their minds.'

*

They made up the time caused by the delay and sixteen hours later, at nine thirty on Monday morning, Blake and Palmer finally touched down at London Gatwick. With no luggage they were able to swiftly navigate their way through the airport and into the arrivals hall. Blake was relieved to see Kathryn Bennett and Danny Brown waiting for them.

'I'd been preparing myself for a big show from the press,' admitted Blake as he approached them.

Bennett shook her head. 'Inspector Phillips has kept them busy. For the moment they're only interested in Nash and the other astronauts. You're going to owe her big time when this is all over though.'

The two detectives waved away Brown's offer to carry their bags. Blake reached inside his and brandished a small bottle instead. 'Didn't manage your vodka last time so you get this instead,' he said, handing it to him. 'We ended up having several hours to kill in Beijing airport. It was that or a teapot.'

'Baijiu?' said Brown, reading the label. He looked at Blake, grinning. 'Thank-you, sir. I'll save it until you've solved the case then we can all have a shot to celebrate.'

He led the way to the short stay car park, all running across the road to avoid a sudden downpour, and they all piled into the waiting car. As Brown drove them out of the multi-storey, windscreen wipers on overtime, Bennett filled the others in on developments since the previous day's press conference.

'You were probably better off having a nice long sleep than being here. It's all gone mental. Good news first though. Jim managed to get a video call with Velasquez before he found out about Mr Nash's accusation. He did a good job of damage limitation. I sat in and Velasquez took the news as well as can be expected. Even managed to joke that the press will no doubt give his adoptive father a hard time so, as he put it, every cloud and all that. As far as he's concerned he's happy to stay far away from it all, and it doesn't get much further than where he is, so no hard feelings.'

'Good work,' said Blake. 'No doubt his email and twitter accounts will take a hammering but if he's sensible he'll just keep his head down. What else?'

'Well, the Chief's pissed at the whole thing but there's not a lot she can do about it and you weren't there anyway so you're off the hook on that one. Doctor Maddix has been doing his best to make up for his part in it by running interference and keeping Mr Nash away from the cameras. The one you will have more of a problem with is Lomax. He's livid that one of his team has been accused and has been giving Director Higgins a hard time. You might want to brace yourself for a call from him.'

'Yeah, we figured as much when he left us stranded. Okay, I'll cross that one when it comes to it. How about Mary?'

'Smooth as you like, to be honest sir. She's been drip feeding information to the press and has kept them off our backs. It's been business as usual for us, other than a greater sense of urgency. I've been looking into the accusation against Daley and the alleged incident in Botswana. As you know there was nothing in his Lunarsol file to suggest he'd ever even been there, and Lomax supplied the official report of the incident which mentions a manager called John Leeson. I cross checked him against Solarcorp's HR records and he was there. Dismissed after the hearing. Everything tallies.'

'Okay, at least that's one thing cleared up,' Blake answered.

'Not quite. I tried contacting the family of the victim, Harry Pepper, but they seem to have vanished. That made me curious so I called their local sheriff's department. They're in a small town in Montana and were really helpful. I said I was a relative in the UK and was worried that I'd not been able to get hold of them, and they agreed to call round. When I phoned back a couple of hours later they said the Peppers weren't at home. But, they'd spoken to a neighbour and apparently they'd won a holiday to Vegas a couple of days ago and had flown straight out.'

'You think the timing is a bit suspect?'

'Don't you? Almost as if they've been deliberately moved out of the picture. I figured trying to track them down now will be a needle in a haystack, so I concentrated on the Botswana end instead. I started by going through news articles from the time. That's when I hit the jackpot. One of the local papers covered the incident, and they do refer to a John Daily who was alleged to have been implicated. Both names spelt incorrectly which is possibly why they haven't come up in any of our searches. It's suspicious though, and definitely doesn't refer to the Leeson mentioned in Lomax's report so something's fishy.'

'Either the paper got the wrong name, or Lunarcorp have doctored the reports,' Blake summarised. 'Nice job detective, keep on it. What about Ellis? Have the laundering guys had any joy finding out who put the money in her account?'

'Not yet. Whoever transferred the money knows how to cover their tracks. Bob Fisher in Fraud has been working on it but said not to get our hopes up, this one's looking like it might end up being untraceable.'

'Could be Lomax, trying to take the heat off his guys,' said Blake.

'Or the Russians. Same reason,' suggested Palmer.

'True,' Blake admitted. 'Okay, we can't prove it either way at the moment so we'll leave Bob to do his thing.' He closed his eyes briefly but jerked his head back slightly as he realised he had almost fallen asleep. 'Christ, I'm tired.' He looked out of the window at the rain hammering down on the queue of traffic ahead, the red blurry brake lights of the cars in front dissolving quicker than the wipers could refresh them. 'I've changed my mind,' he said. 'Perhaps being on the moon isn't so bad after all. I wouldn't miss this.'

24

Chris Lonnen added a sachet of milk powder to his coffee and turned to look at the common room. Unusually for breakfast time all the astronauts were up early and seated at the table. He opened the seal on a croissant, one of his rare treat rations, and went over to take his place between Ellis and Wrycroft.

'A big day,' Yuridov commented, bringing the quiet conversations to an end.

Velasquez looked at his plate of food. 'I'm too nervous to eat.'

'You need to get something down, you've a long day ahead of you,' Yuridov advised. The first solar array was ready. Cheng had fitted the final cell into the frame the previous evening and completed the diagnostic tests. Everything was performing at peak expectation. They'd done this thousands of times on Earth, and would soon be rolling several hundred more out with monotonous regularity, but this first one had everyone feeling an anxious anticipation after everything it had taken to get them this far.

'Big day,' echoed Cheng. 'This should be a good news day for the planet. Shame the press have found out about Nash, it has detracted from the occasion somewhat.'

'How can you be so cold?' Ellis asked. 'I wish Richard was here to see this.' Since the first day after Nash's body had been discovered, the astronauts had unofficially adopted an unspoken agreement between themselves not to talk about the murder or who the murderer might be. Speculation would only serve to feed the paranoia and unpleasant feelings they were all experiencing. Avoiding the subject as much as possible had so far proven to be a successful way of getting through the week.

'Doctor Nash's death remains our over-riding concern,' Yuridov said. 'And, it's only right it overshadows your achievements here. I don't know how the investigation is going but hopefully we'll have answers soon. In the meantime, please don't undervalue how much you've all accomplished, in what has turned out to be very challenging circumstances. Despite everything that's happened you've accomplished something remarkable, something many people thought would not be possible. This is a momentous day for our world, and you deserve recognition for what you've pulled off. Well done, everybody.' He raised his coffee mug in a mock toast. 'Mr Velasquez, is everything ready?'

Velasquez nodded. 'The array is loaded onto the lunar buggy. Eric will come with me and help me move it into position. It's a one man job but we're not taking any chances on this first deployment. Too many people will be watching. Part of me wants to wait until this evening when the second array will be ready. It'd be nice to have a backup just in case anything goes wrong.'

'It won't,' Daley said. 'You've all prepared for this and rehearsed it plenty of times. It's just the thought of an audience that's got everyone on edge but you know it'll be fine.' He paused, then added, 'That's the theory anyway. I wish I felt as confident as I sound.'

The others laughed nervously. 'Alright Gabriel,' Yuridov added, 'you're ready. The rest of the Lunarsol team are scheduled for base duties today. I know none of you want to miss this. Doctor Ellis, Commander Medvelev, I'm sure you're just as keen to witness this moment so your schedules have been cleared for this morning as well. Mr Velasquez, it's over to you. Good luck. Or as we say in Russia, oodahchi!'

*

The astronauts gathered around the control consol. Commander Yuridov and Daley were seated with the others stood around behind them. Yuridov pushed his chair back and gestured for Daley to drive.

'This is your project, Jon. It's only right that you run things from here.'

Daley reached forward, flicking a switch to broadcast the comms link to the room. He crossed his arms and leaned both elbows on the desk. 'Rover Two, this is Moonbase. Gabe, how's it looking?'

There was a short burst of static then Velasquez's voice came over the speaker. 'We're good. We've reached the site, no problems en route. It was a smooth ride and the panel is secure. I'm performing a final check of the location then we'll move the panel into position.'

In truth there was very little for Velasquez to do. He'd already drilled a base plate into the surface ready for the solar panel to be mounted, and the cabling to transmit the energy to the storage units at the base was all in place. The site was ready. He moved round to the back of the lunar buggy where the panel was held and looked at Wrycroft. Their spacesuits were unwieldy but both astronauts had spent a lot of time in them over the last four months, more than anyone else at the base, and they were as prepared as they'd ever be to perform this final task.

'Okay, let's do it,' he said to the Australian. They each reached and took a firm grasp of the handles on either side of the panel, and Velasquez pressed a button to release the clips holding it in place. 'One, two, three!' As he said the final count they both lifted the panel and slowly bounded over to the mounting plate. The design was deliberately as simple as possible due to the ungainly nature of performing tasks in their suits. It was a simple case of sliding the unit down onto the bracket. Velasquez felt rather than heard the connection click into place, and a green light came on automatically to indicate the panel was now live.

Daley's voice came through their ear pieces. 'Congratulations gentlemen. I'm showing a successful docking on our instruments here. Standby for positioning.'

The two astronauts stepped back. 'Affirmative,' Velasquez advised. 'We are clear of the array. Go for it.'

There was a delay of a couple of seconds then the whole panel turned smoothly to one side and angled up to face the sun. The whole face lit up as it found the optimum position.

'Looking good base,' confirmed Velasquez, grinning. 'She's lit up like Christmas.'

The two astronauts heard claps and cheering coming over the intercom as the rest of the team in the base whooped excitedly at the successful installation. Velasquez turned to Wrycroft who held up a hand to high five his colleague. They followed it up with an unsteady, low gravity embrace that nearly sent the two of them sprawling.

'We're up and running boys,' said Daley happily. 'It'll take some time to register any results so get yourselves back here before we drink all the champagne.'

*

Blake and the others had been back at the investigation room for ten minutes when Higgins called. She asked to be put on speakerphone so the whole team could hear.

'Thought you'd like to know, inspector. The Lunarsol team just went live with their first panel. It's now official. They've successfully manufactured and installed a solar farm on the lunar surface.'

'That's impressive,' Blake replied. 'It's nice to get a positive news story for a change.'

'It is. We can't get too carried away, it's a very small pilot phase at the moment, but they'll expand rapidly from here on. Over the next twenty days or so they should be able to get a further fifty units into position. By the time of the next lunar sunrise the base will be fully powered and there'll be enough surplus to start sending some to Earth. That really will be an exciting moment for them.'

'I can't help feeling a lot of what we're doing might end up jeopardising the whole thing,' Blake admitted. 'It's a pity to put a dampener on everything they've achieved.'

'I know,' Higgins agreed. 'But we can't let that distract us. Someone up there murdered Richard and, unfortunate as it might be for the solar project, we can let Mr Lomax worry about the commercial implications. You just concentrate on finding out who did it and bring them to justice.'

'We will, you can rest assured of that.'

'How did it go with Tse?'

'Very useful,' Blake admitted. 'A lot of what he said was off the record but it was worth the trip. I see what you mean about him, he's a good man.'

'Glad to hear it. Please, keep me updated with progress.' She ended the call, leaving Blake with his three original team members.

'Alright. It's a bit of a mess but let's see what we can salvage from this. The press publicity means we don't have to pussyfoot around anymore. When we talk to people we can be up front about the investigation and that gives us a bit more leverage. Let's look at what we do know. Doctor Nash was murdered some time during the night or the following day. Cheng's testimony, if it's to be believed, suggests it was during the night, although that's uncorroborated.'

'I'll try to set up a call with him today,' said Palmer. 'We need to get the detail on exactly what time he was there and what he saw.'

'Good,' Blake agreed. 'Everything points towards Nash having been injected with this drug Sux that caused total muscle paralysis while leaving him fully alert. He was then manoeuvred into position with his head inside the fish tank, unable to move, and he was left there to drown. He was a swimmer so probably had a good lung capacity, but not enough to last until the effects of the drug wore off.'

'He wouldn't have been far off apparently,' Hamilton commented. 'I've been reading up on suxamethonium chloride. It's fast acting but also wears off pretty quickly. Nash may even have been starting to regain some small movement in his final seconds. He would have been agonisingly close to regaining his motor abilities. Not enough to lift himself out of the tank, but enough to have breathed in the water. His body would have been desperately trying to get some oxygen but he would have known that as soon as any sensation returned he wouldn't be able to escape the drowning. I guess the killer would have had to stay and watch to make sure. We're dealing with someone unusually sadistic here. They must have really hated him.'

'Which suggests to me it is more likely to be related to something in his past,' Blake added. 'This wasn't an impulse thing. Nash might have crossed paths with one of the other astronauts before they left for the moon and they've been waiting for their chance to get their revenge ever since.'

'In that case the pendulum swings back towards the American and Russians,' commented Hamilton. 'They've known Nash longer. Both Medvelev and Yuridov are difficult to read, but it's not hard to imagine either of them being cold and dispassionate. Personally, from what we've seen of her I'm finding it harder to picture Ellis doing it, but it's not an out and out impossibility. You have to be pretty single minded to become the first woman to walk on the moon.'

'The first NASA astronaut of any gender in fifty years don't forget,' Bennett pointed out. 'It must have taken some fairly ruthless moves to get to the number one spot.'

'If you ask me you need some massive balls to even sit in one of those rockets,' said Hamilton. 'She clearly knows how to play the game though to get into that number one spot. She'd have had to impress not only the NASA bods but also the private companies funding some of her research. Maybe there is something in those payments to Bermuda. It wouldn't take much for her to tweak a result here or there to make some investors a lot of money.'

'And you think Nash got in the way?'

'He could have stumbled onto something and threatened to go public with it?' suggested Palmer. 'It would have totally undermined all her other work. Like you said, she must be ruthless to have got this far. She'd do anything to hold onto that.'

'They're all driven,' Blake agreed, 'but it's an interesting idea. Let's keep this one between us for now though, I don't want another astronaut being accused publicly. There's still a seven in eight chance she's innocent.'

'I'll see what I can find out,' said Hamilton. 'Quiet like.'

'Okay, the Russians,' said Blake. 'Thoughts on how to crack them?'

'Greschenko won't give us anything incriminating,' Hamilton offered. 'I'm sure Lomax would if only to deflect from his people, but I wouldn't trust it. Especially not in the mood he is at the moment. Our best bet is probably talking to others around the programme like your mate at the swimming pool. They'll have seen a side to the astronauts that others might not have. Maybe we should track down that technician who had his ass chewed off by Medvelev?'

'Do that,' said Blake. 'And keep asking around at ESA for anyone who trained with Yuridov. Or any of them. Don't forget there's still the possibility one of them was ordered to do this, you'll need to look into any political angles as well. It still feels a little strange they're now both in charge of the operation up there.'

25

'Cheng's heading to the camera room now,' Hamilton announced ten minutes later.

'Thanks Jim,' Blake replied. 'I'll take this one, you guys carry on.' He picked up his mug of tea and carried it next door. The screen was already on with Cheng sat facing him.

'Morning Mr Cheng, thanks for seeing me so quickly.'

'That's ok. Is there a problem? Your colleague didn't say why you wanted to speak to me.'

'Well, it appears you haven't been entirely honest with us. I'd like to revisit some of the aspects of our conversation from the other day. Specifically with regard to your nocturnal wanderings.' Cheng's eyes opened wide, so Blake added 'I spent yesterday in Beijing and received the full tour.' Blake left it at that, not wanting to mention Tse's name since he'd passed the information on in confidence.

'So you know?' Cheng said finally. 'About my work for

the Chinese?'

'I know. I understand why you're doing it, and it's not my place to judge. You haven't been accused of any wrongdoing, and even if you had I'm not investigating that. If it's unrelated to the murder investigation then it need go no further. Everything you tell me today is strictly between us, I assure you.'

Cheng bowed his head slightly. 'I think Mr Lomax may suspect me already, but I'd rather not confirm it. Very well, inspector. I apologise for not being fully truthful when we spoke previously. I'm all yours, what would you like to know?'

'Talk me through your visit to Lab Two. What time did you get up, what did you see, everything.'

'I left my room at 4.30am. I've done it once before. It's not the lack of sleep that's the problem, but the risk of bumping into one of my colleagues. Any earlier and it would certainly look more suspicious. At that time if I were to be seen it's more believable that I simply woke and was up and about earlier than usual. Doctor Nash has been doing some interesting work on background radiation and magnetic fields in microgravity and I wanted a closer look. I was going to allow myself thirty minutes max in his lab, no more. As it was, I spent less than five.'

'What did you see?'

'Exactly as Doctor Ellis described, Richard on his knees, bent over with his head inside one of the tanks. There didn't seem to be any need to tell you as you'd heard it already.'

'All we had was Doctor Ellis's word for it though,' Blake explained. 'She might have been lying. Your independent testimony is vital to corroborate her version of events.'

'I see your point. Yes, I should have told you.'

'Okay, so talk me through what happened next.'

'I ran over and shook Richard's shoulder but it was obvious it was too late.'

'Obvious,' Blake asked. 'In what way?'

Cheng hesitated before replying. 'He'd soiled himself. That's one of the first things to happen after death as the muscles relax. His eyes had clouded over as well. I don't think he'd been dead for long. As far as I could tell rigor mortis hadn't set in so it may even have been less than an hour, but he was definitely deceased.'

'So you touched the body?'

Cheng looked down at the desk. 'Yes. When I first ran up to him I lifted his head from the water. That's how I was able to see his eyes. I should have raised the alarm immediately, I know. I'm not sure why I didn't, something made me hesitate. I'm ashamed to say I panicked. I wasn't supposed to be there, remember. I froze, just holding him in my arms as I tried to decide what action to take. Finally I decided it would be better if someone else made the discovery and that I should make sure to be nowhere nearby. It already felt like I'd been in there too long although in reality it was only a few minutes. I gently lowered him back into the water in the same position I'd found him. I'm afraid I'd made a bit of a mess. My clothes were wet, and I'd stepped in a puddle caused by water splashing when I lifted Nash out, so I removed my shoes and backed away as quickly and quietly as possible. As soon as I was out of the room I hurried back to my quarters where I changed into something dry. Then I just sat and waited for someone else to find him.'

'Which didn't happen. Okay, Mr Cheng, let's go back to the laboratory. Did you see anything else unusual?'

'Only as I was leaving when I noticed the foam all over his desk. It was a strange sight and didn't make sense but it was of less importance than Doctor Nash obviously. I didn't give it much thought.'

'So that's it? You didn't see or hear anything else?'

'No. And I can assure you I was completely alert. I spent a good hour terrified someone would burst in on me any second. I was listening for the slightest sound but there was nothing. Each of the living quarters contains three bedrooms. Mine is shared with Wrycroft and Lonnen. I didn't hear a thing until 07:15 when Chris went to breakfast. He was humming some dreadful country and western song, I remember thinking it wrong that someone could be so cheerful while I felt so scared. I still didn't move though. Shortly after there was a knock on my door but I didn't answer it. I just sat there in the dark, hoping they'd go away.'

'Ah, yes, Sergei Medvelev was looking for you I believe,' Blake said.

'Yes, he found me later. Something to do with the printer robots. I think that's what he said anyway. I spent the whole conversation nervous that he was going to accuse me of killing Doctor Nash. Anyway, I decided I couldn't hide away forever so joined them for breakfast shortly after the knock on my door. Other than that there was no sound. If either of Wrycroft or Lonnen did it they were back in their room before I had even left mine at 04:30.'

'Okay Mr Cheng, I'll let you go for now. Please let me know if there's anything else at all which occurs to you. And don't lie to me again, my patience only goes so far.'

Cheng gave a small nod and leaned forward to switch off the camera. Blake rejoined his team and called them over to a whiteboard where he drew a long horizontal line.

'Right, sequence of events. Doctor Nash was last seen by the group in the common room at eight thirty pm.' He made a vertical slash on the far left of the line, wrote the time and scribbled "Nash at dinner" beneath it. 'Doctor Ellis then went to visit him in his quarters a few minutes later. According to her.' He made a mark and wrote "Ellis → Nash. His room"

'Next up is Velasquez, again visiting Nash in his quarters,' said Hamilton. 'According to him,' he added.

Blake marked Velasquez's visit, then added 'Last seen alive' below and underlined it. 'Do we have an exact time?'

'Around eleven o'clock,' Hamilton replied. 'He then went straight to Ellis's, leaving hers at two am.'

"02:00 Velasquez → his room" went up on the board.

'According to Cheng, he then went to snoop around Lab Two at four thirty, where he discovered Nash's body.' Bennett raised an eyebrow so Blake quickly gave an overview of the conversation he'd just had.

'Again, we just have his word for the timing.' Blake looked at the board. 'I should have used different coloured pens for confirmed events. Never mind. He was back in his room before five o'clock, then we have the others starting to wake up and move about from five thirty onwards. Yuridov and Ellis first, then it gets a bit sketchy after that.

'So,' Palmer concluded, 'Nash was killed sometime between eleven pm and four thirty am. It's still a fairly big window.'

'I think we can discount the first couple of hours,' said Blake. 'The murderer would have wanted to be sure everyone was fast asleep before making their move. I'd say it's more likely to have happened between two and four.'

'Velasquez?' Palmer suggested.

'Maybe,' Blake replied. 'He was ideally placed. But if it wasn't him then we're looking at an even smaller window. The killer may have heard Velasquez come back, so would probably have waited a while longer to be sure he was asleep too.'

'Or heard him leave,' Hamilton pointed out. 'I still have my suspicions about Ellis.'

'Either way, same window of opportunity,' said Blake. 'Let's say the killer waited half an hour. Two thirty. They would have had to go to the laboratory first to set things up. All that would have taken time. At least half an hour, maybe more. The tank would have needed to be moved onto the floor and its lid removed for one thing, plus there's that strange business with the chemistry gunk which I'm guessing was done to lure Nash. There he is, fast asleep, when he's woken by someone shaking his shoulder. "Richard, wake up, there's something going on in your lab." He doesn't bother getting dressed, but does slip on his trainers. Didn't I read somewhere they're weighted to help counteract the low gravity? They pass quietly through the accommodation wing and common room, not wanting to wake the others. When they get to Lab Two, Nash enters and sees his worktop overflowing with some kind of strange gooey substance. As he's stood there looking at it, trying to fathom what the gloop might be, he feels a scratch on his arm. His initial reaction is confusion. He might have looked at his arm first to see what it was, then turned to face whoever had led him there. All costing vital seconds. At this point he's still trying to make sense of it as he feels his legs going weak. He's gently ushered a few steps to the side of the desk, and only now does he notice someone's removed the lid from the fish tank. By now his legs have given way and his muscles are becoming unresponsive. He's a smart guy, he realises what's happening, so he takes a big gulp of air while he still can. Then, totally unable to resist his attacker, he's slowly lowered face first into the water.'

No one spoke, all picturing Nash alive but helpless. Eyes open but unable to even blink. Palmer shuddered, causing Blake to look up. He realised he'd been lost in that world, and had really only been talking to himself out loud. 'It fits, doesn't it?' he asked, receiving a few silent nods from the others in response.

'Right. So, now we're looking at the murder happening between three thirty and four am. Probably. We've a lot of assumptions in there but it feels the most likely. Whoever it was is lucky they didn't bump into Cheng coming the other way.'

'Unless it was Cheng,' said Palmer.

'Or the killer could have already been in the lab doing the prep work while Velasquez was changing bedrooms,' suggested Bennett.

Blake looked at the timeline he'd drawn and sighed. 'Yes, that's possible. Feels too tight though, doesn't it? The chances of being caught are high, either by Velasquez at two or Cheng at four thirty. The smart money says the murder happened sometime between that pair's night time wanderings. The question is, does it tell us anything?'

'That they'd have been tired the next day?' said Palmer. 'I'm a mess if I don't get my full eight hours.'

'You're young though,' Hamilton pointed out. 'Us oldies are up twice a night. You get used to it.'

'And these are highly trained astronauts,' Blake added. 'They ought to be able to cope with a couple of hours lost sleep. Plus whoever did this would have been supercharged with adrenaline. That would have helped them get through the next day no problem.'

'Just thinking out loud,' Bennett said. 'Is there a chance the killer might have been prevented from making it back to their room because they heard Cheng approaching?'

'Go on,' said Blake.

'Well, say the murderer has put Nash in the tank. They've then had to sit and watch for ten minutes to make sure he's not getting up again. That drug is a quick hit, remember. Knocks your muscles out almost instantaneously but doesn't last long. Nash was fit, he could have potentially survived a couple of minutes. The killer would've needed to stick around to be sure Nash didn't regain enough movement to get himself out. By then, if your timeline is right, we're getting close to the time Cheng set off. The murderer would have been stranded, unable to get back to their own quarters while they could hear someone else wandering about. Even less able to get back afterwards as there was a good chance Cheng would have been looking out for anyone suspicious. They might have had to hide out somewhere until breakfast then make their appearance as if nothing had happened.'

'I like it,' Blake said, nodding. 'Definitely worth more

attention anyway.' He walked over to a large printout of the base itself. 'The bedrooms lead onto the main common area here, then off to the laboratories here. This is Lab Two where Doctor Nash worked.' He tapped the blueprint. 'There's a backdoor though. This access tunnel leads from the rear of the laboratory wing to the Lunarsol manufacturing plant. If the murderer couldn't get back to the living quarters this would have given them an escape route. After that it was just a simple case of hiding out anywhere in these pods until breakfast.' He swept his hand around the Lunarsol wing of the base. 'Yes, it fits. Phil, Kathryn, can you go back over all of the transcripts with the astronauts, see if any of them said anything which might add weight to that scenario. We're getting close on this one, I can feel it.'

26

As he'd not seen his family since abandoning them at the Parkrun on Saturday morning Blake decided to take the opportunity to escape the office. It was three pm so he called Emily and said he'd pick Sophie and Olivia up from their after school club early and they could all go out for a pizza. As a treat he'd take them to their favourite place on North Street. Emily said she'd get the bus and meet them there.

In the summer he would have taken them to the park for a bit first but at this time of year it was already cold and dark, the drizzle adding to their desire to get indoors as quickly as possible. Fortunately the girls both had wellies and umbrellas so they were happy enough splashing through the puddles on their way to the restaurant. By the time they got to Pizza Workshop it was half past four, but at that time on a Monday there was no problem getting a table near the window. Blake ordered some lemonades and a Deli Board to pick at while they waited for Emily to join them.

'So, how was school?' he asked them.

Sophie, his eldest, just shrugged. 'Can't remember.'

'Come on Soph, think. It was only a couple of hours ago. What was the best thing you did today?'

She sat there looking into space for a minute. 'Oh, we rehearsed the Christmas play!' she said suddenly as the memory came back to her.

'Great! What part are you playing?'

'I'm one of the teachers. We're, like, doing this thing where the teachers have been told to organise a nativity, so we have to, like, audition the children for the different parts. So the play is actually us doing the auditioning.'

'Clever. I'm looking forward to seeing it,' Blake said. 'How about you Livvie?'

'I painted a robin this morning they're going to turn it into a Christmas card then we had playtime then Mr Perkins read us a story about Jack Frost then we had dinner and I had shepherd's pie then we had playtime but Reuben pushed Molly over and she cried and he got told off by Miss Lewis then we did numbers that add up to ten this afternoon then playtime then recorders.' She took a deep breath. 'Then the bell went and we went to after school club but it was too wet to play outside so we did some junk modelling and then you came!'

Blake smiled. It had never been a problem getting a breakdown of Olivia's day. 'A robin?' he said in his best excited voice. 'That sounds epic.' He'd noticed epic seemed to be their favourite word at the moment. 'Have you drawn your Christmas card yet Sophie?'

His daughter looked up at the ceiling. 'I don't know, I can't remember. Stop asking.'

Blake grinned. The other parents in Sophie's class had told him their children were exactly the same. 'Like getting blood from a stone' was a phrase he'd heard more than once.

'Shall I tell you about what I've been up to the last

couple of days?' he asked them.

'Mummy said you had to go on a plane to China,' said Olivia. 'Is that where china comes from?'

'Um. Yes, probably,' Blake replied, caught off guard. 'You know, I think it probably does.' He made a mental note to check later. 'I didn't go there for the pottery though. I was talking to some people about spaceships.'

'I thought you went to Russia?' said Sophie.

'Ah, not quite. I went to somewhere called Kazakhstan, but you're right I did meet a Russian.'

'Was that to talk about spaceships too?'

'Er, yes, we did a bit. I even saw one.'

'Oh. Are they going to rescue the people on the moon?' asked Sophie.

'Rescue them?' Blake said, curious about where this was going.

'Yes, it was on the telly at the weekend. You must have missed it because you were away. The astronaut on the moon has died. They think one of the others did it. Do the people in China need to fly up to bring them back? Or the people in Kakadan?'

Blake looked at her, momentarily lost for words. 'I don't think they know what's going to happen yet,' he said finally. He was spared any further explanation as Emily burst in, pushing her hood down and shaking herself in the doorway to get some of the rain off. The waiter hurried over and offered to take her coat.

'Yuck!' she said as she sat down. 'It's horrible out there.' She leaned over and gave Blake a kiss. 'You smell,' she added.

'Nice to see you too. Sorry, I feel grubby, I could do with a shower.'

'And a shave. Don't worry, food first. What are we having?'

'Pizza!' both girls chimed. The waiter appeared with their drinks and the starter, plus a couple of children's menus with games on for them to colour in. Both girls dove into the crayon pot and set to work on a join the dots and a word search. Emily asked for a lemonade as well, then as they all knew what they wanted ordered the pizzas.

'Good trip?' Emily asked once the waiter had left.

'Long,' Blake replied, tucking into a mini stuffed pepper. 'And tiring. But yes, worth it. I think.'

'How's the case going?'

Blake shrugged. 'Sometimes it feels like we're making real progress, then other times it seems as if we're getting nowhere. I'm sure there's something I'm missing but can't put my finger on it.'

'It'll come to you, it always does.'

The waiter returned with the extra lemonade. 'We could have done without the accusations at the press conference,' Blake added once they were alone. 'Although away from the media circus the fallout hasn't been as bad as it could have been. I appear to have lost my executive jet privileges but other than that things are going about as well as can be expected.'

'It's all the Sunday papers talked about,' Emily said. 'I got a copy of each in case you need them although I guess you know it all already. I found it all fascinating reading them yesterday. There's a lot about the moon base itself but most of the focus is on Richard Nash and Gabriel Velasquez. Is it true what Nash's father said? Did Velasquez do it?'

Blake took a sip of his drink then placed it carefully back on the table. He glanced at the girls but they were both lost in concentration colouring in a pizza on their sheets. 'It could have been any of them,' he said finally. 'We really haven't been able to rule out a single one yet. The Russians are impenetrable, and the Lunarsol crew are being protected by the parent company. I'm starting to wonder if anyone really wants us to solve this case.'

'What about the NASA astronaut? Ellis?'

'As likely as any of them,' Blake replied. 'Who knows? Maybe Nash's experiments contradicted her own and she was paid off by a corporate sponsor to silence him. Or perhaps she just didn't like the way he walked. It's a strange environment they're in, all locked away together up there. If the psychologists got their aptitude tests wrong and have inadvertently grouped a bunch of people together who really can't get along then it's not surprising the whole thing has blown up in their faces.'

'Is that what you think's happened?'

Blake shook his head. 'No. This goes back further than the moon mission. There's something in one of their histories which ties all this together. That's why the Velasquez thing sounds so convincing in the papers. Twisted the right way, his father dying at the hands of the British comes over as a very strong motive.'

'That's sad,' Olivia said quietly.

Her parents looked over as she diligently continued to colour in a tomato. 'What's sad sweetie?' Emily asked.

'The astronaut whose daddy died. He must have cried for a long time.'

'Oh, it happened before he was even born darling,' Blake told her. 'He never even knew about it until much later.'

Olivia thought about this. 'I guess that's okay then,' she decided. 'It would be more sad if you knew your daddy and then he died.'

'It would sweetie, it would,' Blake said, but she wasn't listening. Having reached a satisfactory conclusion her head had dropped back down and she was once again absorbed in her crayoning. He reached across and took an olive and a piece bread. As he slowly chewed it he realised Emily had been talking.

'Huh? Sorry love? I was miles away then.'

'I said do you have any more exotic trips planned?'

'Not planned. Jim was trying to wangle a trip to Bermuda but now we've lost the jet I don't think we'd get the expenses signed off. Long story,' he added, when she raised her eyebrows at him. 'Can you excuse me a minute?

I just had a thought, need to give Jim a quick call.'

She watched as he grabbed his coat from a peg and stepped out into the rain. Peering through the condensation on the window she could make out her husband talking into his mobile for a couple of minutes before he hung up and came back inside, just as the pizzas arrived at their table.

'Perfect timing,' he said, removing his coat and accepting the waiter's offer to take it. 'Let's eat.' He put a slice on each of his daughters' plates then helped himself to a couple, the cheese stretching satisfyingly back to the plate as he pulled them away. The conversation moved on from the case for the rest of the meal as they discussed Christmas presents for family and friends, and who was going to sleep where when Emily's parents came to stay.

'You can make your red cabbage with the cider,' Emily suggested, 'but for the rest of the morning your only job is to keep everyone else out of the kitchen. So long as these two aren't on the naughty list and Santa actually brings them the bikes they've asked him for, then maybe you could take mum and dad out with you while they try them out.'

'Or, I could just take your dad to the pub?' Blake offered. 'A bit of father-in-law bonding. Your mum and the girls can help you with the turkey then.' He ducked as she pretended to throw her scrunched up napkin at him. 'You're lucky we're in a public place, inspector, or you might find yourself the victim of a murder.'

'Can I help?' asked Olivia. 'I can chop the vegetables.'

'Thank you sweetie,' Emily replied. 'But I'm sure you'll be busy opening your presents.'

'I don't mind. I'll get up early and get the food out of the fridge then I'll wait for you.'

Emily glanced at Blake who had turned pale. 'Are you ok?'

'Say that again,' Blake said, looking at Olivia.

'I'll get the food out of the fridge.'

'No, not that bit.'

'Um. I'll get up early?'

Blake slapped his palm onto his head. 'Idiot,' he said to himself. 'It's been staring me in the face the whole time.'

'What has?' asked his wife.

Blake was prevented from replying by his phone ringing. Seeing Hamilton's name on the display he apologised and leaned away from the table to answer it. A minute later he hung up. 'Sorry love, I need to dash. Don't wait up. I might be late.'

27

All eight of the astronauts were gathered in the diary room when Blake walked in with Mary Phillips and the rest of his team. Whiteley, Higgins and Maddix followed, having been summoned by Blake, and took their seats along the wall. The overall effect was that both rooms, hundreds of thousands of kilometres apart, were unusually congested.

'Not enough space,' quipped Blake, unable to resist the temptation to use the pun. 'Thanks for coming everyone. There has been some progress on the investigation and I thought it might be easier if everybody was able to hear first hand where we are rather than pick things up via Chinese whispers.'

He shuffled his notes. 'Chinese whispers,' he repeated, almost to himself, then looked back up to the large screen. 'You know, it was something you said Mr Cheng that got me thinking.' A couple of the astronauts turned and looked at the muscular Lunarsol scientist.

'I'll come back to that. Let me start with what we know,' Blake continued. 'Firstly, Doctor Nash's body was discovered in Laboratory Two. Secondly, he had been lured there by his killer some time during the night.'

Yuridov leaned slightly towards the camera. 'Can you be sure about that?'

'I think so, yes,' Blake replied. 'It's very unlikely he would have been killed somewhere else. Even in low gravity moving a body is a difficult, cumbersome business. The killer would have run a very high risk of being caught. Much safer to set off a simple chemistry experiment as bait. Once Nash had been drawn into the trap, distracted by what he discovered, the murderer could carry out their plans.'

Yuridov nodded his acceptance of this logic.

'What we don't know,' Blake added, 'is when, or even if, the killer then went back to their own room.'

He waited while a few of them exchanged confused looks. A similar scene was being played out among the audience in his video room. He held up a piece of paper. 'I have here a plan of the base. I'm sure everyone is well acquainted with the layout. There are two routes from the murder scene back to the sleeping quarters. Either the shorter path directly into the main living area, or through the passageway which leads to the four pods of the Lunarsol manufacturing plant. It's a more circuitous route but would still have brought the murderer into the common room, albeit from a different direction. In other words, both options would have meant going through your central hub to gain access to the bedrooms. But, if they had found themselves cut off it would at least have given them a way out, and plenty of places to hide until morning.'

'What does that tell you though?' Cheng asked. 'I'm not the only one who can get into the solar plant. I may spend my whole day there but we all have access to the entire base. Anyone could have used that route.'

'True,' Blake replied. 'But it's useful to get an understanding of what might have happened, particularly when we look more closely at the timing.' Blake looked to Cheng's left. 'Mr Velasquez. We know that at some time during the night you were up, moving around the living quarters.'

'Ah, now wai–' Velasquez started, but was cut off by Blake raising his palm.

'You must admit,' Blake went on, 'the finger points to you. There's the incident with your father for one thing. The fact his death is connected to the Falklands conflict gave you a very real reason for hating the British. If anyone might wish him harm, it's you.'

'That's ridiculous,' Velasquez spat angrily. 'I never even knew my father. Even if I did, he was a petty criminal, he knew the risks. And I certainly don't blame the British for what happened.'

'There's more to your childhood though isn't there,' Blake said. 'Your mother remarried and you ended up being the victim of a very unhappy upbringing. You escaped and found safety in G. Dolman Construction, but then Chase Lomax took that family away from you as well. You have every reason to hate Lomax. Damaging his great lunar project might be sweet revenge. Having a dig at the British into the bargain is the perfect result for you.'

Velasquez slammed his hand down on the table angrily. 'Rubbish. All of it. Yeah, it was sad to see the old man's business get swallowed up, but it was bound to happen one day, and Lomax has always been good to me. I owe him a lot for how my life's turned out, including getting to come here.'

'And then of course,' Blake went on, 'we also have your relationship with Doctor Ellis to consider. You knew, or suspected, that Doctor Nash also had feelings for her, and that she was particularly friendly with him. You're often out on your own, all day long, while she and Nash were back at the base. It wouldn't be unreasonable for you to develop jealous feelings towards him. Or perhaps you objected to something Nash said, or did, Doctor Ellis?' Blake finished, turning to look at the NASA scientist.

'Me? You can't seriously think I would have wanted to kill Richard?'

'Why not? The love angle feels like a stretch, but there is the work rivalry. Maybe his findings conflicted with your own. Professional jealousy is not uncommon, especially if you were receiving payments from an external source to doctor your results.'

'To do what?' she cried. 'That's outrageous!'

'The fact you were the one to discover his body is also suspicious. You could have easily removed any vital clues before the others got to you. Plus you had ample opportunity to do it during the night. Knowing of Mr Velasquez's movements leaving your room, and that our focus would have been on him, you could have waited and then easily enticed Nash to the laboratory and injected him with the suxamethonium chloride.'

'That's horrible. I can't believe you would think that,' Ellis replied, her eyes reddening.

Blake paused. 'I don't,' he said in a reassuring voice. 'I apologise for upsetting you doctor. I don't believe you did this, or Mr Velasquez. I only brought it up as I think some of it might be relevant.'

Velasquez and Ellis looked at each other then back at Blake. 'In what way?' asked the engineer.

'Let's take you first Mr Velasquez. Your argument with Doctor Nash the previous evening was very public,' Blake explained. 'As you yourself suggested, if the murderer had been waiting for the right time to carry out this crime, then the scene between the two of you could have set the clock ticking. From that moment on, Doctor Nash was on borrowed time. Your relationship with Doctor Ellis was a bonus. If you were in the habit of returning to your quarters in the middle of the night, and the killer knew that, then they could have waited to carry out the crime at a time when all indicators would point to you.'

Velasquez glanced around at his fellow astronauts. Blake continued his summary of events. 'And just for the record, Doctor Ellis, we're fairly confident the payments recently made to an account in your name did not originate from some mysterious lobby trying to bribe you into producing false results.' Blake could tell by the blank look on Ellis's face this was the first she'd heard of any payments. 'My suspicion is someone at Lunarsol has been attempting to sidetrack our enquiries. Rest assured I'll be taking that up with Mr Lomax later.

'So,' he went on, 'your bedroom habits may have given the killer the start time of their window of opportunity. What they wouldn't have known was Mr Cheng would also be taking an early morning stroll. I think that closed the window prematurely. By our reckoning, there's a good chance they wouldn't have made it back to their room before they heard Cheng approaching. The murderer would have been forced to retreat down the access passageway and would then have had to hide out somewhere in the Lunarsol plant.'

'But they could still have made it back round to the living quarters by taking the longer route round to the common room,' pointed out Cheng.

'True,' Blake said. 'But they wouldn't have known what you were doing or how long you would be. If they'd hurried they might have just made it before you came back from Nash's lab. Would they have risked it? I don't think so.'

Ellis looked at Cheng. 'What were you doing in Richard's lab?'

Cheng looked at the floor. 'I have some explaining to do.'

'You do,' Blake interrupted. 'But that can wait. And as it happens I've just had a call which may redeem you partially. Of course, if you'd raised the alarm at the time this whole thing might have been solved then and there. It would have been obvious straight away if the killer had been seen coming from the other direction, unless they somehow managed to slip in amidst all the confusion.' Blake shrugged. 'It's a moot point anyway. You didn't wake the others so the guilty party was in no immediate danger. However, getting back to their room would have been risky in case you were on the lookout, which you say you were.'

'I was. And I didn't see anyone.'

'So you say,' Blake replied. 'In which case, the killer didn't make it back to their room at all.'

Again, the astronauts looked around amongst themselves. Ellis was the first to respond. 'It must have been the first person at breakfast then.' She turned to Yuridov. 'Commander?' she questioned, weakly.

'It was not me,' Yuridov replied emphatically. 'I was the first one into the common room but I came directly from my sleeping quarters. I didn't go near Doctor Nash's laboratory.'

'No, and nor did anyone else apart from Doctor Ellis who we've already discounted, and Mr Daley who you saw coming from the laboratory wing as he returned from the Lunarsol plant.'

'Me?' asked Daley. 'You don't think I did it?'

'No, I don't,' replied Blake. 'For one thing you didn't have the luxury of setting up the distraction. Without that it would have been harder to catch Doctor Nash off guard. Secondly you wouldn't have had time to move the fish tank onto the floor. That would have had to be ready so Nash could be lowered into it as soon as the drug took effect, otherwise it might have worn off before he even got near the water. Those facts alone mean this must have happened earlier before Doctor Nash would have normally started his work for the day.'

Yuridov realised everyone was looking at him. 'I say again, it was not me.'

'Interestingly,' continued Blake, 'it was your colleague,

Commander Medvelev, who said something which first made me suspect the culprit.' Medvelev raised an eyebrow at the mention of his name. 'You told me how you've been trained to control your emotions. Because of that you believed it could not have been one of the pilots, as you put it, but rather one of the others. But that's how this murder came across. It wasn't spontaneous in a fit of anger or passion. It was cold, calculated. Executed clinically. So it struck me, contrary to what you thought, it was, if anything, more likely that one of the pilots could have done it.'

'But what possible motive could we have had?' Yuridov asked.

'You tell me, Commander. Your job is to follow orders. It might look odd to an outsider that, with Doctor Nash no longer there, you and Commander Medvelev now hold the two top ranking positions at the base. Could that have been part of some directive from above?'

'If it had been then it is one order I would not have followed,' Yuridov stated. 'Richard was a good man. A friend. There is no way I would have done such a thing.'

'And you, Commander Medvelev?' Blake prompted.

'I am same,' Medvelev replied. 'Except Richard and I were even closer. I would not hurt him.'

Blake paused. 'No, you wouldn't,' he said finally.

Medvelev looked back at him with a mixture of surprise and relief, while the remaining astronauts unconsciously looked around at each other.

'But you said it was one of the pilots,' Daley protested. 'Was it them or not?'

'You may or may not know that doubts were cast over all of you. But there's only one person who ticked all the boxes. Someone with military training who is able to control their emotions and act clinically. Someone who was up early, wasn't seen at breakfast, and yet was ready for work before the others. And someone who, as my colleague Sergeant Hamilton has recently established, might just hold Doctor Nash's family responsible for the death of his father. No, not you Mr Velasquez,' Blake said as the engineer opened his mouth to object. 'Your colleague. Eric Wrycroft.'

All eyes turned to look at the Australian. Wrycroft stared dispassionately back at Blake.

'You did a good job of playing down the effect your father's death had on you. But you were nineteen, away from home for the first time. Out a lot, having fun. Not calling your folks as often as you should. And then bang, he's gone. A strut fails, the mine caves in. Those who are trapped don't have long before water from the lake above breaks through and fills up the cavity. Twelve men, dead, including your father and uncle. All because of a weakness in a support brace made by William Nash's construction company.'

'Accidents happen,' said Wrycroft dismissively. 'Goes with the territory.'

'Perhaps. But it wasn't just your father and uncle was it? Nor was it the other ten miners, who I'm guessing you knew like family. It was your mother too. That accident destroyed her, didn't it? Yeah, there was money from the company, although not a lot, not really. Not enough for her to live comfortably and to support you through uni. Must have been difficult for you, working odd jobs between classes to get by. I'm guessing you had to give up the flying too for a bit, can't afford a luxury like that. All the time surrounded by loads of rich kids who had it so easy. Kids like Richard Nash who, let's face it, grew up with everything handed to him on a plate. First rate education, fancy holidays, you name it. The money wasn't really the issue though. She never recovered from losing him, your mum, did she? Withdrew into herself, rarely left the house. She just gave up. That's what got to you more. You could handle what had happened to you, but not how it broke her. I see she died a couple of years later while you were on active duty. Do you feel guilty you weren't there for her? Is that why you couldn't go back? Is that why you've harboured a grudge against the Nash family for all these years?'

There was silence as everyone looked at him. The Australian held Blake's gaze, then looked away, rubbing his chin with his large hand.

'Realising you have a strong motive is one thing,' Blake continued. 'It's not proof you did it. Mr Cheng gave us that.'

Wrycroft looked at the Chinese American, along with everyone else in the room.

'Me?' asked Cheng. 'But I didn't see anyone.'

'It's not what you saw. It's what you heard. Or didn't hear to be precise. You told me you were up during the night and discovered Doctor Nash already dead. You could have lied, of course, to cover your tracks if you were the murderer. I'm inclined to believe you, but it wasn't that which finally made everything fall into place for me. We had a lot of questions in our scenario of the timeline. Did the killer see to Nash then get back to their quarters before you left yours, or did they get trapped by your unexpected appearance? You said you got back to your room,' Blake glanced at his notes, 'terrified someone would burst in on you, I think your words were. You stood by the door listening out for anyone who might come to get you next, is that right?'

Cheng nodded, glancing briefly at Wrycroft then back to Blake.

'And remind us, Mr Cheng. The pod where your quarters are. Who else do you share that with?'

Cheng looked at the astronauts to his left. 'Chris and Eric.'

'You told me you heard Mr Lonnen heading off to breakfast at seven fifteen, is that right.'

'That's correct.'

'Mr Lonnen, would you agree?'

'Yes, sir, that would'a been about right.'

'Did you hear Mr Wrycroft leave his room Mr Cheng?' asked Blake.

Cheng thought for a moment then shook his head.

'Commander Medvelev. I believe you went looking for Mr Cheng in his quarters. You knocked but he didn't answer, too afraid to open his door. Did you pass Mr Wrycroft at any point?'

'Nyet, I did not.'

'Mr Lonnen,' went on Blake. 'Did you see Mr Wrycroft, either in your accommodation pod or in the main common room for breakfast?'

Lonnen looked at his friend, clearly still reluctant to believe what he was hearing, then back at Blake. 'No, sir. The first time I saw Eric was when I got to the rover. He'd already run through the safety checks for our EVA.'

'So Mr Wrycroft. Would you care to explain how you managed to get from your bedroom, past Mr Cheng and Mr Lonnen, past Commander Medvelev and anyone else who was in the common room getting their breakfast, and into the lunar rover without being seen? The only way you could have got there is if you didn't come from your own room at all. You had to have come from somewhere else in the base, where you'd been hiding out after killing Richard Nash in his laboratory.'

All eyes were on the Australian. He shook his head and gave a small laugh.

'Fucking Cheng,' he said to himself. 'You don't know how close I came to killing you too.'

There was an audible gasp in both rooms and the astronauts all noticeably leaned away from him.

'Man, I was wired,' Wrycroft continued. He'd clearly kept everything bottled up and now it was out he saw no point in holding back. 'Came out of Nash's lab, my heart still pounding, then you appeared out of nowhere, creeping through the common room in the dark. My only option was to backtrack up the tunnel. No way I could make it back to my room with you in the way. Thought about jumping you then and there. With two dead astronauts they'd have had to bring us straight back, and the chances of anyone proving anything would've been much slimmer. At the very least I'd have had more time to make myself scarce.'

'What stopped you?' asked Cheng quietly.

'It would've been risky. Without the drug you could have put up more of a fight, and I didn't want to wake the whole base. I didn't think you'd seen me, but I couldn't understand why you didn't raise the alarm. That bought me time to hide, but I was worried you might have witnessed something. The opportunity just hadn't come up to deal with you yet.'

Daley looked at Wrycroft. 'This wasn't even about Richard. You wanted revenge on his father.'

'He was cutting corners,' Wrycroft said simply. 'Cheap steel, nowhere near strong enough to handle the pressures of a deep mine. Somehow the bastard managed to pin it on the mining company, got off without a single person going to court. Thirteen lives lost. You're right, Mr Blake. He's as guilty of killing my mother as he is of any of the others. Her slow, drawn out death was painful to watch, but theirs hurt just as much. They were good men, hardworking men. Drowned because he was saving himself a few dollars.'

'And that was enough to inflict the same death on William Nash's son?' Blake asked.

'It's regrettable. Richard was a nice enough guy. But his father had to know. Had to feel it. I wanted him to go through what we all went though. Knowing our family had suffered, alone, in the dark. Realising as the water rushed in they only had a couple of minutes to live and there was nothing they could do about it. That's haunted me for the last twenty five years. Now he can do the same for the rest of his life.'

'So you lured Doctor Nash into the laboratory and injected him with the suxamethonium?'

257

'Exactly as you called it, inspector. I kept the syringe. Didn't want to make it too easy for whoever investigated this. Thought there might even be a chance no one would work that bit out if the traces of the drug had left his system before anyone was able to check. I took it out on an EVA later the same day. It's buried about fifteen kilometres away at the site Chris and I went to, somewhere deep in the centre of the crater.'

'Then when the autopsy did go ahead you tried to cover your tracks by setting the fire?'

'That was the plan. I wasn't sure what we'd be asked to do, or what we'd find. Have to admit I panicked for a moment there. I'd hidden the phosphorus and solvent in my room in case I needed it. Doing chemistry at uni has its uses. I didn't know if I'd be able to plant it, but when the Commander had his back turned at the end I took a gamble. Picked up my jacket and left the mixture hidden under the table. I guessed it would take a good twelve to fifteen hours for the solvent to evaporate, so by the time the phosphorus was exposed to the air I'd be far away.'

'And the gunge on Nash's desk?'

'An insurance policy. He was no fool, and stronger than he looked too. I needed a distraction so he wouldn't see what was coming until it was too late.'

Blake looked around at DCS Whiteley who nodded. 'Eric Wrycroft,' Blake said, turning back to the screen. 'I am arresting you for the murder of Doctor Richard Nash. You do not have to say anything, but it may harm your defence if you do not mention when questioned something which you later rely on in court. Anything you do say may be given in evidence. Do you understand?'

'Whatever,' replied Wrycroft. 'It's not as if I'm going to be in court any time soon. What are you going to do? Lock me up? Here? What use is that to anyone?'

'He has a point,' said Yuridov. 'What happens now?'

'Nothing, that's what,' said Wrycroft. 'You can't abort the project, you'd need to bring us all back and you'll have a fight on your hands from Lomax if you try that. Nah, the way I see it, you keep me up here. You know where I am, you might as well have me working. I can face trial in two years when we get back.'

'And until then you're a free man?' asked Blake. 'I don't think so. No, until we decide what to do with you you're confined. Mr Yuridov, please lock up Mr Wrycroft somewhere secure. If that takes two years, so be it.'

Yuridov stepped towards Wrycroft and held out his arm to the door, gesturing for him to lead the way. Wrycroft made to go, then looked back at the camera. 'Fuck that,' he said, whipping a fist round and catching the Russian hard on the side of his head. As Yuridov crumpled, Wrycroft bolted for the door. The rest of the crew were momentarily stunned but Daley and Medvelev were quickest to react. Blake and the others watched helplessly as they set off in pursuit.

28

Daley charged out of the room and was immediately floored by another hammer blow from Wrycroft. Medvelev dove over the falling Lunarsol leader and landed a punch of his own, but Wrycroft rolled with it and slammed the Russian into the corridor wall. He set off down the corridor as Medvelev scrambled to get up, nearly colliding with the remaining astronauts as they came through the doorway and took up the chase.

'Give it up Eric!' called Lonnen. 'There's nowhere to go!'

Wrycroft didn't slow as the others raced after him, through the common room and off towards the Lunarsol plant.

'Eric, wait!' Lonnen shouted again as he ran. Arriving in Lunarsol Pod 1, the five astronauts checked themselves. Wrycroft was standing on the far side of the pod, the inner airlock door opening behind him. He stood facing the others.

'I can't be locked up guys. I'd hoped no one would pin Nash on me, but now they've figured it out there's no way I'm spending the rest of my life in a cell.'

'Don't do it, Eric,' pleaded Velasquez. 'It's like you said. They can't abort the whole project. You're safe up here while they figure out what to do. After that, you get home, you do your time. You move on.'

'You think they'd ever let me out?' Wrycroft laughed. 'Not a chance. If I go back that's it. They'll make sure I never see the outside world again. I might as well be dead.'

'It might not happen like that,' Velasquez continued. 'Your father, mother, the rest of the miners. They'll take that into account, a jury will understand you weren't thinking straight.'

Wrycroft shook his head. 'The whole thing was premeditated Gabe. I laid the trap, lured him into it, murdered him in cold blood. I know that, they know that. It's a fair cop, they got me. Maybe if I'd got to Cheng I could have covered my tracks, we'll never know.'

He stepped backwards into the airlock.

'My old man ran out of air when the mine flooded. Nash went the same way. Now it's my turn.'

He pressed the button to close the door as Velasquez and Cheng dove for the opening. Ellis and Lonnen shouted in vain but the sound didn't carry. They were too late. The door had closed, locking automatically to prevent a breach. They could only look on helplessly as Wrycroft gave them a little wave through the porthole then turned to face the outer door. He took a few deep breaths, seemingly hesitant about whether to go, then slammed his hand against the decompression button. With a hiss the air was sucked from the chamber. They watched his shoulders drop as he blew out his last breath. A light came on to confirm it was safe to open the outer door. Wrycroft reached forward, lifted the handle and pushed. The shock of being exposed to the vacuum of space caused him to stumble slightly, then he stepped outside.

'No!' screamed Ellis as Wrycroft stood with his back to them, looking to the horizon as he awaited his fate.

'He's got fifteen, maybe twenty seconds,' said Cheng shaking his head. 'There's nothing we can do. With the outer door open we can't re-pressurise to get out there, we'll need to take one of the other doors.'

Wrycroft swayed drunkenly for a second then dropped to his knees, his palms resting on the lunar surface. Then suddenly something changed. He turned his head to his right and they were just able to make out a confused expression on his face. A shadow appeared, closely followed by an alien being in one of the crew's spacesuits.

'What the –' said Velasquez.

'It's Commander Medvelev,' came Yuridov's voice behind them, breathing heavily from running to join them.

A few of them spun round to look at him. 'What?' asked Lonnen.

'Look!' shouted Velasquez as he continued to peer through the porthole. The astronauts whirled back round to see Medvelev dragging a now unconscious Wrycroft back into the airlock. He pulled the door closed behind him and hit the re-pressurisation button.

'I'll explain later,' said Yuridov. 'Get the resuscitation equipment.' They looked at him, momentarily stunned. 'Quickly!'

Cheng grabbed the defibrillator and pads and handed the emergency medical kit to Ellis.

'Come on, come on,' said Velasquez impatiently as the air rapidly hissed back into the chamber. An agonising few seconds passed before the green light came on and Velasquez yanked open the door, pulling Wrycroft's limp body into the main pod. Ellis took over, as Yuridov went to help Medvelev who was bent over, his hands on his knees, recovering from the race to get to the Australian before it was too late.

'How is he?' called Yuridov as he released Medvelev's helmet. The younger Russian nodded to confirm he was fine.

'I've got a heartbeat,' said Ellis. 'Breathing is weak and he's still unconscious. Administering adrenaline now.' She pushed the syringe into Wrycroft's thigh. A few moments later Wrycroft's eyes opened wide and he took a deep breath. He looked around wildly, gasping heavily as he tried to sit up.

Velasquez and Cheng quickly leaned in and pinned Wrycroft's arms to the floor as Ellis continued to check his vital signs. 'Keep hold of him guys,' she said. 'I'm sure Sergey doesn't want to go back out there after him again, and I can tell you I'm not keen to have to go through this for a second time either.'

*

'We have him,' Yuridov said to the camera when he returned ten minutes later. The rest of the crew were with him, except for Medvelev who'd remained with a now restrained Wrycroft to monitor his recovery.

Blake slumped back in his chair and looked at the ceiling in relief.

'What happened, Commander?' asked Higgins.

'I was a little slow to follow the others out of the room,' replied the Russian, rubbing the side of his head where he'd been hit. 'When I made it to the corridor I could see them going after Mr Wrycroft, but then Commander Medvelev turned and headed for the airlock off the common room instead. He'd guessed what Eric was planning to do. I followed and helped Sergey into his suit. I understand he'd spent a lot of time practicing this manoeuvre again and again with Doctor Nash after one of their practice sessions at ESA went wrong. We bypassed all the safety checks, the under layers, the life support monitors, the LCG.'

'Sorry, the what?' asked Blake.

'My apologies, inspector. That's the liquid cooling

garment, an under layer needed to regulate temperature. Commander Medvelev didn't have time for any of that, just the outer suit, helmet and gloves. In an emergency you can get dressed very quickly. While the others kept Wrycroft talking, Sergey was able to exit the base and make it round to the Lunarsol airlock just as the door opened.'

'So Mr Wrycroft exited the base without a spacesuit on?' asked Blake. 'Wouldn't he freeze?'

'No. In a vacuum you don't lose heat. There are many other dangers of course. It's not advised.' He gave a small smile. 'On this occasion it appears he got away with it. He lasted around fifteen seconds outside before collapsing into unconsciousness. Fortunately Commander Medvelev arrived in time to pull him back in. We'll have to wait and see if there's any lasting damage but he's lucky to be alive.'

'Well done, Commander,' said Whiteley. 'That goes for all of you. And please pass our thanks on to Commander Medvelev.'

'I'm not sure we've helped things,' Daley commented. 'If Eric had successfully killed himself that would have solved the problem of what to do with him next.' Ellis gave him a disapproving look. 'Hey,' added Daley. 'I'm just saying.'

'We'll work something out,' said Higgins. 'You're two crew members down now. I don't imagine there's any appetite within Lunarsol to abandon the project but there is now more of a case for sending the rescue rocket with a relief crew. ESA will select one of our astronauts to replace Doctor Nash. Whether Mr Wrycroft is replaced by one of Lomax's reserve team or by another astronaut can be decided after this call. If any of the rest of you wishes to come home then now's your chance.'

'Very well,' answered Yuridov. 'I suspect I know what everyone will say since we've already had this conversation, but we'll discuss it and I'll get back to you in due course. Now, if you'll excuse me, I'd like to go and check on

Sergey and the prisoner.'

'You go ahead, Commander. Everyone else, please take some time to digest everything that's happened today. We're here if you need us.'

Yuridov bowed his head and left the room. Blake watched as Daley and Lonnen sat down and started talking quietly, clearly still coming to terms with the revelations. Ellis was listening to Cheng who looked crestfallen, but she reached out and rubbed his forearm then leaned in and gave him a hug. Velasquez, watching, turned to the camera. 'Looks like he's forgiven. Thank-you, inspector. For solving this. For believing in me.'

'Don't thank me Mr Velasquez. I've been worried all the way through that cracking this one could bring about the end of the cheap solar energy you've been promising us. Just go and make sure it works now will you?'

Velasquez smiled. 'Yes, sir. I'd been wondering if we should give the solar farm a name. Now I know. I'll have the Nash Array up and running by the next sunrise. It seems a fitting tribute, don't you think?' He leaned over and switched off the camera. As the screen went black, Blake leaned back in his chair and closed his eyes.

'Mary,' he said. 'If you're quick you might make the deadline of the morning papers. They're all yours.'

NOTE

I've tried to be as factual as possible throughout the novel. The science is real. I watched a terrific BBC documentary called Do We Really Need the Moon? with Dr Maggie Aderin-Pocock, British space scientist and co-presenter of The Sky at Night. There was a segment where she looked at the possibility of putting solar panels on the moon and beaming that energy back to Earth as microwaves. When I looked into it further I discovered several organisations from different countries around the world are looking seriously into this technology. With no atmosphere, no weather and almost constant sunlight, a solar array on the lunar surface would be significantly more efficient than anything we can assemble here on Earth, and with the advances in 3D printing there's no technical reason we can't do it. We just need to start going back to the moon.

My one slight deviation from the facts, that I'm aware of at least, is when I send Blake to meet his friend McHugh at the deep dive 'Neutral Buoyancy' astronaut training pool. This pool does exist (indeed, there are several around the world as NASA, Roscosmos, ESA and the CNSA all have their own). ESA's is in Cologne though, not Boscombe Down in Wiltshire. I just couldn't quite get the timeline to work by jetting Blake off to Germany for the morning. It was possible, but there are enough flights in the story already so to avoid repetition I used a bit of poetic license and relocated the pool. For those who spotted it I hope it didn't detract too much from the storyline.

Mark Robinson

ABOUT THE AUTHOR

Apparently everyone has a book in them. Whatever happens next at least I can now say yes, I wrote one once. I signed up to a 'Write Your Novel' course at the Bristol Folk House in the autumn term of 2016 without really having much of a plan on what my story would be about. I think I'd finished the first draft of Murder on the Moon by the following August, but it then took almost as long again to work my way through several revisions.

The whole writing experience has been fascinating. Fun at times, with inevitable hurdles along the way and many, many late nights, it feels immensely rewarding to have got this far. I now also know a lot more about the moon than I did two years ago, and find it more captivating every time I glance up and see it. It seems incredible that we haven't been there in my lifetime. At least now we seem to have a renewed appetite for space adventure so perhaps that will change within the next few years.

If you enjoyed the book then I'd really appreciate it if you could take a moment to leave a review. It's hard as a new author to get noticed, particularly having self-published, and reviews go a long way towards helping with that.

Thanks,
Mark

Printed in Great Britain
by Amazon